"Say what you have to say so I can get out of here."
She wouldn't think about the possibility that Sparkle
might not intend to release her. But just in case, she
scanned the area for a weapon. Whips, chains, and a
bunch of other torture implements. Hmm. She could
do some damage with that small ax.

Sparkle laughed. "Give it up, Cinn. The only real
things in here are the chains keeping Dacian from
trying to suck us dry."

Cinn slanted a quick glance at Dacian. Who knew
that eyes so black could look like they were burning?
She swore she could almost see the flames behind his
enraged glare.

"So here's the deal. Yes, vampires do exist, along
with lots of other nonhumans. Edge and I are cosmic
troublemakers. My specialty is creating sexual chaos
throughout the universe. Edge is the cosmic troublemaker in charge of death. You can guess what he does.
Bain is a demon, and yes, Holgarth is a real wizard."
She held up her hand to stop Cinn from interrupting.
"Let me finish."

Cinn had no intention of interrupting. No way
could she talk with her jaw dragging on the floor.

"I sense a kindred spirit in you."

# NINA BANGS

# My
# Wicked
# Vampire

LEISURE BOOKS 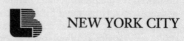 NEW YORK CITY

*For Brenda and Billy Trapani, my awesome neighbors.
No need for me to go to Vegas, because I won the neighbor
jackpot when I moved in next to you.
Thanks for being the best.*

A LEISURE BOOK®

October 2009

Published by

Dorchester Publishing Co., Inc.
200 Madison Avenue
New York, NY 10016

ISBN 10: 0-8439-5955-X
ISBN 13: 978-0-8439-5955-0
E-ISBN: 978-1-4285-0747-0

The name "Leisure Books" and the stylized "L" with design are
trademarks of Dorchester Publishing Co., Inc.

Printed in the United States of America.

10 9 8 7 6 5 4 3 2 1

Visit us online at www.dorchesterpub.com.

# My Wicked Vampire

# *Prologue*

"Freaking."

"Pain in the ass."

"*Vampire.*"

Ganymede punctuated each comment by heaving another shovelful of hard-as-concrete West Texas dirt over his shoulder. What the hell was he doing here when he should be home watching whatever crappy movie was on TV and finishing off that carton of Rocky Road ice cream?

"She couldn't send me out to dig up his undead carcass on a warm sunny day. No, it had to be in January in the middle of a bitchin' blizzard." He hauled back his foot and kicked the empty coffin waiting by the open grave. It flew through the air and landed among a pile of boulders a hundred yards away. Snow immediately started to cover it. "The hell with a coffin. I should just drag him out of his Motel Dead and dump him into the light. Then I could warm my toes by the bonfire his burning butt made."

A really entertaining thought, but not doable. Sparkle wouldn't see the humor when he brought back a pile of ashes in her nice new coffin.

He went back to digging . . . until he broke his third shovel in the hard ground. He hurled the pieces after the coffin. He was the most powerful cosmic troublemaker in the universe, and damn it, cosmic troublemakers *never* did the grunt work. They had magic or minions for that. But here he was, in human form and digging this guy up.

"How'd you do it, Dacian?"

Night feeders didn't dazzle with their awesome supernatural skills. They were the pissants of the vampire world. So where did this one get the mojo to keep paranormal power from working near his hidey-hole?

"You're testing my kind and generous nature, bloodsucker." By now he was snarling each word. If it weren't for Dacian's damn protective ward, he could sit at the top of the hill and blow a football-field-sized crater right here and wipe out the problem along with any evidence he had ever existed. The thought of violence made Ganymede feel all warm and fuzzy for a minute, and then he exhaled deeply as he picked up another shovel.

And all for a woman. But what a woman. She'd owe him for this. Big-time. He smiled at the thought of how he'd collect. Then he yanked his hood forward to block out more of the driving snow and dug faster.

Finally, he stopped to glance at his watch. Plenty of time before the bloodsucker rose. Even ancient night feeders—not that many of them survived long enough to qualify—couldn't rise before full dark.

He leaned on his shovel. Damn, he was sucking wind. He'd gotten soft lying around the Castle of Dark Dreams, watching TV and chowing down on chips and dip.

Okay, only a few more shovelfuls and he'd be able to jerk Dacian's undead ass out of his grave. He went over to retrieve the coffin. Once the vampire was inside, he'd nail down the lid so he wouldn't have to put up with any crap on the way back to Galveston.

A minute later, with a final grunt of effort, he flung the last shovelful of dirt out of the hole he'd dug . . .

And found himself staring into the wide-open eyes of one really pissed bloodsucker.

*Oh, shit!*

# Chapter One

"We're all about team at the Castle of Dark Dreams, Cinn." Sparkle seemed to think that needed an explanation. "A year ago those words wouldn't have passed my lips. I only cared about sex, clothes, and manipulating other people. I was a 'me' kind of person." She smiled wistfully. "Those were the good old days." She stopped smiling. "Forget I said that. Anyway, then I almost lost the love of my life, Mede. Something like that changes a person. I decided he deserved a honey who was more caring, less self-absorbed, someone worthy of him. So now I'm totally committed to the team, and I'm as happy as I can be."

Cinn could've sworn Sparkle forced that last sentence through clenched teeth.

"You're one of us now, so it's time you met the team managers." Sparkle glanced at her watch. "The guys will be here any moment. They make sure the castle runs smoothly. Of course, I'm the team owner, so I have the final say." She sipped her drink as she watched the entrance to Wicked Fantasy from her perch on a bar stool. She crossed her legs and her short black dress rode higher on her smooth thighs. Every man in the club inhaled at the same time.

Cinn tried not to think too hard about the weirdness of having a boss named Sparkle Stardust. She concentrated instead on the ordinary. This was a small intimate club in a fake castle. The fake castle was part of an adult theme park dedicated to fulfilling fantasies. There were a pirate ship, a Wild West Main Street, and a bunch of other settings that encouraged role-playing. It was just a Disney World for grown-ups. A clever marketing idea, but it didn't wander far from ordinary.

While she contemplated the complete *ordinariness* of her new job, three men entered the club. Two of them were so gorgeous they could bring tears to the eyes of the most dedicated man-hater. The third? Not so much. His blue robe decorated with gold moons, stars, and assorted other celestial bodies matched his tall conical blue hat. The hat added about a foot to his height, so he didn't look too much shorter than the others. Okay, she got it. The castle was for role-playing, so he was either a customer who liked to live his role or the castle's resident wacky wizard.

She forced her attention back to Sparkle and the team thing. "The team concept is great, but come on, I work with plants, Sparkle. What's the point? Plants don't have team spirit. We're loners. We don't do group activities."

Sparkle raised one perfectly shaped brow. "Now you're scaring me, sister. *We?* Please don't tell me you're one with your plants."

"No, but what I meant was that I won't be working with anyone. It'll just be me and my plants out there in that little greenhouse you set up. Oh, and thanks for connecting it to one of the kitchen doors so I don't have to run between the raindrops in bad weather."

Sparkle's amazing amber eyes widened. "Wherever did you get the idea that you'll be working alone? I'm sure lots of people will be fascinated by your plants. They already love Jessica and Sweetie Pie." She slid the tip of her tongue over her full bottom lip as she reached back with both hands to run her fingers through her heavy fall of red hair.

The bartender's Adam's apple bobbed at warp speed as he watched the lift and thrust.

"The castle is a hotel as well as a place to role-play. Hordes of guests will be interested once they find out what your plants can do." Sparkle grew thoughtful. "I bet mobs of tourists will sign up for a tour of your greenhouse. You can give them a brief rundown of your plants' talents."

"Hordes? Mobs?" Cinn went into panic mode. "Wait. I thought I was just here to develop a few plants with interesting traits for the castle. I didn't think I'd have to *talk* to anyone."

Sparkle's expression hinted she was doing a few mental eye-rolls. "I told you that Jessica and Sweetie Pie were huge hits. Everyone will want plants like them in their rooms. Get over your hermit complex, for heaven's sake. You're brilliant. Revel in it. Milk it for all the attention you can get."

Damn. Cinn opened her mouth to argue over her job description, but before she could get a word out, the three men she'd seen enter a moment ago reached the bar.

"Let's go somewhere a little more private." The one with the thick tawny hair jerked his thumb toward an empty corner table.

The guy was big. Toe-to-toe, Cinn would have to look up a long way to meet his gaze. Not that meeting his gaze was on her to-do list. His eyes were the same shade of amber as Sparkle's and had the same predatory gleam. But that was where the similarity ended.

Cinn would bet that Sparkle hunted men for a whole different reason than the guy staring at her now. He wore a short-sleeved T-shirt that exposed a grim reaper tattoo on one muscular bicep. It fit. She wouldn't want him hunting *her*.

Sparkle didn't argue. She slid from the bar stool and motioned for Cinn to follow her. Even though her boss hadn't said a word, Cinn got the feeling that Sparkle wasn't a huge fan of Mr. Big-Bad-and-Scary. Strange. She'd swear it wasn't team spirit zinging back and forth between these two.

Before Cinn could slide from her stool, strong hands lifted her and placed her firmly on the floor. She gasped and turned to look at the man beside her. "Thanks, I . . ." Forget the first man. Now *this* was wicked in its most basic form.

He smiled, a flash of white teeth in a face otherwise dedicated to darkness. She didn't know why she thought that. His eyes were deep blue, framed by long sooty lashes. His mouth was a sensual treat. She didn't usually notice men's mouths, but his was hard to ignore. And his face . . . What to say about it? His features were beautiful, and all that smoky-dark hair framing his face made it . . . not real? Dumb thought. Of course it was real. She was staring at it. But something hungry crouching behind all that beauty made her uneasy. Evil wearing that face would be deadly.

"You're the plant lady." His voice was warm and welcoming with a touch of sinister hiding in the bushes.

As she let him guide her to the corner table, she decided that his voice could convince sane women to do insane things.

Once seated, Cinn watched all of them watch her. The wizard leaned forward. She'd bet he intimidated lots of people with his narrowed gray eyes and long pointed gray beard.

"You, madam, are a pervert." He glared at Cinn.

Cinn blinked.

"Oh, stuff it, Holgarth." Sparkle sounded more resigned than shocked.

The wizard didn't back off. "You take perfectly nice plants and turn them into cheap voyeurs feeding on sleazy sex."

Okay, he'd gone too far. Cinn didn't look for trouble, but an attack on her plants brought out every one of her maternal instincts. "Now I know why you wear that hat. It's the only one that'll fit your pointy head." Fine, so she was acting immature, but this man triggered her inner brat. "If you knew anything, you'd know I expand my plants' horizons. I give each plant more options in life than just growing and dying." She dismissed him with an angry huff. "Some of them probably have higher IQs than you, but then that wouldn't be much of a stretch."

"Sleazy sex?" Sparkle hadn't gotten past those words yet. "I can't believe you said that, Holgarth. I've experienced some amazing sleazy sex."

Holgarth sniffed. "I'm sure you have." He turned his attention back to Cinn. "As the attorney for Live the Fantasy, I've advised Sparkle against turning mutant plants loose in the park. They're a lawsuit waiting to happen."

"*Mutant* plants?" This guy was Sparkle's *lawyer*?

"Exactly. Leafy savages capable of inflicting mental anguish on unsuspecting guests. And I wear many *different* hats, Ms. Airmid. I also oversee the managing of the castle." The threat was implicit—*Work here and I'll make your life miserable.*

"Look, we're wasting time." The guy with the grim reaper tattoo glanced at his watch. "Someone, somewhere needs to die, and I have to make sure it happens. So let's get the intro over. I'm Edge."

He reached across the table and offered his hand. Cinn automatically took it even though she was still trying to make sense of what he'd just said. His large hand engulfed hers. A little more pressure and he'd snap a few bones. He evidently wasn't in a bone-snapping mood tonight, because he released her. She dropped her hands into her lap, where she tried to rub away the numbness.

"Sparkle will fill you in on the details." Rising, he strode from the club.

"I'm Cinn . . ." Her voice trailed off. He couldn't hear her. She turned to Sparkle. "What did he mean by—?"

"That Edge, always joking." Sparkle's laughter sounded forced.

Doubts poked at Cinn's determination to make this job work. The offer had seemed like a great idea when Sparkle made it. With her family all in Oregon, Texas seemed like the perfect place to escape from their constant visits. She was tired of fending off demands that she abandon her experiments and fall in with family tradition. Airmids had always worked with plants, but not the way she did. Generations of Airmids had become horticulturalists, run landscaping businesses, and owned ordinary greenhouses.

Cinn was the exception, the only one who dared to tweak Mother Nature's nose by developing plants that went beyond accepted plant behavior. Mother Nature would eventually bring her hammer down, or at least that's what Cinn's family thought.

"Well, now that you've met Edge, we can move on to Bain." Sparkle's determined cheerfulness was fraying around the edges.

Bain smiled, and Cinn's train of thought derailed.

"Unlike Edge, I don't have places to be and things to do."

The sensual twist of those lips promised that if he did have things to do, they'd be a lot more interesting than what Edge had in mind.

Cinn grasped at something she understood, something familiar. "Intriguing name. The baneberry is an herb with poisonous berries. That's why *bane* means something that causes death or destruction." And here she'd promised herself she wouldn't bore people with plant stuff. But she refused to feel guilt. She'd bet this man could turn most women into babbling idiots.

He seemed to be giving her comment serious thought. "Different spelling. I spell my name with an *a-i-n.* Death and destruction, huh?" The idea evidently amused him, because his smile widened. "I like your spelling better."

What did he mean by that?

He leaned back in his chair. "I think your name's a lot more interesting than mine, though. How can a man resist a woman named Sin?"

If any other man handed her that line—and they had—she'd pencil him into her uncreative-jerk column. But there was something about the way the word *sin* rolled off his tongue, as though it were a gooey chocolate treat, one that he'd savor slowly and then lick off his fingers so he wouldn't miss one drop. It was that kind of feeling. She took a deep breath and tried to wipe the image from her mind. You couldn't tell anything about a man from the way he said one word. Could you?

She handed his answer back to him. "Different spelling. I spell my name with a *c* and two *n*'s."

"So Cinn is short for . . . ?"

"Cinnamon." She wanted to relax and smile, but she was having trouble doing both, with the chocolate image still clogging up her brain.

Sparkle tapped an impatient rhythm on the table with one shiny red nail. "Fine, so you're both named after herbs or spices or whatever. Awesome. Let's move on."

Cinn chose to ignore her. She was still focused on Bain. His lips and eyes weren't on the same page. Once again she was sure those gorgeous eyes hid darkness, a darkness completely separate from the polite interest he was showing in her. "My parents named my sisters and me after healing plants—Ginger, Belladonna, Willow, and me."

He tilted his head to study her. "Belladonna? Nightshade. Deadly."

"And also a medicinal extract." For the first time during this little meet-and-greet session, Cinn managed a sincere smile. "Many things wear two opposing faces." And if he took that personally, so be it.

His gaze sharpened and then his smile widened into the real deal. No hidden messages or sensual signals. "Very perceptive, Cinn. We'll get along fine." He glanced at his watch. "I lied. I do have someplace to be. I'm acting in the first fantasy."

Sparkle nodded absently, not even bothering to watch as he left. She was staring at Holgarth. "What's wrong? Only a few halfhearted insults? So not like you."

Holgarth took a moment to straighten his hat before answering. "You're right, of course. I have more serious things to think about than a woman who grows plants that feed on sexual energy." He exhaled wearily. "I'm considering retirement, Sparkle."

Sparkle sighed as though Holgarth was heading down a well-worn path. "You just won't let it go. Get this through your head: Ike wasn't your fault. This was a hurricane so huge it almost filled the Gulf of Mexico. Even you can't stop a force of nature that massive. You did what you could."

"That's precisely the point. I couldn't do enough. I saved the castle, but I couldn't help Bolivar Peninsula." Holgarth closed his eyes as if in pain. "I couldn't save the Balinese Room. All wiped away." He shook his head. "I heard Frank Sinatra sing at the Balinese Room." His hat slid to the side, but he didn't straighten it. "It was my pride. I thought I could do it all. I should have called in Ganymede to help. I'm too old, too weak to carry on my duties as the castle's wizard."

Okay, this was officially too far out there even for Cinn. This guy wasn't joking. He thought he was a real wizard. She wondered about the contract she'd signed. Maybe she should've read it a little more closely. Was there an escape clause?

Sparkle reached across the table to put her hand over his. "Of course you're not too old. The castle would be so much less . . . dynamic without you."

From the little she'd seen, Cinn thought the castle would do a happy dance if Holgarth left. But that was just her.

Holgarth opened his eyes. "No, you're not changing my mind. Starting tomorrow, I'll begin interviewing possible replacements—a nearly impossible task—for my job." Pushing his chair back, he stood, wrapped his robe more tightly around him, and swept from the room.

Sparkle turned troubled eyes Cinn's way. "Hurricane Ike devastated him as well as Galveston Island. Before the storm he was so secure in his power." She sounded like she actually believed all the wizardry talk. "Now he's just a shadow of his former self. Would you believe that you're the first person he's worked up the energy to insult since the storm?"

"Yay for me." Cinn didn't know if Sparkle heard her

muttered sarcasm, because her boss was already standing to leave.

"Well, the intros didn't go exactly as planned." She guided Cinn out to the hotel lobby and toward the door that would lead to the castle's great hall. Sparkle held the door open for her.

Cinn marveled at how guests could step back in time just by passing through this door. Behind it was an authentic-looking great hall complete with a massive fireplace, a long banquet table set on a dais, and stone walls covered with tapestries and ancient weapons, among other things. Customers could really get into their fantasies here. She knew from the brochure left in her room that several other areas of the castle were also reserved for fantasy sessions. Cinn hadn't been here long enough to explore anything but her room, the castle's restaurant, and Sparkle's Wicked Fantasy club.

But as exciting as everything around her was, Cinn's common sense was telling her there was something really weird going on. She needed to find somewhere else to work with her plants. "You know, now that I've had time to think, I've decided that maybe this job might not be the perfect fit for me."

Sparkle didn't seem surprised. "Look, I know the guys didn't make a great first impression, but I want you to meet one last manager. Then if you want out of your contract, you can give me the usual two-weeks' notice."

"Two weeks?" Not good. "I can still send you my plants no matter where I go, so why can't I just leave? I know you spent money on the greenhouse, but I can pay for that." Eventually. With many, many monthly payments.

"I've already put you on the castle's list of attractions. I'll need time to replace you." Sparkle attempted to look aggrieved while casting Cinn a sideways glance. "By the way, a good stylist could do wonders with your hair, and a few sexy outfits would . . ." Her voice faded away and she stood staring at nothing for a moment. Then she smiled as she returned her attention to Cinn. "I'm in control again. It's tough to break the habit of centu—, uh, years."

The mystery of what the hell Sparkle was talking about followed Cinn across the great hall to a dark doorway and down winding stone steps—lit only by wall sconces—that ended in a shadowy hallway. "Why wasn't this manager at the meeting?" Not that Cinn cared. She was counting on Sparkle releasing her from her contract before the two weeks were up. Then she'd get on the phone and beg for her old job back. Her family would be thrilled if she were once again close enough to harass daily.

"He has a few emotional issues right now, so he's pretty much keeping to himself." Her gaze skipped away from Cinn's. She stopped in front of a heavy wooden door. "This is the dungeon. We use it in our fantasies, but it's off limits until Dacian feels able to cope." She pulled out an old-fashioned key and shoved it into the keyhole.

This didn't sound promising. Emotional issues? Cope? Cinn noted the click of the lock. To keep Dacian in or others out? "Umm, maybe I should wait to meet him until he's feeling better."

"No, now is the right time."

Shadows played across Sparkle's face as she pushed open the door and stepped aside for Cinn to enter. Cinn barely registered Sparkle following her in, relocking the door, and then coming to stand beside her, because shock had frozen her in place.

A man was chained spread-eagled to the stone wall. No, not a man. Nothing human had fangs like that or eyes completely black with no white showing. Whatever he was, he was tall and muscular with long matted hair and wore nothing but what looked like a black silk scarf around his hips. A light sheen of sweat threw every straining muscle into relief, highlighting the scars criss-crossing his chest and stomach. Not bullet wounds. These had been slashing wounds. She shuddered.

He lifted his lips away from his fangs in a silent snarl. No need for him to make scary noises. He was already the star of her next fright fantasy.

"He's a big man." Sparkle slid her gaze the length of his body, lingering where the black scarf slowly slipped lower, inch by torturous inch. "And oh so dangerous. Dangerous men are sexy." She glanced at Cinn. "Don't you find that's true?"

Cinn's heart began beating again with a solid thunk. She turned to face Sparkle. "Okay, you got me. I bought into the reality for a moment. But if I were going to fantasize about a vampire, I'd make damn sure he looked better than that." She refused to turn to look at "that" again.

Something in Sparkle's smile made Cinn swallow hard.

"You're right. Most vampires are gorgeous, but I guess there's always the exception to the rule. Although who knows what he really looks like under all that hair, dirt, and scars? Mede brought him here directly from his grave." She moved closer to the "vampire." "He's a little crazy right now. I hope he comes out of it soon." Sparkle sighed. "I hope he comes out of it at all. He has a brother, Taurin, who's searched for him a long time. In fact, Taurin and his wife have just finished running down another false lead."

Behind her, the fake vampire hissed, and Cinn controlled the urge to bolt. Things were getting a little too bizarre for her.

"Mede got a tip on Dacian's location three days ago and went to check it out. He showed up at the castle with Dacian a few hours ago. We're not quite sure where Taurin is right now, so we can't give him the news. Considering Dacian's condition, maybe it's better this way. Taurin and his wife will be back at the castle in a few days."

"Uh . . ." No words came. Sparkle wasn't joking. She was freaking *serious*.

"Then Mede and I will have to make a decision." Sparkle's expression said it wasn't a decision she looked forward to. "If we can get Dacian coherent and cleaned up, we'll reunite him with his brother."

"And if not?" Cinn didn't know why she was whispering. A quick glance at the guy—she would *not* accept that he was anything else—didn't show any awareness gleaming in those scary black eyes.

"We'll destroy him." Cold and emotionless, this was a new face of Sparkle Stardust. "Right now he's a danger to himself and anyone near him. It would devastate Taurin to see his brother like this." She shrugged. "It would be kinder to allow him to keep searching and to never find Dacian."

Cinn felt like Sparkle's words had sucked every bit of air from her lungs. Her boss was calmly discussing murder. "You can't kill him." She edged toward the door. If she escaped, she wouldn't stop running until she got to the police station.

Sparkle looked puzzled. "Of course I can't. He's already dead. I can destroy him, though. If nothing's left of his mind, it would be a kindness to Taurin and to him." She watched Cinn's slow creep to the door. "I wouldn't bother if I were you. The door's locked, and I have the key."

Cinn ignored her in favor of yanking on the door. Right. Locked. She pounded on the wood and shouted, "Help! I'm locked in here with a maniac. Someone get me out!"

"The wood's a foot thick and the room is sound-proofed. No one will hear you," Sparkle offered help-fully.

Cinn abandoned the door. She pulled her cell phone from her pants pocket and blessed the habit that never allowed her to go anywhere without it. Frantically, she hit 911.

Sparkle had a patient expression pasted on her face. "You won't get a signal down here."

Cinn shoved the useless phone back into her pocket. She eyed Sparkle. The woman was taller than her, but Cinn was in good shape from digging, planting, and toting bags of fertilizer.

Sparkle smiled. "Don't even think about it, sister. You along with all your friends and family couldn't take me down. But hey, if you want to try, knock yourself out."

Cinn wanted to try. She flung herself at Sparkle. About a foot from her goal, she smacked into an invisi-ble wall. She couldn't see it, but it was damn well there. After pounding her fists on it and delivering a few kicks that only served to hurt her toe, she backed away from Sparkle.

"Good. Now that you've gotten that out of your sys-tem, we can get down to business." Sparkle hopped onto a table with a bunch of ominous-looking straps. Cross-ing her legs, she motioned for Cinn to join her.

Cinn shook her head. "I'll stand." She tried to quiet her frenzied thoughts so she could think. But her mind refused to stop circling the invisible wall. "Say what you have to say so I can get out of here." She wouldn't think about the possibility that Sparkle might not intend to release her. But just in case, she scanned the area for a weapon. Whips, chains, and a bunch of other torture implements. Hmm. She could do some damage with that small ax.

Sparkle laughed. "Give it up, Cinn. The only real things in here are the chains keeping Dacian from trying to suck us dry."

Cinn slanted a quick glance at Dacian. Who knew that eyes so black could look like they were burning? She swore she could almost see the flames behind his enraged glare.

"So here's the deal. Yes, vampires do exist, along with lots of other nonhumans. Edge and I are cosmic troublemakers. My specialty is creating sexual chaos throughout the universe. Edge is the cosmic troublemaker in charge of death. You can guess what he does. Bain is a demon, and yes, Holgarth is a real wizard." She held up her hand to stop Cinn from interrupting. "Let me finish."

Cinn had no intention of interrupting. No way could she talk with her jaw dragging on the floor.

"I sense a kindred spirit in you." Sparkle dangled one lethal-looking stiletto from her toe as she swung her leg back and forth.

"I don't think so." Somehow Cinn had ended up between Sparkle the psycho and Dacian the undead. At least Dacian was in chains, so she took a step back toward him.

"Cinn, Cinn." Sparkle shook her head. "Self-deception is always sad." She leaned forward.

Cinn took another step back. She thought about the

weird things that Edge, Bain, and Holgarth had said. Now Sparkle seemed just as crazy. Mass delusions? *Uh, remember the invisible wall? Felt sort of real.* Nope, couldn't be real. She slammed shut the door in her mind that might be open to possibilities and folded her arms under her breasts to keep her pounding heart from leaping out of her chest and bouncing around the dungeon. How the hell was she going to get out of here?

Sparkle laughed, a soft husky sound that right now seemed pretty threatening to Cinn.

"Calm down. All I want you to do is to hear me out and then think about what I said. I intended to do the big reveal gradually so I wouldn't scare you to death, but now that you want to quit I don't have a choice. When I'm finished with what I have to say, you can leave the room."

Sparkle tried to look harmless, but Cinn figured Sparkle never had a harmless minute in her life. "Fine. Spit it out and then I'm out of here." Right now her pushy family was looking good.

As Cinn waited for Sparkle to spout more lunacy, she felt a tentative fluttering in her mind. It was questioning and unsure, but it was a definite presence. Vince? Was it possible? Had he sensed her fear over the distance between the dungeon and the greenhouse? Had her fear finally driven him to reach out?

"I'll try to say this in a way that won't terrify you." Sparkle pursed her full lips, making the act of thinking into an erotic invitation. "But there are some things that just have to be said with no sugarcoating."

There it was again. Stronger this time. Cinn held her breath as the fluttering became a careful probing. Vince was trying to analyze her emotions. She was sure of it. She forced herself to relax, to send peaceful thoughts his way. And after a few seconds the presence receded and was gone.

"You, Cinn Airmid, have supernatural powers given to you by your family's namesake, the Celtic goddess Airmid." Sparkle held up both hands. "Now don't start crying and going hysterical on me. Let me explain . . ." She frowned. "Why are you smiling? You're supposed to be overcome with panic and disbelief."

Cinn shook her head, bemused by the wonder of what had just happened. "I'll be overcome with panic and disbelief in a moment. Something incredible just happened."

Sparkle didn't look happy. Evidently she'd been hoping for a lot more frenzy and fear.

"Vince just connected with me mentally." Cinn knew she must have a silly grin pasted on her face. "He sensed my emotional turmoil."

"Vince? Is he an assistant? I don't remember agreeing to pay an assistant." She looked outraged at the thought.

Cinn's breath caught at the wonder of it all. "Vince is my vinca minor."

Sparkle looked blank.

"A periwinkle, Sparkle. He's one of my *plants*."

# *Chapter Two*

The routine was always the same. Dacian struggled free of the madness even as he silently cursed his maker. After the cursing came the questions. How long had the rage lasted this time? Had he killed anyone along the way? He seemed to remember reaching Big Bend National Park before Stephan had mentally hit him with the usual demand: *Come back to me.* Yeah, like that was going to happen.

And then when Dacian had refused, Stephan took his mind and twisted it into uncontrollable patterns of anger until his head felt ready to explode with his need to kill. That was where Dacian's memories stopped until he emerged from the long dark tunnel of his insane fury.

Careful not to give any hint of returning awareness, Dacian took stock. Chained to a freaking wall. No windows. Big-ass door. Probably locked. Two women. Unarmed.

For the first time, he felt like smiling. He didn't have a clue where he was or why two unarmed women were in the room with him, but if he could break the chains, the unarmed part would give him a huge advantage.

"Wait. You said I have *supernatural* powers from Airmid?" The woman facing away from him took a step backward. "That's crazy. In fact, all this paranormal stuff you and the rest of your people have spouted tonight is crazy."

He sensed a silent, *"You're* crazy," in there some-where.

"Come on, Cinn, stop fooling yourself."

The woman facing him had long red hair and strange amber eyes. Perched on a table decorated with enough restraints to hold down King Kong, she practically oozed sexual power. Nonhuman. Amazing that this Cinn woman couldn't sense it.

"I don't know what you're talking about. I do a little experimenting with plants. So what? People blame lots of things that happen on the supernatural. Then scientists find a perfectly logical explanation." Cinn sounded as though she was trying to convince herself. She took another careful step backward.

He controlled his urge to lick his lips. When she got close enough, he'd throw everything he had into one effort to escape his chains. Then he'd grab the little plant experimenter and heave her at the red-haired bitch. While they were trying to untangle themselves, he'd rip the door from its hinges and deal with what was on the other side. He had to get out of here fast so he could find Taurin.

"Let's get things straight, sister." The redhead sounded pissed. "You supply plants that feed on sexual energy to the Castle of Dark Dreams. A plant in your greenhouse just stuck its vine into your mind. That is *not* normal. And there isn't any damn scientific explanation for what you do. So stop thinking there is. No amount of splicing and fertilizing could produce the babies you have out in that greenhouse. Wake up and smell the supernatural."

*The Castle of Dark Dreams?* How the hell had that happened? Not a coincidence. He didn't believe in them. But he wasn't going to question fate. This was where he was supposed to be. Now all he had to do was get free, find Taurin, and haul his ass to somewhere safe, somewhere Stephan couldn't reach him.

Not as easy as he made it sound. From the chains, he'd guess there were nonhumans—because humans alone couldn't have done this—who didn't want him to leave. He hoped they didn't work for Stephan. No way did he want to be delivered to his maker wrapped up like some preholiday present.

Cinn took another step back. "Why are you doing this, Sparkle? As long as I deliver the plants you want, why does it matter how I feel about my work?"

Sparkle? He stopped himself from snorting. The woman with the great ass and warm brown hair—that was all he could see of Cinn from this angle—sounded almost scared. Not that it mattered to him. All he wanted from her were a few more steps back.

"Because I want you to be more than you think you can be. And yes, I speak in clichés, because they tend to be true. I want you to feel safe to talk about your work, knowing that everyone around you understands the woo-woo aspects of what you do and respects you for it."

"*Woo-woo* aspects?" Cinn sounded outraged.

Damn, she didn't step back this time. He guessed Sparkle's comment had cemented her to the floor.

Sparkle shrugged. "Admit it: your family doesn't appreciate you. I bet you scare the crap out of them with some of your experiments. Don't you think I know why you accepted a job in Texas? I've been around for thousands of years, sister. Not much gets by me."

Thousands of years? Dacian upgraded the possibility that this Sparkle might turn into a pain in the ass. Someone who'd survived that long must have serious powers.

*"Thousands* of years?"

Shock drove Cinn back those two final steps he needed. Dacian concentrated his power on the chains attached to the cuffs around his wrists and then yanked. The chains were strong, but there was always a weak link. In all things. And not much could hold him when he focused his energy. Both chains broke. And before either woman could react, he'd bent down and snapped the chains holding his legs.

Between the moment he freed himself and the one in which he prepared to spring at Cinn, two things happened. Cinn turned to stare at him. He had an instant impression of warm brown hair shaded with blonde and big hazel eyes wide with horror. He couldn't see her mouth, because she'd clapped a hand over it, probably to hold back a scream of terror. She had it right. He was a thing to be feared. And if there was a flash of bitterness in the thought, well, it didn't matter. Only his freedom mattered.

And Sparkle spoke. "Uh, Mede, I think now would be a good time." She sounded mildly concerned.

Distracted from his attack for a second, he glanced at Sparkle and then followed her gaze to a shadowed corner of the dungeon where a big black-and-white cat padded into view. It had the same damn eyes as Sparkle, a weird amber color. And that was all he had time to observe before he heard the voice in his head.

*"Okay, big guy, time to cool it and listen to what I have to say."* The cat glanced at Sparkle. *"The trolls guaranteed those chains would hold any vampire on Earth. They ripped you off. Return the weak-ass suckers and ask for a refund."* Then he turned his attention back to Dacian.

Dacian had to make a decision: attack or listen. There were now two nonhumans in the room, and he had no idea what waited outside that door. Not good odds. If they'd wanted him dead, they could've destroyed him while he was helpless. And he was in the castle where Jim had said he'd find Taurin. He paid the guy good money to keep track of his brother, and he had no reason to doubt him.

Jim was a retired CIA agent, so when he'd gotten wind that Taurin was in danger, that Stephan had found his brother's location and would kill him to punish Dacian for refusing his maker's call, Dacian didn't hesitate. Time was important. If he managed to escape, he'd have to flee the building and then figure out how to contact his brother. His decision made, Dacian dropped his clawed hands and backed away from his attack. "So talk."

Cinn had turned panicked eyes toward the cat, so he must be broadcasting his mental message to everyone. Not an easy thing to do.

"Chat with the vampire *after* you let me out of here." Her gaze skittered between the cat and the door. "And I can't believe I'm talking to a cat."

The plant lady was making a real effort to keep her voice from shaking, but Dacian's enhanced hearing picked up the faint vibrations. If he weren't such a heartless bastard, he might even feel sorry for her.

"So you can run away?" Sparkle didn't seem upset by the thought.

"Yes."

Sparkle shrugged. "Okay, go. Although if you give yourself some time to think about this, you'll realize that working here is best for you. Not only will you be able to work without having to explain yourself to nosy relatives, but you might be able to expand your experiments beyond the plants."

"How?" Cinn's expression said she asked the question against her better judgment.

The plant lady's spark of curiosity might be her undoing. Dacian sensed Sparkle beginning to close her net.

"Well, for one thing, you might be able to help Dacian here. And I might be able to turn you into a sensual woman." Sparkle frowned. "Forget that last comment. I don't do that anymore. I keep forgetting."

Cinn swallowed hard as she shifted her gaze to Dacian. She'd taken her hand from her mouth. God, the woman had a great mouth. It was a testament to how hot those lips were that he could even notice them in this situation. But then, he hadn't had sex in a long time, so any woman's lips would look great.

She didn't say anything, but he figured she thought sticking with her plants would be a safer bet. She'd be right.

Ignoring all the negative vibes ricocheting off the stone walls, Sparkle forged onward. "He's a vampire. Human medicine can't help him control whatever spell turns him into a dangerous animal."

Spell? Cinn would think that just *being* a vampire made him a dangerous animal. No spells needed.

"But you have power given to you by Airmid. You might be able to find a way to help him. Maybe whip up an herbal cocktail that could stop the episodes before they started." Sparkle looked hopeful.

Cinn blinked. "I doubt it. Now can I go?"

Heartless bitch. Even as Dacian passed judgment on her, he admitted she was probably right. Stephan was the only one who could stop his episodes.

"I know this is all overwhelming, Cinn. I wanted to ease you into the more . . . interesting aspects of the castle, but," Sparkle tried on a regretful expression, "things didn't turn out the way I'd planned. I'm sure when you get to know everyone, you'll feel right at home here."

"No."

Sparkle ignored her. "And once Dacian takes a shower and puts his fangs away I'm sure you'll find that he's a really nice guy."

"I'm *not* a nice guy. I've *never* been a nice guy. And if someone doesn't start explaining what's going on, I'm going to tear out a few throats."

"*Shut up, bloodsucker.*" The cat hissed at him.

"No." Cinn was standing firm.

"Well, I wasn't going to mention this, because hey, I didn't want to scare you . . ."

"Could've fooled me." Cinn's muttered comment was meant to be heard.

Sparkle forged on. "But Airmid has gotten wind of what you've been doing, and she's really pissed. In fact, she's on her way to your home in Oregon right now to put a major hurting on your plant-mutating ass. That's really why I brought you here now. We can protect you." She shrugged. "Just letting you know."

"You're lying." But there was a note of uncertainty in Cinn's voice. "This whole thing is one giant con. I don't know how you did it or why you did it, but I want out."

Sparkle glanced at the cat and nodded. The cat stared at the door and it swung slowly open. Without a backward look, Cinn almost ran from the dungeon. Dacian was tempted to follow her out but decided at the last moment to stay. He'd take the chance that they didn't intend to separate his head from his shoulders. According to Jim, Taurin worked at the castle, so they'd know where he was. Dacian watched the door swing shut and heard the click of the lock.

*"Not too smart, cuddle-bunny."* The cat's gaze returned to Sparkle.

Cuddle-bunny? Dacian almost laughed, but he controlled the urge. It was a matter of survival. You didn't laugh when you wanted to convince the enemy you were a bigger badass than they were.

*"You went to all that trouble to get her here, and now you're letting her walk away. And she'll talk."*

"No one will listen." Sparkle hopped off of the table and walked over to stand in front of Dacian.

The sway of those hips qualified as a lethal weapon. And like a weapon, she used it deliberately. He sort of liked how Cinn moved better. Just as sexy, but not calculated. He let a frisson of anticipation warm him. He'd like to taste Cinn, in all ways. Then he banished the thought. Sex didn't have a place in his business here.

*"But she's* leaving." The cat couldn't get past that fact. *"I would've made her stay."* He twitched his tail, and the gleam in his cat eyes suggested he would've enjoyed the whole making-her-stay process.

Sparkle sighed. "She's *not* leaving. I had her little greenhouse locked down tight right before I met her at Wicked Fantasy. Cinn won't go anywhere without her precious plants."

The cat joined her. *"Hmmph. Might work. I like the direct approach better. Threaten her with a slow agonizing death if she doesn't stay. No, I've got something even worse. Lock her in a room with Holgarth. She wouldn't last a day."*

Sparkle's laughter was soft and sexy. "I'm doing something almost as delightfully cruel. At the same time I locked down Cinn's plants, I ordered Asima to stay with her at all times." Her eyes gleamed. "They'll both hate it. A double scoop of mean from Sparkle Stardust. It doesn't get much better."

The cat coughed. *"Umm, sweetie, you asked me to remind you if you were wading into shallow water again."*

Sparkle frowned. "Oh, of course. I'm not supposed to enjoy the misery of others." She sighed. "I'll try not to have too much fun watching them poke holes in each other."

She reached up to brush a strand of hair away from Dacian's face. He showed fang as a warning.

"Mmm. Aggressive. I like that in a man." She smiled as she dropped her gaze to the cloth around his hips. "I'm sorry all you have to wear is my itty-bitty scarf. But the black silk matches your eyes. At least you're color coordinated. Take care of the scarf, because I want it back."

The cat snorted. *"Give it a rest, Sparkle."* He offered Dacian a man-to-cat stare. *"She wants me to stop her when she starts acting like the old Sparkle Stardust: a manipulating, fashion- and sex-obsessed, all-around shallow bitch. Personally, I think she was a lot more fun when she was dedicated to eternal shallowness. But that's just me. I need a cookie."* He glanced longingly at the door.

Enough of this crap. Dacian speared each of them with a hard stare. *"Who* are you? *What* are you? And why did you bring me here?" *And where the hell is Taurin?*

Reaching down, Sparkle picked up the cat and cuddled him between her impressive breasts. The cat's expression brightened. A lot. He didn't mention the cookie again.

"I'm Sparkle Stardust and this is Ganymede. We're cosmic troublemakers, powerful beings in charge of—"

*"Everything."* The cat managed to look superior even peering out from between her breasts. *"At least I am. I'm the most powerful of the troublemakers."*

"Edge thinks *he* is," Sparkle reminded him.

Ganymede's whiskers twitched. *"He's nothing next to me. For tens of thousands of years I've created chaos throughout the universe."*

Dacian narrowed his gaze on the cat. Probably a shifter. "What are you when you're not being a cat?"

*"Anything I want to be, bloodsucker. But I like being a cat. Cats can sneak around and find out things. People aren't afraid to tell secrets in front of cats."* He wiggled his butt into a more comfortable position. *"Usually I'm a black or gray cat, but I decided on black-and-white this time because I'm feeling conflicted about Sparkle's nutty plan to make herself into someone she's not."*

Sparkle's deep sigh made Ganymede's eyes glaze over for a second. He recovered quickly, though.

*"Okay, enough of me. This is about you. Here's the deal. Your brother's been looking for you for a lotta years. Since he works for Sparkle, we've sort of kept an eye out for info about you.*

*"A tip came in a few days ago from someone who said he worked for you. He claimed that you'd paid him to keep an eye on Taurin. He swore he was telling me this because it was the right thing to do, that he wanted to reunite you guys. Figured he was playing me, but I decided to check things out anyway. He said you'd holed up in Alaska. Couldn't give me an address, but I'm an awesome tracker. I found where you'd been, but you weren't there anymore. Trailed you to Big Bend National Park."* He paused to study Dacian. *"Remember anything about what happened there?"*

"Nothing." How had Ganymede tracked him over all those miles between Alaska and Texas? And why had Jim contacted him? Jim hadn't seemed like a sentimental kind of guy.

*"Good, uh, I mean, that's tough."* His cat eyes gleamed.

*"You'd dug yourself a nice cozy grave and put up some half-ass puny ward. I took my human form and used my amazing power to blow you right out of that grave. You were out of your head crazy, but with my preternatural strength, I slung you over my shoulder and lugged you back to the castle."*

Sparkle did some serious eye-rolling. "Last year I would've let that lie scoot right past me, but since I'm trying to build character this year, I have to be honest. My sweetie had to dig you up with a shovel and then fight you every inch of the way back here. He never could get you into the nice new coffin I sent along."

Ganymede hissed at her. *"I liked you a lot better when you had zero character."*

"And you did all this out of the goodness of your hearts?" Call him cynical, but Dacian figured most people had an angle.

*"Taurin will owe me. Besides, Sparkle wanted you, and I always give my evil lady what she wants."*

Okay, that was Ganymede's angle. Now for Sparkle.

"I'm trying to be less shallow, so I guess my quest for personal depth starts with you." She offered Dacian a smile that should've melted the chains right off the wall.

It didn't. He wondered what Cinn's smile looked like. His thoughts turned sour. She probably only smiled when she was planting seeds. "Why'd you chain me to the wall?"

Ganymede's tail whipped back and forth. *"You're kidding, right? No way could we turn a berserk bloodsucker loose in the castle."*

Sparkle added, "The tourist board would take away our five-star rating like that"—she snapped her fingers—"if they found drained guests littering the halls. This was the only place secure enough to hold you. Mede broke a sweat chaining you to the wall. Your clothes—and I use the term loosely—were bloody and torn. Mede had to cut them off you because you were too out of control to unchain. I contributed my scarf to the cause in case of visitors." She smiled. "What a shame to cover what is definitely your best feature."

Ganymede hissed.

Sparkle put her finger over her lips. "Oops. Sorry. That was the old me. The new me didn't even notice your excellent package."

Dacian had to say something in his own defense. "I feed from animals most of the time." Except when he needed a power boost. Like now.

Sparkle held up her palms. "See, there you are. An immediate problem. How would we explain all the missing shape-shifters?"

Okay, time to change the subject. "Where's Taurin?"

*"Away. Somewhere in Europe. He'll be home soon. But we need to know what you've been doing for the last couple of hundred years before we let you join our happy family."* Something dangerous moved in the cat's eyes.

Dacian thought about how much to tell them. Bare bones. That was all they needed to know. "I've been trying to avoid my maker."

"Why?" Sparkle leaned forward, and Ganymede sank deeper. He purred.

Dacian thought Sparkle's excitement didn't bode well for him. Just a feeling. "Stephan has a god complex. Nothing short of world domination will make him happy. He's been trying to call me home to help him. I don't want to go."

*"Bastard,"* Ganymede commiserated.

Sparkle looked like she wanted to ask more questions, but Dacian didn't give her a chance. "Can I get out of here?"

*"Do you know where 'here' is?"* Ganymede sounded wary.

"The Castle of Dark Dreams. Your informant was right about me keeping track of Taurin."

Ganymede just nodded. Dacian could read all of the cat's unasked questions in his eyes. He had a few of his own. But now wasn't the time for any more questions or answers. He needed to feed so he could think clearly.

Ganymede glanced at the door and it opened. *"I've sent for Holgarth. He'll take you to a room. We'll send something up for you to drink—from a bottle, not the hotel employee. Can we trust you not to go wacko on us while you're here?"*

"I get some warning. If I feel anything coming on, I'll let you lock me back up."

*"Good enough for now. We'll talk again later."* Ganymede glanced up at Sparkle. *"You can put me down now, babe."* He sounded sad about that.

As Sparkle set the cat on the floor, a short thin man wearing a blue robe decorated with stars and a matching pointed hat stepped through the doorway. His long pointed beard almost quivered with distaste, and his eyes were frosty with disapproval.

"Oh, goody, the demented undead has a moment of lucidity." He strode over to hand Dacian what looked like a monk's robe. "Put this on. When I take you through the great hall everyone will think you're part of the ongoing fantasy." He sniffed. "Ah, the sweet scent of Mother Earth. May I suggest you shower as soon as you get to your room?"

Dacian was just wrapping the robe around himself when Sparkle reached out and whipped the scarf from his hips. "Pure silk. I'm still shallow enough to want this back."

Holgarth huffed his disdain. "Well, at least I can't criticize your taste in clothing because you have no clothing. And I've never seen a vampire with scars like yours. Where . . . ?"

Dacian didn't give him a chance to finish his question. Pulling the robe tightly around him, he strode from the dungeon, forcing Holgarth to follow him.

Sparkle narrowed her eyes as she watched the vampire leave. "There's a lot he didn't tell us."

Mede leaped onto the iron maiden and began washing his face. *"I'll root around in his mind later. He's powerful, but he won't be able to keep me out when I want in."*

"He's a night feeder, so why is he so powerful? They're usually the jackals of the vampire world, strictly scavengers. No night feeder should've been able to snap those chains." She was intrigued, and she hadn't felt this energized since she'd decided to become a woman with depth and character. "And all those scars." She allowed herself a delicious shudder. "They're kind of sexy in a primal savage way."

Before Mede could open his mouth, she waved his comment away. "I know. Thinking about sex was the old me. The new me should get past it. Well, climbing out of the shallow end of the pool is tough. And it's not fun." She pursed her lips in a pout. Her puckered lips always drove Mede crazy. Too bad. Let him suffer the way she was suffering.

*"I need a cookie."* He held her with a fixed stare.

She knew her smile was taunting and sensual, but she didn't give a damn. She'd climb back on the character-building wagon tomorrow. "I just bet you do."

He glanced away. *"I think the bloodsucker was headed here when I dug him up. Why? He went to all that trouble to fake his death in that fire two hundred years ago. He never contacted Taurin in all that time. Now he's resurrecting himself from the dead. Gotta be something important.*" Ganymede's expression said he hoped the reason involved death and destruction.

"I wonder what kind of sex life Cinn has?"

Mede blinked at the sudden change of subject.

"Oh, I know it shouldn't matter to the new me, but I just . . . wonder." Sparkle was having a tough time suppressing the meddling instincts she'd honed to a razor's edge over the centuries. "Not that it's important." She forced her thoughts elsewhere. "I can't wait to explore possibilities with her plants. I bet I can guide her research in all kinds of interesting directions." She hurried to correct any false impressions. "Not sexual. Umm, maybe her plants could help to foster world peace."

Mede snorted.

"Just saying." She shrugged.

Mede had evidently had enough. He leaped from the iron maiden and padded to the door. He paused before leaving. "*Give it up, babe. Look at you, you're miserable. You weren't meant to have character depth. You're the freaking cosmic troublemaker in charge of causing sexual chaos in the universe. You can't escape your destiny.*"

"But I—"

"*And if you're doing it for me, forget it. I liked the old you. I miss the whining over a chipped nail, the rush you got from a sale at the mall, the constant nattering about sex.*" He looked mournful. "*I really liked the sex talk. And I long for my old playful sweetie who loved finding two people who were completely wrong for each other, exciting them into a sexual frenzy for each other, and then tearing them apart. You were fun back then.*"

If she hadn't known better, Sparkle could almost believe that it was overflowing emotion making his eyes glisten. But Mede didn't believe in tears.

"*Forget character. I have the character of a gnat. It's just not an important quality for a cosmic troublemaker to have.*" He ended with a heartrending plea: "*I want my evil woman back so we can live the wicked life together again. It's lonely being bad alone.*"

Sparkle stood staring at the doorway long after he'd padded away. *She* had nothing against tears, at least not nowadays. She hadn't cried for thousands of years, and now she couldn't seem to stop. She swiped at her eyes. Good thing she hadn't given up waterproof mascara.

She sighed as she walked toward the door. What to do? Mede wanted the old Sparkle back, but the Big Boss had used the old Sparkle against Mede. And the Big Boss was in charge of them all. She couldn't give the Big Boss an excuse to interfere in their lives again.

She brightened a little. Maybe she'd do some compromising. Why couldn't she build character at the same time she did a little meddling? God knew that both Cinn and Dacian needed an upgrade in their quality of life. She could do that.

With renewed purpose, she strode from the dungeon. And if sex happened during her meddling, well, was it her fault? Of course not.

She hummed "Wicked Game" as she made her plans.

# Chapter Three

Murder was an option. She'd claim justifiable homicide. No jury in the country would convict her. Cinn took a deep breath before once again rattling the greenhouse door. Yep, locked. The witch. No wonder she'd been so calm when Cinn had left the dungeon. See, now Sparkle had overplayed her hand. She'd had Cinn scared witless, but fury had pushed the fear aside for the moment. No one kept her from her plants.

She'd backed her truck up to the greenhouse, ready to load her plants, so now she climbed into the cab, looking for something she could use to break a window. She came up with a hammer. Good. She'd free her plants and then maybe she'd use the hammer on Sparkle's head.

Returning to the greenhouse, she flung back her arm, ready to crunch some glass.

*"This is all very entertaining, and I certainly don't want to interfere with your breaking-and-entering plans, but I would like to point out that Sparkle will prosecute. And since there are security cameras everywhere, Holgarth will have all the proof he needs. Even he couldn't lose this case."*

The voice in Cinn's head swung her around. *Not* Ganymede's voice. This voice was light and feminine with a built-in snootiness. This woman—she looked down—this *cat* sounded just as superior as the other cat.

Cinn was too angry to feel intimidated. "Let me guess. You're Ganymede's sister."

The Siamese cat widened her almond-shaped eyes in horror. *"What a dreadful thing to say to someone you just met."* She sniffed a delicate cat sniff. *"And here I was, trying to help you."*

Cinn didn't care about the cat's bruised feelings. "Look, the plants inside this place are mine. I'm reclaiming my property."

*"I don't think the judge will see it that way. And if he does, Ganymede will change his mind. Literally."*

If what Cinn had seen so far at the castle was real and not a hallucination brought on by eating the castle restaurant's medieval meat pie—huge, and no, she hadn't needed a doggy bag afterward—then the cat was right. Reluctantly, she resigned herself to a less violent solution. "Who are you?" Amazing that she could ask that so calmly.

*"I'm Asima, messenger of the goddess Bast and the only devotee of the arts in this whole castle."* She sat and wrapped her tail around her elegant body. She stared at Cinn with deep blue eyes. *"Dare I hope that you're interested in the theater or perhaps the opera?"*

"I've seen a few Broadway plays." Why was Cinn standing here talking to another cat? She had to get her plants away from this freak show. Once she drove across the causeway to the mainland, she was never coming back. "What do you want from me?" Because she had a feeling everyone here wanted something.

Asima lifted her finely chiseled, aristocratic head so she could meet Cinn's gaze. *"I'd like to be your friend."* She glanced away. *"And Sparkle told me to keep an eye on you."*

Aha! "You're a snitch."

*"I prefer intelligence agent."*

Cinn knew she should just get in her truck and leave

now, but she couldn't abandon her babies to Sparkle. No way would anyone but Cinn know how to care for them. They'd die. And that *wasn't* an option.

Besides, Cinn had signed a contract. Now that she was calmer, she realized if she drove away, not only would she owe Sparkle for the greenhouse, but she'd also have to pay back the money Sparkle had advanced her to make the move to Galveston. She didn't have that kind of cash to lose.

With a sigh, she surrendered to the inevitable. She'd give Sparkle her two weeks' notice. And if after that Sparkle didn't honor her agreement, Cinn would hire a lawyer. One who *didn't* have a pointed hat with celestial bodies on it.

*"Well?"* Asima sounded impatient.

"Okay, you can tell Sparkle she won. For two weeks. After that I'm out of here." Cinn resisted the urge to bend down and touch the cat, just to make sure she was real. No touching, no thinking, no reacting until she was safe in her room. Well, as safe as she could be in this hotbed of weirdness. Then she'd try to wrap her mind around the whole bizarre night. She turned toward her truck.

Climbing in, Cinn reached for the ignition key.

*"Personally, I prefer a luxury vehicle. During the few times a year I return to human form, I rent a Lexus."*

With a startled squeak, Cinn jerked her gaze to the passenger side. Asima sat there. Her aloof expression implied she was a queen riding on a hay wagon.

"How the hell did you get in here?"

Asima yawned. *"I go where I wish to go. Not that I wished to go here, but a good intelligence agent goes where she must."*

Oh, boy. Cinn tried to ignore the cat as she parked the truck and then took the elevator up to her room. She wasn't in the mood to climb the winding stone steps to her floor.

Cinn stopped at her door. Wicked Intentions. Every room in the castle had a name, and they all began with the word *wicked*. After meeting Sparkle, she found it fitting.

She looked down at Asima, who stared up at her expectantly. "No, you can't come in with me. If you beam yourself into my room without my permission, I'll crack your little head with a lamp."

Asima made a disappointed mewling sound. *"Well, if you're going to get violent, then I suppose I'll have to wait outside your door. In the cold, cold hallway."*

"The hallway is warm."

*"And sleep on the hard, hard floor."*

"It's your choice."

*"You're a cruel . . ."*

Wait for it, wait for it . . .

*"But I suppose technically Sparkle is the cruel, cruel woman."*

"What a crappy day." Cinn paused. "No, make that a crappy, crappy day." Unlocking her door, she stepped inside and closed it in the cat's face.

Flinging herself onto her bed, she covered her eyes with her hand while her brain feverishly played back what had happened tonight. She could keep the Good Ship Denial afloat for just so long before it sank beneath the weight of piled-up proof. Right now she was sinking fast.

Okay, she could dismiss Edge, Bain, and Holgarth because they hadn't *done* anything. Talk didn't mean anything. But the other stuff . . .

If Dacian's fangs and eyes were fake, then whoever had made them was a genius. She'd gotten a close-up of the fangs. They were too long to be human teeth filed to a point, and she would've been able to tell if they were fakes. And his eyes . . . She shuddered. The last time she'd looked at him, all the rage in the world lived in those eyes. Nothing phony about them. So put a check in the real column for Dacian.

Next, Sparkle. No matter how much Cinn wanted to believe that the invisible wall hadn't been there, she couldn't. She'd pounded and kicked it. Another check beside real.

Finally, the two cats. Even if the cats had been wired for sound, no one could make cats act the way they had. Cinn knew cats. They didn't take direction well. Another check beside real.

Cinn wouldn't examine what Sparkle had said about Airmid. She'd accepted all her mind would allow for the night.

The bottom line was that she was stuck here for two weeks. She'd spend as much time as possible with her plants and as little time as she could with the people living in the castle.

With that decision made, she climbed from the bed, peeled off her coat, and dragged herself into the bathroom.

A short time later she emerged wearing her warm nightgown and her fuzzy slippers. The comforting familiarity of both made her feel better. Climbing into bed, she propped herself up and buried herself in the latest plant journals. She hoped she'd read until she fell asleep.

An hour later, she'd read exactly four pages and felt as though she'd never sleep again. At least not in this place. What if the people she'd met were just the tip of the iceberg? What if strange beings were staying in the next room, the room across the hall?

But out of everyone she'd met tonight, it was Dacian's image that was superimposed over every page she tried to read. He was the primal scream that lurked in the darkest corner of her mind. He was the ancient symbol of man's primitive fear. He was the ultimate terror that stalked the night. And yet . . .

She shook her head. No, there was nothing else. Cinn refused to even try to look past the horror of what he was. *Vampire.*

Finally, she gave up. Reading was impossible. She glanced around the room. An authentic-looking castle chamber: dark woods, rich colors, old tapestries, and a canopied bed. All it needed was the ancestral ghost. She peered into the shadows. Maybe you paid extra for the ghost.

Putting her journal aside, she slid under the covers and closed her eyes. And no, she wasn't turning the light out tonight. If she had to visit the bathroom in the middle of the night, she didn't want to open her eyes to a spirit perched at the foot of her bed. And yes, she was a giant wuss.

When Dacian was finally able to drag Taurin away from this madhouse, maybe he'd bring the whole pile of stones down around all of their ears as a parting gift. He could do that when he was at full strength. And he was just pissed off enough to want to.

He hated taking orders. Stephan already knew that. Sparkle, Ganymede, and the sarcastic wizard would find out soon enough. But for now, he'd pay for his stay here by doing what they wanted.

Powered by a string of silent curses, he took the last few strides to Cinn's door. He smiled. Scaring the crap out of her would improve his mood a little.

*"Please watch where you put your big feet. I'm guarding this door."*

Dacian glanced down. A cat was curled up in front of the door. What was with all the cats? "You're kidding, right?"

The cat looked insulted. *"I'm a ferocious guard. No one gets past me. Oh, and don't step on my tail, please."*

"Then maybe you need to move your furry little butt out of the way."

The cat hissed at him. *"My beautiful, elegant butt is staying right where it is."*

Impasse. Dacian was looking forward to picking up the cat and depositing her in a nearby trash bin when she uncurled herself, stood, stretched, and yawned.

*"On second thought, I'm tired of sleeping on the floor when I have a nice soft bed waiting for me. Sparkle can hire another intelligence agent to work the night shift."*

"Intelligence agent?" This place got more bizarre by the minute.

*"Sparkle wanted me to keep an eye on Cinn to make sure she didn't sneak off with her plants in the dead of night. But I think my shift is finished."* She glanced at him over her shoulder. *"Who are you?"*

"Dacian."

Her eyes widened. *"Taurin's brother?"*

He nodded.

*"What an intriguing reunion that will be. I mustn't miss it."*

"Whatever." If he were lucky, he'd have Taurin out of here before any of them knew what was happening.

*"Did Sparkle send you?"*

"Yeah."

*"Good. You can take the next shift."* She padded toward the stairs, her tail waving in the air.

"And you are?"

*"Asima. I hope you like sleeping on the floor. Cinn threatened me with violence if I tried to come into her room."*

Before he could ask her anything else, the cat disappeared. Frustrated, he turned back to the door. Threatened her with violence, huh? His smile returned. He'd just see about that. He pounded on the door.

No answer. Even if she were sleeping, she would've heard his knock. He glanced around. It was late. He didn't want to call attention to himself by shouting through the door at her. Sure, he could get inside in a number of other ways, but he didn't want her screaming the place down.

He snarled his frustration. Dacian liked the direct approach. But in this case he'd go the kinder and gentler route. Focusing, he reached into her mind. *"Open the damn door before I blow it off its freaking hinges."*

He felt her horrified reaction right through the door. Okay, maybe he needed to tone it down a little. *"Please."*

All he could sense from her was panicked indecision. When in doubt, lie. *"Sparkle sent me. She has info about your plants that you need to know."*

Evidently mentioning her plants did the trick, because a few seconds later she flung open the door.

"What about my plants? What has she done to them?" Her eyes were wide and fearful. But the fear was for her plants.

He stared bemused for a moment. Her long nightgown covered her from the neck down. The only things showing were the tips of her toes. Her toenails were painted a pale pink. Feminine. Personally, he liked bold colors. "Nothing about your plants. I just needed you to open the door. But Sparkle did send me."

"Who . . . ?"

He didn't need to be in her head to follow her thought processes. She was adjusting his cleaned-up version to what she'd seen in the dungeon. He sensed the exact moment she made the connection.

"Vampire!" She tried to close the door.

"Dacian." He kept it open with his foot.

"No!" Her gaze shifted to a nearby lamp.

"Yes." He stepped inside and caught her as she made a dive for her weapon of choice. "Asima warned me you had a violent streak."

Dacian almost smiled. He liked females who weren't afraid to bash a few heads. Amazing how she'd improved his mood.

"Turn. Me. Loose." Each word was forced through clenched teeth.

"Or?"

"Or I'll scream loud enough to shatter your undead eardrums. There have to be some normal people in this place who will come to help me before you can drain me dry."

He was tempted to let her scream. Throwing a few bodies around would release some of his pent-up emotion. But then he decided against it. Ganymede might try to toss him out, and he needed to last at least until Taurin came home.

"I'll let you go, but first look into my eyes. I'm safe to be around now." A lie. He was never safe to be around.

She kept her gaze averted. "Uh-uh. I know the score about vampires. I look into your eyes, and you glamour me."

He snorted his contempt. "Where'd you get all this knowledge?"

"I read a lot." She sounded a little defensive now.

"I don't care what you've read. I can't glamour you." Another lie. The truth? He didn't bother to glamour anyone when he could achieve the same result by more physical means. Why drain his power when a punch to the jaw accomplished the same thing?

She was still twisting and turning, trying to escape. A startled hiss escaped him. The pressure of her body moving against his was having an unexpected effect. Unexpected because sex was the last thing on his mind right now. But someone had forgotten to tell his cock.

He released her. "If you'll look into my eyes, you'll see I'm back in control." Dacian prepared to move if she made a grab for the lamp. He could take it out of her hands without touching her, but he'd rather not scare her with his various talents any more than he already had.

She took a deep calming breath, and he noted the lift and thrust of her breasts beneath the shapeless gown. He stomped on his body's attempt to react. Now wasn't the time.

"What do you want?"

Her voice sounded calm, but he could hear the fluttering panic of her heartbeat, the breaths coming too quickly. Her reaction didn't bother him. After six hundred years, you got used to the terror of others.

She still hadn't looked into his eyes, but he decided not to press the issue. He strode over to one of the chairs in her sitting area and sat. Maybe if he were lower than she was, she'd relax a little. He gestured toward the chair opposite him. "Sit."

As expected, as soon as he moved from the door, she made a dash for it. He exhaled deeply. Humans were so predictable. With a flick of his mind, he slammed the door shut and locked it. She yanked and pulled, but to no avail.

Cinn turned and pressed her back against the door. "I could scream."

"I could stop you." Without his permission, Dacian's

gaze fixed on her lips. He had many ways to stop her, some more enjoyable than others.

Finally giving up, she firmed those surprisingly full lips and marched over to the chair he'd indicated. She sat. Then she looked into his eyes. He made sure he didn't blink.

Frown lines formed between her eyes. Those lines fascinated him. How many centuries had it been since he'd had human reflexes? Now his face was a smooth mask, never betraying emotions, unless he was using those emotions to manipulate others. Truth was, he had few emotions left other than rage and lust. Good enough for him.

"Your eyes are dark blue, almost black. They look normal." She didn't try to hide her shock as she took a closer look. "And no fangs?"

Time to ease her worries with a little charm. "No fangs." He smiled, the smile he'd used on women for six hundred years to get what he wanted from them. "You saw me when I was a little . . . upset." Try really pissed.

Her gaze slid across his face, and then she looked away. He knew what she was seeing.

"I choose to keep the scars."

She was startled into looking back at him. "Why?"

Dacian shrugged. He should've let it go. No need to get into things she didn't have to know. But now that he'd brought it up, he'd finish it. "I can heal without scarring, but I chose not to. I kept them to remember." He stopped.

*Remember what?* The question was written all over her face. He didn't answer it.

Suddenly, she seemed to realize she was talking to him as though he was an ordinary guy. She stiffened. "What does Sparkle want? And what happened to Asima?"

"Sparkle wants me to guard you from Airmid during my waking hours. And if Asima is the Siamese cat, she got tired of lying outside your door. She went off to sleep in her soft bed."

Cinn's lips lifted in a brief smile, and Dacian's interest rose.

"You mean her soft, soft bed."

"What?"

She waved the comment away. "An inside joke. And I don't need a vampire protecting me from anything. I don't even know if I believe this Airmid exists. Sparkle would tell me anything to keep me here."

He didn't know why. What could a woman who grew plants have to offer Sparkle? But he didn't really care. "Doesn't matter. She says to protect you, so I protect you."

She drew those sexy lips into a thin line of disapproval. "I already have Asima keeping an eye on me."

He got up, opened the door, and made a big production of looking up and down the hall. "Talking cat gone. I'm here. I'll stay here until someone takes over at dawn."

"A vampire is not staying in my room with me. You want to guard me, you can do it from outside the door." She studied him closely. "Other than being a little pale, you don't look like a vampire. Not like you did down in the dungeon."

"I'm glad you find me almost human." He walked back to the couch and lay down. "That way you'll be able to forget I'm even here. Oh, and I've fed, so you're safe."

He watched the horror bloom in her eyes. "Bottled blood." Sort of a before-dinner cocktail. He'd go hunting for his main course tomorrow night. "No bellboys died in the making of my meal. And no, I'm not going to curl up outside your door. If you want to take a shot at bashing my head in, go for it. But it won't do any good."

Cinn was ready to suggest that *she* sleep outside her door. Or maybe at the hotel down the street. "I can't sleep in the same room with you." Was that wimpy voice hers?

For a moment she could've sworn bitterness shone behind those blue eyes, but then he smiled. Not the same kind of sexy smile as a few minutes ago.

"You'll sleep if you're tired enough." He reached into the pocket of his jeans and pulled out a key. He swung it back and forth. "The key to the greenhouse. Sparkle said I could let you work there at night as long as I stayed with you."

She took a deep breath. Sparkle knew exactly what buttons to push. Cinn would accept the devil himself if he got her into that damn greenhouse. Jumping up, she grabbed the clothes she'd peeled off a few hours ago and headed for the bathroom. "I'll be out in a minute. I need to see my plants."

Cinn didn't glance back for his reaction. Once inside the bathroom, she leaned her forehead against the closed door and shut her eyes. The cool smoothness of the wood grounded her. This was really happening, so she'd better accept it. All that mattered now was making sure her plants were happy and comfortable. She'd come to terms with her vampire protector later.

Straightening, she quickly dressed. The longer she put this off the harder it would be. A few minutes later, she emerged from the bathroom and looked around. Maybe he'd left. Maybe he'd never existed. Maybe she was just crazy. Right now, crazy would be a good thing.

She found him by the window, looking into the night. He turned when he heard her.

"You seem pretty anxious to go out into the dark with

an insane bloodsucking abomination." He said the words with no inflection.

Cinn raised one brow. "Insane bloodsucking abomination?"

"One of my kinder titles."

"Do you *want* me to be afraid of you?"

He seemed to think about her question as he moved back into the room. "It makes things easier. No false expectations."

She sighed. "I'm too tired for this garbage. Okay, consider yourself feared. Now, let's go see my plants."

Without comment, he led her from the room. He didn't take the elevator. As she followed him down the winding stone staircase, she allowed herself to really see him for the first time without her sight being clouded by terror.

She already knew he was tall and muscular. Even in the midst of her panic down in the dungeon, she'd noticed that body. Her gaze slid across his firm and nicely rounded butt showcased in worn jeans.

He'd washed and trimmed his hair, because it fell shiny and clean almost to his shoulders. But he must not have bothered with a brush. Looked like a finger comb to her. But the mussed look suited him.

Okay, reality check. Unless she woke up in a mental health facility pretty soon, she was actually following a *vampire* down the steps. Why was she even noticing his body and hairstyle? Probably the human mind trying to explain the unexplainable by searching for familiar points of reference.

She shifted her gaze to the steps in front of her. Wouldn't do to trip and go splat after surviving what she had so far since coming to the Castle of Dark Dreams.

Instead of using the outside entrance to the greenhouse, he led her through the kitchen. "Sparkle showed me both entrances." He unlocked the greenhouse door and stood back for her to enter first.

Cinn slipped past him. Close enough to realize what a truly big man he was. She glanced around. And how really alone they were out here. "These . . . episodes you have. Like the one in the dungeon. Um . . . do you have them often?"

His laughter was low and—maybe it was just her—sounded a little menacing. He'd moved up close behind her, and she shivered as awareness drew a thin line of goose bumps down her arms. No, not awareness. Probably just static electricity.

"I have them whenever my maker calls me to him, and I don't come. Stephan has visions of world domination with his loving children at his side. Me? Not so much. So each time I turn him down, he sends a killing rage my way as punishment." No lines of worry or nervous eye tics hinted that he was even a little worried about his episodes.

Well, *she* sure was. Against her better judgment, she gave in to her curiosity. "Why does he think that particular punishment will change your mind? And what would he want you to do if you gave in and joined him?" Did she really need to know this? Knowledge was power, so yes, she probably did.

He remained silent for a few heartbeats too long. *Her* heartbeats. Maybe his maker wanted him to slaughter every botanist he found alone and unprotected.

"After I came out of the first rage, I realized I'd killed people. Lots of them."

He might think his expression gave nothing away, but self-loathing lived in his eyes.

"People I knew." He shrugged. "So I went away to a

place where there weren't any people. And Stephan would want me to destroy anyone who opposed him."

He moved a little closer, and she swallowed hard. Wow, that static electricity was doing a prickly dance up and down her spine. "Yes, well, let's hope he doesn't make a call while you're here."

"Don't worry, I'll get warning and make myself scarce."

Cinn nodded and then tried to look casual as she moved along the rows of her plants. She stopped beside Sandy. A little droopy. She leaned over the succulent and stroked it. "Feeling puny, sweetie? Guess the long trip was pretty stressful."

She pretended not to hear the snort of derision behind her. With head high, she moved on to the next plant. She'd covered half of the greenhouse, examining plants and offering some encouraging words, when Dacian interrupted.

"Son of a bitch! This plant bit me. What the hell is it?"

Cinn closed her eyes and drew in a deep breath of patience. She should've warned him before he entered the greenhouse, but she'd been too anxious to see her plants. She turned to look at him.

"That's Carla. She has aggression issues." Cinn winced. Dark blood dripped from his finger. But even as she watched, the wound closed and the bleeding stopped. "I thought you encouraged scars."

"I choose the scars I carry." He spoke through gritted teeth. "Now tell me about Carla before I rip her up by her roots."

Anger blazed in her. "Is that how you solve everything? Kill?"

"Works for me."

She tried to calm herself. Cinn didn't doubt he could destroy every one of her plants if he went on a rampage. God, she hoped her fear didn't show in her eyes. She felt the brush of his mind a moment before he spoke.

"You're crazy, do you know that? You're more afraid for these plants than you are for yourself." He shook his head at what he'd consider stupidity beyond understanding. "Now tell me about Carla."

"Carla is a Venus flytrap."

"I've seen pictures of Venus flytraps, and this isn't one."

"Yes, well, she grew a little bigger than normal."

"You think? She's at least six feet tall." Dacian glared at the plant. "She's dangerous."

"Pot, kettle?"

His smile was merely a baring of his teeth. "But you *expect* me to bite you, sweetheart." His smile eased into something more sensual. "I always like to rise to those kinds of expectations."

She refused to react. Okay, how to explain Carla and the rest of her rejects to someone who probably never had a soft feeling in his entire life? "I made mistakes with a few of my plants. They weren't as calm and friendly as I'd hoped. But I couldn't destroy them. They were alive. They didn't want to die." She realized she was twisting the bottom of her T-shirt nervously and stopped. "I keep them in a corner of the greenhouse. They're my weed warriors."

He didn't smile. "Better put up a warning sign." Then he *did* smile. "On second thought, don't. I'd like to see the face of the first person who leaves with Carla's teeth marks in him. I'd like to follow him outside and listen as he tries to explain to his friends how he got the bite."

Cinn didn't register anything after that smile. Sure, he'd smiled before, but this was a *real* smile.

And for the first time she got a glimpse of the beautiful man he must've been before bitterness, cynicism, and probably just being a vampire had leached all the emotion except rage from him.

She took a deep breath. Something monumental had just happened. For just a nanosecond, she'd forgotten the vampire part and thought only of the human. Not a good thing. Because it was the vampire part that could kill her.

# *Chapter Four*

Dacian watched the play of emotions cross Cinn's face and enjoyed them vicariously. They were part of her humanity, something he hadn't been able to claim for six hundred years. Emotions were a blessing and a curse. They'd made him feel alive, but they'd also made him vulnerable. And in the end, they'd killed him. Stephan had seen to that.

Thinking about Stephan soured his mood. He turned his back on Cinn and strode over to the corner, where Carla squatted with her merry band of misfits. If he hadn't known better, Dacian would swear the plant was smirking.

"Wipe the grin off your . . . whatever before I do a little pruning in here." That should put her in her place. He scanned the other five plants behind the Jaws of the greenhouse. "I don't know what you guys do, but mess with me and you'll be going to the great compost heap in the sky. I'm here to protect Cinn, so we're working on the same side." And talking to a bunch of plants was about as weird as it got.

Just before he turned back to Cinn, he felt a tentative probe of his mind. What the . . . ? The touch wasn't feminine, and it didn't have the feel of Stephan. Then who . . . ?

He swung toward the door. Whoever it was wouldn't be far. "Someone is tapping on my mental door. I need to track them down." People who tried to breach his thoughts weren't usually friends. Yeah, so he didn't have any friends.

Dacian had flung open the greenhouse door leading to the courtyard and stepped out into the night before Cinn caught him.

"Wait. That's probably Vince."

He glared into the darkness. "Fine. Who's Vince? And he better have a good reason for poking around in my head."

She sighed. "You won't like this."

He turned his glare on her. "Lady, I haven't liked *anything* that's happened to me since I got here. So let's hear it."

"Vince is my vinca minor, the common periwinkle plant to you. He senses that I'm upset and is trying to figure out why. He's harmless." She swallowed hard.

She was really afraid he'd destroy her plants. *Isn't that what you wanted? Her fear?* Somehow the reality didn't make him feel quite as good as he'd thought it would.

Dacian forced back his first impulse, to threaten. He didn't know why. She wasn't anyone special in his life. And as soon as Taurin came back, he'd never see her or her plants again. Still, he supposed there was no need to play rough with her or her freaking plants.

He stepped back into the greenhouse, quietly shut the door, and locked it behind him. "Look, your plants will be safe. I'm just interested, okay? Let's meet Vince."

She nodded and then led him over to a long vine with dark green leaves. Then she hovered.

"I drink blood, Cinn. I don't eat plants. So stop looking as if I'm about to make a tossed salad out of your Vince."

She nodded, but her expression didn't change.

He huffed his frustration before turning his attention back to the periwinkle plant. It looked too normal, too much like plants Dacian had seen crawling along the ground in the shadows of ancient keeps, for him to believe it could crawl into his mind as well. But Dacian had experienced too much in his long existence to dismiss the possibility. Besides, one of her plants had bitten him. Proof that she was a lot more than just a nice lady who grew plants.

*Nice* lady? He slid his gaze the length of her body. Full breasts that would fit perfectly in the palms of his hands. A round little ass that called to him with every step she took. Long sexy legs she could wrap around him as he plunged . . . He shook the thoughts away. Bottom line? Nice wasn't the right word. Hot was a much better one.

Dacian forced himself to focus on the plant. "Here's the deal, Vince. Stay out of my mind. I'm a private person. I don't make polite with anyone dropping in uninvited. Got it?"

"He doesn't understand words, just emotions." She moved closer to Dacian, her warm and sensual scent playing havoc with his concentration.

"Then he's out of luck, isn't he? Because I'm not into emotions, except for the occasional insane burst of rage or uncontrollable bout of lust."

Instead of moving away from him as he'd expected, she just looked puzzled. "Why do you do that?"

"Do what?"

"Try to scare me by playing up your negatives."

He couldn't stop his surprised bark of laughter. "Lady, I don't have anything *but* negatives. Believe it."

She didn't respond. Instead her expression smoothed out and she closed her eyes.

"What're you doing?"

She didn't answer for a moment, and then she opened her eyes. "I was sending Vince calm and peaceful feelings. It'll reassure him."

"Right. Reassure." God, he hoped Taurin hurried home. Or maybe Airmid really would show up. Kicking goddess butt might keep him sane.

Cinn glanced around the greenhouse. "Well, I think everyone's fine, so we can leave." She headed for the kitchen exit, but paused with her hand on the door to glance back at him. "I can introduce you to the rest of the plants tomorrow night."

"Wonderful." He didn't think she heard his muttered sarcasm.

Suddenly she grinned at him. It was playful and teasing and so sexy he almost groaned. Had he warned her about his uncontrollable bouts of lust? Sure he had. The exaggeration might turn out not to be an exaggeration at all. Maybe he'd spent too long in the Alaskan wilderness, because Want was wearing a capital *W* and coming up fast in his rearview mirror. He couldn't let it gain any traction, because he had serious stuff to deal with. He couldn't afford any side trips.

"My friends run and hide when I start talking about my plants. You can't. I'm looking forward to having a captive audience. The life of a bodyguard sucks lemons, doesn't it?" Her soft laughter was an expression of real amusement.

No one had shared that kind of laughter with him for a long time. She'd never know what a rare treat it was. And because he could almost feel his hard edges turning to mush, he strode through the kitchen, determined to put some space between them.

Dacian was already halfway across the great hall and

headed for the stone steps that would take him back to her room when he remembered. He'd forgotten to lock the greenhouse door. He glanced behind him. He'd also forgotten to bring her with him. Even now she could be grabbing her plants to load into her truck. *Damn*.

When he got back to the greenhouse, he found her waiting for him, holding Vince all cozy in his pot.

"I decided to take him up to the room with me. He'll be less nervous if I'm nearby." She didn't ask why he'd rushed off, and he didn't offer an explanation.

Her narrowed gaze told him she was ready for his contemptuous comments. So he didn't make any. "Great. Take him with you. Let's get back to your room." He thought about offering to carry the plant for her, but decided against it. The thought of one of her leafy charges in his undead clutches would horrify her too much.

He did compromise by taking one of the elevators in the hotel lobby up to her floor instead of climbing the stairs. She'd never know how much it cost him to stand in that small enclosed box. Whenever he camped out in a national park, he simply slept in a cave or the ground. No coffin for him. He could dig himself out of the earth. He'd never let himself be trapped again.

Once back in front of her door, she simply stared at him. He met her stare and held it. He'd protect her whether she wanted it or not.

"Give me some space, Dacian. I need to spend tonight alone in my room without you or Asima crowding me."

He understood the need for alone time. And so he decided to compromise again. Damn, he hadn't done this much compromising ever. He'd always been a my-way kind of guy. He nodded. "For tonight. I'll hang around in the hall. I'll know if someone gets into your room."

She looked troubled. Evidently the thought of Airmid being able to simply materialize in her room bothered Cinn. It should. You didn't mess with goddesses. He'd found they were a lot more dangerous than the gods because they held grudges longer.

"Thank you."

Her relief that he wouldn't be sleeping on her couch sort of ticked him off. Yeah, it was all about ego. Because even with his scars and his attitude, he'd never had problems attracting women when he wanted them.

As she closed her door behind her, Dacian once again felt the light brush against his mind that he could now identify as Vince. Only this time it wasn't quite so tentative.

*"Got it."*

The shock of hearing the voice stopped him dead. He reeled back his memory, trying to remember what he'd said to Vince. *"I don't make polite with anyone dropping in uninvited. Got it?"* Holy shit. The plant could talk, or at least it was learning to talk. Maybe Cinn needed to think about what she was creating out in that greenhouse. For now, he'd keep his mouth shut about Vince. If the plant wanted to talk to her, it would. It wasn't any of Dacian's business.

No way could he settle down outside her door. He had too much suppressed energy, so he started to pace. He moved silently, but he wasn't worried about other guests discovering him. They'd all be asleep.

Every time he passed Cinn's door, he saw the room's name, Wicked Intentions. By the time he'd passed it for the hundredth time, it had become his mantra. What he wanted to do with her had no goodness and light attached to it. He'd had plenty of time to let his imagination run amok, and what he had planned for the plant lady would scare her shitless.

He was working on the second hundred trips up and down the damn hall when he sensed the presence. Its power wrapped around him and he had to exert all of his own strength to keep it at bay. What the hell was it? Airmid? Possibly. She'd want to take out any possible protectors before going after Cinn.

The presence was also mounting a massive attack on his mind. This was no tentative tapping. Dacian strengthened the wall around his thoughts with reinforced concrete and tempered steel. Nothing would get in. Then he stilled as only a vampire could and *felt*.

It was climbing the steps toward him. He could've charged down the stone stairs to meet it, but he didn't like fighting in confined spaces. If it came to violence, the hallway offered more maneuvering room. Whatever it was didn't seem to care if he sensed it. So he stood in front of Cinn's door and waited.

A man emerged from the stairwell. Big, with sandy-colored hair that reminded Dacian of a lion's coat, and a grim reaper tattoo on one bare bicep, he would've looked formidable even if Dacian hadn't sensed he wasn't human.

As the guy drew closer, he slowed, and his amber eyes grew colder in direct proportion to his power push.

The hell with him. This wasn't Airmid. But even if it had been the goddess, Dacian didn't take crap from anyone. He gathered his power and did some pushing of his own. At the same time, he tried to jump into the stranger's mind. No deal. He wasn't really surprised, but he wanted the man to know that two could play the same game.

The guy stopped several yards away from him and just stared.

"Seen enough?" Dacian kept his voice quiet, but he put all the threat he could into the question.

The other man didn't answer for a moment, and then he nodded. "Yeah, I guess I have. I had a few things to do tonight, and I just got back. Decided I'd come up to make sure you really were guarding Cinn. I take over the guard duty at dawn."

Dacian knew his smile was no smile at all. "Don't trust me? That's okay, because I don't trust anyone, especially someone who hasn't told me his name."

The big man shrugged. "Names don't matter, vampire. But if you need to know, I'm Edge. I'm one of your fellow 'managers,' which is just a fancy term Sparkle uses for the men she's trying to manipulate at the moment. Right now it's you, me, and Bain. The three before us were Eric, Brynn, and Conall. They've moved on to other projects."

Dacian figured Edge was using the small talk to work up to something bigger, so he didn't say anything.

Edge smiled. "Wait, I think you know Eric Mackenzie. At least he says he knows you. I called him as soon as I found out that Ganymede had dragged your ass back to the castle. Eric says he'll be here as fast as he can. Seems you two have some old times to talk over." His smile widened, but it didn't make him look less dangerous.

Dacian didn't let Edge see by even a blink how this news shook him. Hell, he didn't need Eric complicating what was already a tangled mess. "I'm looking forward to seeing Eric again. So what's your part in this game? And what's your real name?"

Edge shrugged. "Hey, I'm just an interested observer. I've been here while Taurin searched for you. It takes a cold bastard to let his own brother think he's been dead for two hundred years. But then, I admire someone who doesn't let his emotions rule him." His smile grew a little warmer. "That's from one cold bastard to another."

Dacian didn't let the slight warming fool him for a moment. Edge would smile just like that as he tore off your head. "Your *real* name? Because you seem to be the kind of guy who would have a behind-the-scenes name." A guess, but he figured more than likely it was true. "Oh, and you have the same eyes as Sparkle and Ganymede, so I'm guessing you're another cosmic troublemaker. Never heard of you guys before, and now I'm tripping over you everywhere I go. Weird."

Edge moved a little closer, and Dacian made sure his back was to the wall. Words masked intentions, and since he couldn't read Edge's mind, he'd have to go with body language. And Edge's body language said he was putting himself in a position to attack.

"My real name? *Finis.* The End. I'm the cosmic troublemaker in charge of death. You deserve it, I bring it. I've done my thing for tens of thousands of years." He wasn't smiling now. "From what I've heard, you deserve a dropkick into hell more than most. And if it wouldn't upset Taurin and make Sparkle all pissy, I'd take you out right now."

"And you think you could do it?" Dacian made his voice casual and only slightly interested. But he gathered his powers around him. Ready.

Edge seemed surprised. "Sure. Why not? Look, you're a night feeder. And everyone knows night feeders are at the bottom of the vampire power rankings. I could destroy you in my sleep." His expression said it was only a matter of time before he tried.

Dacian was almost enjoying himself now. The troublemaker was underestimating him, just like Stephan had underestimated him. Stephan had thought because he was older than Dacian that he would be the one in control. Over the last two hundred years he'd found out differently.

"Try." He hissed the challenge, positive that Edge had too much ego to turn it down.

Edge glanced up and down the hall and Dacian could almost hear him mentally calculating how much damage he could get away with inflicting on this nothing vampire.

Dacian saw it in his eyes a second before Edge struck, and he flung up his shields. The blast of power rocked Dacian, but his shields held and the blue flash bounced away from him and dissipated.

This was the part Dacian lived for. Edge's eyes widened in shock and then his lips thinned in concentration.

"Well, well. Looks like I'll have to work a little harder. Your point, bloodsucker. I wasn't expecting any resistance." He tried to look unconcerned. "Of course, I wasn't trying to fry you, just lay a hurting on you. Like the hurting you've laid on your brother for so many years."

Low blow. That made Dacian mad. Because it was true. It drove him to retaliate instead of just protecting himself as he'd planned.

Without trying to control his power, he lashed out at the other man. A whiplash of energy snapped Edge's head back. A red welt pulsed angrily along his jaw.

"Son of a bitch." Edge's comment was one part surprise and three parts fury.

He backed away from Dacian and then let him have it. Slivers of glass drove at Dacian from every direction. Dacian's shield shook and wavered under the onslaught.

Dacian had to give himself time to strengthen his shield, so he retaliated. Rivulets of fire crept across the floor, converging on the cursing troublemaker. The streams of flame crept over his shield, looking for a crack, a place to slide through and incinerate the enemy.

The sharp cracks of shattering glass and the sizzle of the flame filled the hallway with noise and smoke. Dacian had lost himself in the battle, and the glare from Edge said he wasn't pulling any punches either.

But Dacian was weakening. The troublemaker was wearing him down. When he couldn't maintain his shield any longer, he'd have to escape. He eyed the window at the end of the hallway. It was a narrow castle window, but if he shifted right before he hit it, he could smash through and be gone.

*Cinn.* Damn. He had to protect her. He'd have to find her window, crash through, and then listen to her scream bloody hell. But he didn't have any other plan, so he'd go with it. The next power play by Edge shoved him hard against the wall and the troublemaker grinned. He sensed victory.

*"What the hell do you think you're doing?"*

Ganymede's roar of anger rattled around in Dacian's head. Edge looked pained. They both froze.

Ganymede stood in front of the elevator, his cat's eyes narrowed, his ears pinned, and his tail lashing from side to side. A man Dacian didn't know stood beside the cat. He was grinning. The bastard.

*"I just had to go into the minds of every guest on this floor and convince them they only dreamed there was glass breaking and a fire in the hallway."*

He could do that? Dacian was impressed.

The cat padded down the hall until he stood between the two men. *"Who started this?"* His whiskers twitched.

Dacian kept quiet. So did Edge. The troublemaker went up a notch in his opinion. He wasn't a finger-pointer.

*"Idiots."* Ganymede nodded at the man beside him. *"Maybe Bain can keep his mind on business. He'll take over*

*for the rest of the night. You two*"—he nodded at Dacian and Edge—"*come with me. Sparkle wants to talk to you.*"

Dacian groaned. Not Sparkle. He'd fight ten Edges and enjoy every second of it before he'd meet with the redheaded witch. A side glance at Edge showed the same expression of dread on his face. Great. Misery loved company.

"I think I'd like to sit in on this meeting."

They all turned to where Cinn stood in her doorway, her favorite plant held protectively against her. She returned their stares. "And yes, he comes with me. No one's taking him away." Her expression dared any of them to try.

Which took a lot of guts, because if she had any sense at all she had to know any of them could take that plant from her without moving a muscle.

Dacian turned on Ganymede. "I thought you wiped everyone's memory."

The cat looked unconcerned. "*I didn't bother with her. It's her butt on the line, so she deserves to know how she's being protected.*" He nodded at her. "*Let's get moving. I think I need a bowl of ice cream to keep from wiping the castle with the two of you.*"

"If you think you can, cat, let's see it." Edge almost vibrated with aggression.

Dacian stared at him, amazed. Dumbass. No way would he take on the cat after going a round with Edge. *Maybe Edge is a lot more powerful than you are.* Yeah, there was that, too. Dacian prided himself on being pragmatic. He wasn't into lost causes. He'd rather live to fight another day.

For a moment, the threat of unleashed power filled the hall with danger. Without thinking, Dacian moved in front of Cinn. If the explosion happened, he'd push her back into her room and take her out through the window.

And then the threat was over. Dacian didn't know who had blinked, or even if anyone had, but the confrontation wouldn't be tonight. Something told him it would eventually happen, though. That was one power struggle he didn't want any part of.

Everyone except for the guy Ganymede had identified as Bain headed for the elevator, and Cinn fell into step beside Dacian. She'd taken the time to pull on jeans and a red top. *But not a bra.* He gripped his lower lip between his teeth to keep from showing fang. When he finally released his lip, he watched her gaze slide across it. She licked her own lips.

Awareness was suddenly alive and well between them. He let his gaze slip to her feet. Safe enough. She still wore her fuzzy slippers. They made him smile. Good. Desire wasn't banished, but at least it was bellowing outside the gates. And that was where he'd keep it for now.

"Do you want me to carry the plant?"

She frowned.

"I mean, carry Vince?" He hated to humanize the plant with a name, but if it made her more at ease with him he'd do it.

She wouldn't let him carry the plant. She didn't trust him. He was the terrifying undead to her. He didn't try to slip into her mind to verify that belief because . . . he didn't want the ugly details.

Cinn hesitated for a moment and then nodded. Reluctantly, she handed him the plant.

He couldn't have been more surprised if she'd handed him a bomb. Dacian took Vince and wrapped his arms around the plant. If she'd put her trust in him to do this, he was going to make damn sure he didn't drop the pot.

She'd had the vine wrapped in a nice neat ball, but now it tumbled loose. Smothering a curse, Dacian gathered up the vine and draped it over his shoulder. Just freaking great. He glanced at Cinn. She was grinning. And suddenly, he felt like grinning, too.

Sparkle and Ganymede had a suite in one of the towers. Ganymede paused in front of the door. *"Understand something. Sparkle did the decorating before she got depth and character. Personally I think this is who she really is, but that's just me. Anyway, the first jerk who makes a crack about it gets a fist in the face."*

"You don't have a fist." Dacian had to point out the obvious.

*"Smart-ass."* Ganymede turned back to the door. *"I have claws, though."*

The door swung open and Ganymede padded in. Dacian, Cinn, and Edge followed him. Dacian and Cinn froze in the doorway. Edge just snorted his opinion and kept walking.

Sparkle swayed toward them. "Welcome. Have a seat."

Her smile was an invite to have much more than a seat, but who was looking at her smile? Her nightgown was long, black, and just short of see-through.

Her smile widened as she studied Dacian. "I made sure I was decent for the meeting. And this gown is a leftover from my shallow days. I've ordered some plain cotton jammies, but they, um, must've gotten lost in the mail." Her expression said she wasn't looking too hard for them.

*"Ouch."* Vince's voice?

Dacian blinked and looked down. He'd tightened his grip until the pot was in danger of shattering. He relaxed. A side glance at Cinn caught her glaring at him.

Interesting. She must not be a fan of Sparkle's night-wear.

Sparkle draped herself across a chaise. Her black gown slithered and slid, forming interesting patterns of skin and silk.

Ganymede ignored everyone as he sprawled next to the remote on the couch. *"Someone put the damn head-phones on me so I can watch the tube while you guys yammer. Oh, and I need my bowl of popcorn. Someone take care of it."*

Everyone looked at everyone else. No one moved.

Finally, Sparkle sighed and unwound herself from the chaise. "Men. Helpless babies." She thought about that. "Or kittens, as the case may be."

She somehow managed to get the headphone buds in Ganymede's ears and then she plunked the popcorn down so hard in front of him that kernels flew in every direction. He ignored her bad humor as he stared un-blinking at the screen.

Cinn dropped onto the couch beside Ganymede. Edge and Dacian sank into twin overstuffed easy chairs. Not the kind of seating arrangement he liked. A straight chair was simpler to spring out of if danger threatened. But Sparkle had stuff piled on the chairs grouped around the small dining table.

"So why are we here?" Dacian wanted to be gone. He intended to take Cinn back to her room, where the Bain guy would presumably guard her until morning when Edge would take over. He'd taken Edge's measure and didn't doubt the guy could handle the goddess. But he didn't know squat about Bain. He'd find out, though. Soon.

"I need all three of you together for just a few min-utes." Sparkle had once again arranged her body on the chaise in a lush display of female flesh.

Only a saint could ignore what Sparkle was, and God

knew, Dacian wasn't a saint. An angry hiss jerked his attention to Ganymede. The cat's gaze was fixed on him with clear intent to do physical damage.

Sparkle's laughter was low and so sexy it would make a man's teeth hurt, along with other body parts. "Ignore Mede. He doesn't understand the game, Dacian."

"Obviously I don't either." Cinn's voice sounded neutral, but her clenched fists suggested otherwise.

For some reason, that made Dacian feel good. He wasn't ready to analyze why.

Sparkle sighed. "You've spent too much time around your plants, Cinn. Everything that happens between a man and woman is a game. And if you're lucky, you both win."

Cinn raised one brow. "Is this the old shallow Sparkle talking, or the new one with depth and character?"

Sparkle's smile was a sly lift of her lips. "It's both, sister. The new me tells the truth. The old me knew the truth. There's nothing I don't know about what goes on between a man and a woman."

"Be afraid. Be *very* afraid," Edge intoned.

She shifted her attention to Edge. "I don't know what game you were playing tonight, but stop it. Dacian is my guest as well as a manager, and you can always be replaced."

Edge narrowed his eyes. "I can always quit."

"But you won't, and we both know why."

Tension hummed between the two, and Dacian watched the interaction. Maybe this was something he could use. He glanced at Ganymede. The cat didn't seem concerned with the back-and-forth, so sex probably wasn't involved. Interesting, though.

"Is that all?" Edge's voice almost thrummed with anger.

"Not quite. My sources tell me that Airmid has been

to Oregon. She knows Cinn isn't there, and now she's
picked up the trail and is headed this way. It won't take
her long to find out where Cinn is. So everyone needs to
keep a heads-up."

Dacian turned to catch Cinn's expression. She was
pale but not panicky. Yet. He'd bet Cinn wasn't sure if
she believed Sparkle. Dacian certainly did.

"*Now*, is that all?"

Sparkle nodded.

Without another word, Edge rose and left the suite.
He didn't slam the door behind him. Great control. Dacian would've slammed the freaking door.

# Chapter Five

Cinn's thoughts were rattling around in her brain like air-popped corn gone wild. Did this Airmid goddess really exist? If she did, how had she found out that Cinn wasn't at home?

Ohmigod, had someone hurt her family? She fought down the urge to lunge for the phone. *Calm down.* She only had Sparkle's word for any of this.

She looked across at Dacian, who'd just set Vince down on the coffee table. Poor Vince. He had to be picking up on her emotions. Not only that, but she'd separated him from the others.

And then there was Dacian. What was she going to do about her thoughts of him? Did she fear him? Uh, that would be a yes. Did she trust him? Sort of. At least until he did something that reminded her of what he truly was. But of all the crazies living in the castle, he was the only one she felt she could depend on. Maybe.

Oh, God, she didn't know how she felt about anything. "Excuse me, everyone. But I have to call my family." She stood.

"Sit down." Sparkle leaned over and picked up the phone from beside her. She passed it to Edge, who passed it to Cinn. "Call someone in your family now. I bet everyone's okay. Airmid can be a bitch, but she wouldn't bother laying waste to your town and family just out of petty revenge. I'm sure she's happy with the rest of your family. They've been good little plant people."

Cinn barely listened as she punched in Willow's number with a finger that refused to stop trembling. She would've called her parents, but she didn't want to upset them if nothing was wrong. She barely waited for her sister's sleepy hello before speaking. "Are you okay? Is everyone in the family okay?"

There was puzzled silence for a moment on the other end of the line. "Sure. Shouldn't they be? I talked to Mom and Dad before I went to bed, and no one's called to say there were problems. Why?" There was another pause. "I just checked the time. If it's late here, that means it's even later in Texas. What's going on?"

Okay, no reason to scare her sister. "I had a nightmare. Seemed a little too real for me. Something about a creepy-looking woman asking questions about the family. Nothing like that happened, did it?" She held her breath.

"Now that you mention it, there *was* someone asking about you." Willow sounded more awake now. "A woman stopped at Dad's greenhouse. Said she was an old friend." She laughed. "Dad said after he told her you'd moved to Texas, she spent at least an hour hanging around and telling him what he was doing wrong with the plants. Strange thing is, Dad said she really knew her stuff."

"Did she give a name?" Cinn had a death grip on the phone.

"Nope. She just told Dad maybe she'd run across you someday when she was passing through again."

"Guess I overreacted to the dream." Cinn tried to sound embarrassed.

"No problem, sis. How's the new job going?"

"Great. Just great." *I've met a vampire, demon, wizard, messenger of Bast, and three cosmic troublemakers all in one day. Oh, and Airmid, the goddess of healing plants, is out to kick my butt. Other than that, hey, everything's fine.* Cinn felt numb. "Look, I'll let you get back to sleep."

She passed the phone back to Sparkle. Cinn would've gotten up to return it, but if she made any sudden moves she'd shatter into a thousand shards of pointy nerve endings.

"Satisfied?" Sparkle looked sympathetic.

Cinn didn't believe that look. She took a deep breath and just nodded. Then she tried to calm herself by focusing on the normal. She glanced around the room. *Normal, normal, normal, where the hell was normal?* Not in *this* room.

Every surface, and every object resting or attached to said surface, was dedicated to the sensual. Erotic paintings hung on walls of deep red. Sexy sculptures rested on furniture with carved scenes of sexual acts. The light from a bunch of candles cast shadows that danced along the walls and the scents filling the room from the candles made her want to . . . want to . . . tackle Dacian, take him to the floor, and commit unspeakable acts of wanton abandon on his yummy body.

Horrified, she looked at Sparkle. "This is the new you?"

Sparkle looked sad. "The old me. The new me has ordered a bunch of white paint and Shaker furniture along with some Norman Rockwell prints. They haven't gotten here yet."

*"If I have anything to say about it, they never will."* Ganymede wasn't as wrapped up in his movie as everyone thought.

"Have you said everything that needed saying?" Dacian sounded impatient.

"Not exactly." For the first time, Sparkle seemed a little

nervous. "Bain had a vision. He gets flashes of the future once in a while. Usually there's not too much detail."

Dacian's gaze sharpened. "This Bain, he was the guy with Ganymede, the one who'll be guarding Cinn."

"A demon." Cinn felt good about being on the telling end of something for a change.

Sparkle nodded. "He saw you chained to a post, Dacian. Oh, he didn't know who you were, because he hadn't met you yet, but I recognized your description." She hesitated.

"Go on." Dacian's expression darkened.

"Another vampire was attacking you. Bain didn't see any way you could survive." She looked away. "He didn't see anything to give a hint of where you were, and he didn't see the outcome."

"In other words, he didn't see me die."

"No." Sparkle sighed and returned her gaze to him. "The other vampire was ordinary looking—average height, slim, short dark hair, no beard or mustache. Recognize him?"

"It's not Stephan. He has long blond hair and a mustache. How accurate are this guy's visions?" Dacian's voice was level and calm, but Cinn could sense his intensity, his anger building. So far he hadn't shown fang, but she figured if he didn't put a lid on his feelings fast, he could boil over and scald all of them.

"Umm, pretty good."

"*How* good?"

"One hundred percent so far." Sparkle hurried to smooth some of the sharp edges from that average. "But no one ever stays at one hundred percent. I mean, this could be the one he blows. And the future is tricky. We have free will, so we can change the future."

Cinn guessed that, like all of them, Sparkle didn't want to be the cause of Dacian having another episode.

Not that Cinn believed ordinary anger would trigger the insane rage she'd seen. But while Sparkle tried to talk the tension out of him, Cinn decided to take a more hands-on approach.

She got up and went over to stand behind Dacian. Resting her hands on his shoulders, she massaged the tight muscles there. "I'm sure everything will be okay." Did she believe that? Absolutely not. But she was treating him the same way she treated Vince, sending him peaceful feelings and hoping he picked up on them.

Slowly, she felt his muscles loosen, and he relaxed a little. She could stop now if she wanted. Only she didn't want to stop. Something about the firmness of male flesh beneath her kneading fingers felt better than it had any right to feel. Falling into a rhythm, she kept going.

Sparkle's anxious expression eased. "I bet if Bain had gotten the big picture instead of just a snippet, he would've seen someone rushing to your rescue."

Cinn thought Sparkle should probably just shut up.

Sparkle forged onward. "But you needed to know. Mede's put everyone on high alert for Airmid and the guy in Bain's vision. At least your maker hasn't descended on us yet."

Ganymede gave them his attention for a moment. "Been wondering about something, bloodsucker. Were you headed here when I dug you up?"

Dacian's expression was shuttered. "I got word that my maker had found Taurin and was going to kill him to get back at me."

*"I don't know what the big deal is. If Stephan shows up here, I'll kill him. Problem solved. And Airmid is a woman. I can handle her."* He went back to his popcorn and movie.

Cinn waited for Sparkle's outrage. Nothing. Huh? "Do you always put up with that sexist garbage?"

Sparkle shrugged. "I let him keep his illusions. Alone in our bed I make the power structure clear to him." She glanced at Ganymede. A small scary smile played around her lips. "And when he really gets obnoxious, I throw out all his treats."

Ganymede's head whipped around. *"Umm, I was only talking about ordinary women, honey-fluff. Not you. You're in a class all your own, babe."* He wrapped his chubby cat body protectively around the bowl of popcorn.

Dacian stood. "Okay, I can't stand any more of this crap. I need to hunt. I thought I could make it till after I rose, but I can't. All this bullshit has made me thirsty." He glanced at Cinn before heading for the door. "And yes, I'm feeding off a few humans." He stared at her to make sure she got the message. And when he left, he slammed the door behind him.

Cinn stared blankly at the door. *Dacian, thy name is volatile.* She'd say he was moody, but that suggested he had a happy moment once in a while. If he did, she hadn't experienced it yet.

She didn't have anything else to say to Sparkle or Ganymede. She guessed she'd go back to her room. The room that was now guarded by a demon. Wow, that was some upgrade. And maybe, just maybe, she could catch a few hours of sleep before the whole merry-go-round started again. Reaching over, she lifted Vince into her lap.

"I'll head on back to my room now. Oh, does anyone have a clue what this Airmid looks like?" She was finally ready to admit that the goddess existed and was out for her blood. But why? Everything she did with her plants was for the common good. Fine, so Carla and the rest of her weed warriors might not be too user friendly. But other than those few, her plants did lots of good.

No one answered.

As she started to rise, Sparkle waved her back into her seat. "Stay for a little longer. We have some things to discuss." She stared at Ganymede until he finally looked at her.

"*What?*" He stuck his face into the popcorn bowl and inhaled a mouthful. Probably strengthening himself for whatever Sparkle was about to say.

"Cinn and I need a few minutes for some girl talk. Why don't you check up on Dacian? We never told him that he couldn't hunt inside the park."

Mede hissed his unhappiness with Sparkle's weak ploy to get him out of the suite, but he finally leaped from the couch, padded to the door, stared at it until it opened, and then left. The door swung quietly shut behind him.

"Now. We're alone." Sparkle looked like she wanted to rub her hands together in glee.

For some reason, this scared Cinn witless. Anything that made Sparkle that happy couldn't be good for Cinn. "This better be important. I'm tired."

Sparkle ignored her comment as she motioned Cinn toward her bedroom. "I have some things I want to show you."

Cinn allowed herself to be led. At least for the next two weeks, Sparkle was still her boss. But she stopped thinking about Sparkle for a moment as she took in the erotic impact of the bedroom.

The bed was a huge four-poster with erotic scenes painted on the headboard. A red velvet bedspread added the final touch. There were more sexually explicit paintings and the prerequisite scented candles. The rugs were black fluffy compromises to the fact that a male shared the room. *Hmm.* She had to know.

"Does Ganymede take human form often?" Cinn's guess was yes, because that big bed would need lots of use to keep it happy.

Sparkle blinked and then smiled. "Your question surprised me. Not many people ask." She pursed her lips as though trying to decide how much to tell Cinn. "Several times a week. Some shifters can change instantly. For cosmic troublemakers, it takes a little more time and effort." She slid the tip of her tongue across her lower lip. "You wouldn't believe Mede in his golden god form. He owns an island in the Caribbean, and when we spend a few weeks there he doesn't take his cat form at all." Her eyes were slitted in ecstasy at the memory. "He's a totally sexual creature, you know."

Cinn couldn't help it; she smiled. Somehow she couldn't picture the cat with his face in the popcorn bowl as a hot guy. The image just wouldn't come.

Sparkle looked like she wasn't sure if Cinn's smile should offend her. "Mede doesn't have sex when he's in his cat form, so he compensates by eating. A lot." She shrugged. "You take the good with the bad."

Cinn had been so wrapped up in the discussion about Ganymede that she hadn't noticed what Sparkle was doing. She noticed now. Sparkle had dragged a bunch of clothes out of her closet and piled them on her bed. Uh-oh.

"I think these will fit you, at least until I get you some of your own." She glanced at Cinn's feet. "A size six I'd guess. I'll have a few pairs for you by nighttime."

Horrified, Cinn stared at the clothes. They were . . .

"Now that I'm abandoning the shallow life, I'll have to get a new wardrobe." Sparkle ran her fingers over a red dress with a short flirty skirt. "You can keep any that fit you. They're all designer labels."

"Thanks. They're . . ."

"I'll have to start shopping at the"—deep, deep, shudder—"big-box stores."

"I really appreciate your offer, but they're a little more wow than I usually wear."

"Sexier? You can say the word."

"Yeah, I guess so. I usually just wear jeans and T-shirts when I'm working around my plants."

"If you're going to meet the public, Cinn, then you have to represent the castle appropriately."

Cinn stared at a purple top that was just a few pieces of cloth stitched together. "Gee, I can use this while I'm repotting my plants. Wait, no, it's perfect for fertilizing."

Sparkle sighed. "When exactly did you miss the name of this place? It's the Castle of Dark Dreams. Visitors expect all things sensual." She paused. "*I* expect all things sensual."

"Fine, I get that, but these clothes are—"

"Your new uniforms. Wear them with joy." Sparkle's gaze grew thoughtful. "Your hair is a pretty color. Those blonde highlights make the color pop, but I don't know about the style. It just sort of lies there."

If Cinn hadn't had Vince in her arms, she would've clamped protective hands over her hair.

"We'll have to do something with your hair." Sparkle's gaze dropped. "And your face."

Cinn opened her mouth to complain.

Sparkle shook her head. "Sorry, but I'm the boss. I'm pulling rank on you. I own the park and you're an employee of the park." Then she smiled. "You'll love how you look."

Cinn firmed her lips in silent disagreement.

Sparkle's expression turned sly. "Even with all his

scars, Dacian is an incredible-looking man." She tried on a sorrowful expression. "I'm sure he hasn't known much love in his life."

"That won't work on me." Cinn wasn't sure if she was telling the truth, though.

"And I wasn't joking when I told you that you might be able to come up with a cure for him. Work on him like you work on your plants. Find some way to block the message that triggers his rage. You can do it. I have faith in you."

*Rah, rah, and sis-boom-bah.* Sparkle would've made a great motivational speaker-slash-cheerleader. Cinn wouldn't be winning any battles here tonight, so she'd retreat to lick her wounds and gather her strength for the next fight.

"You can't carry the clothes and your plant, too, so I'll have the clothes sent to your room." Sparkle's expression said that if it were her, she'd drop Vince and opt for the clothes.

Cinn finally made it out the door. She sighed deeply once she'd reached the relative safety of the hallway. "Do you get a spiraling-out-of-control feeling, Vince?" He might not be able to answer her, but at least he could share her emotions.

*"Personally, I think you're letting the bitch walk all over you. I wouldn't even consider wearing those slutty clothes she's sending to your room. If you need clothes, I have much more tasteful choices."*

For a moment, Cinn thought Vince was answering her, but then she recognized Asima's voice. She glanced down. Sure enough, the Siamese cat was pacing beside her. It was pretty sad when she was thinking of Asima as a friend.

"How did you know what was going on inside there?"

Asima blinked her blue eyes in surprise. *"I listened at the door, of course."*

"And you don't see anything wrong with that?"

The cat looked puzzled. *"No. How else would I find out things?"*

"Point taken." No use arguing. "You said you're the messenger of Bast, so I guess you have goddess connections."

*"Excellent goddess connections."* If she'd had a fluffy coat, Asima would've been puffed up into a round ball of feline pride. *"Bast depends on me."*

"Umm, do you think there's a chance that Bast might intercede with Airmid for me? You know, goddess to goddess?"

Asima looked horrified. *"That wouldn't be possible. Bast only interferes to help her own. I wouldn't dare ask her."*

Well, that solved that. They'd reached the elevator. "Thanks for sharing with me. I'll probably see you around now and then." Preferably then. *Wait.* Cinn had just thought of something. "Dacian said you'd gone to your room to sleep on your nice soft bed." She resisted the urge to add an extra *soft*.

Again, Asima's gaze drifted away. *"Yes, well, I found that I was too excited to sleep. So much has happened. Both you and Dacian arrived. There hasn't been this much excitement in ages."*

Cinn decided against asking for details. She waved good-bye and stepped into the elevator. Thankfully, Asima didn't follow her.

By the time Cinn reached her room, she was tired enough to believe she really could sleep. No wonder. It was only a few hours until dawn. Cinn put in her ear-plugs just to make sure she got at least a few hours of uninterrupted rest. And as she drifted off to sleep a short time later, she realized she hadn't seen her newest protector, Bain, anywhere. Some protector. But she was too tired to care.

Her last hazy impression was of Bain suddenly appearing on her couch. In that halfway state between waking and sleep, she watched him pull out a book and start reading. In the dark. Must be a dream. Dumb dream.

Something wakened Cinn. She didn't know what it was, but she knew this wasn't a normal wakening. She pried her eyes open and then quickly closed them against the glare of sunlight beaming through the narrow arrow slits that passed for windows in the castle. Someone had pulled back the damn curtains.

Cinn pulled out her earplugs as she allowed her senses to settle before opening her eyes again. She felt great for the first few seconds, until memories of the night before slapped her silly. She groaned. Blinking, she turned her head away from the sunlight. A quick glance at the clock on her bedside table told her it was afternoon sunlight brightening the room. She must've been more tired than she'd thought.

Pounding so loud that even her earplugs wouldn't have blocked it interrupted her thoughts. That must have been what wakened her. Sliding her feet to the floor, she stood, stretched, and slipped on her robe. Then she shuffled toward the door.

The pounding continued. "Jeez, I'm coming." She shuffled a little faster. Out of the corner of her eye, she noticed a piece of notepaper on the coffee table. A note? It hadn't been there last night. Had it? She couldn't remember. Caffeine. She needed coffee before she could even remember her name.

Already irritated with the day, she flung open the

door just as Edge was getting ready to pound again. "Okay, okay, I'm awake. Now go away."

Edge grinned, obviously in a better mood than last night. "Just making sure. I went down to eat breakfast and got tied up with some things Holgarth wanted me to do. Need anything?"

"Coffee." She was only capable of short sentences and simple thoughts before her first shot of caffeine. Afterward she could move into the realm of complex thoughts.

He nodded. "I'll get some. Want anything to eat?"

She decided against food. "No, I'll take a shower and then eat in the restaurant." Before she could thank him for the coffee, he was gone.

Turning, she headed toward the bathroom and then paused. Something . . . Cinn frowned. Something wasn't right. Nothing specific, just a feeling of wrongness. She glanced around. As her gaze slid across the table beneath the arrow slit of a window, she froze. *Vince.* He was gone.

Panic made her heart skip a beat. And then as her stomach dropped like a broken elevator she frantically scanned the room. *Gone.* Really gone. *Oh, God. Oh, God.* For a moment, she couldn't think, didn't know what to do first. She was shocked that when she clawed to the surface of her panic, her first coherent thought was for Dacian. But he wouldn't rise until dark, would he? Her next thought was for Edge. He was coming back with her coffee. But she couldn't wait even that long.

She ran to the closet and flung open the door. Only to be confronted by Sparkle's borrowed wardrobe. "Shit, shit, shit." She shoved aside the unwanted clothes, searching for her old jeans and chunky sweater. Gone. The bitch had taken all her clothes.

Almost panting with her fear and confusion, she

grabbed a couple of pieces of clothing and one of the only pairs of flat shoes in Sparkle's offerings, then raced into the bathroom.

She'd just pulled on the silky black top when she heard the front door open and then close. Evidently locked doors meant nothing in this cursed place. She was too worried about Vince to think about who might've come in. If it was Airmid or Sparkle, all the better. *Bring it on, bitch.* And she didn't much care which bitch it was.

She hurried from the bathroom only to find Edge setting a container down on her coffee table.

"I'd let it cool for a moment."

He didn't look at her as he picked up the piece of notepaper that Cinn had totally forgotten about in her panic over Vince.

"It's from Bain. He just wanted to let you know that Sparkle had delivered your new clothes and shoes." Then Edge glanced up.

"Whoa. Talk about a new person." His smile was slow and sexy. "Love the leather pants and silky top. Very hot. I—"

"Vince is gone."

"Vince?" He glanced around. "You had a man here last night? Bain didn't mention it."

She wanted to scream at the time wasted in explaining things to him. "No, no, no. My plant. Vince was sitting under the window last night. Now he's gone."

"Oh." He looked puzzled by her obvious upset. "Bain was here. We can ask him."

"Ask him now."

Shrugging, Edge pulled out his cell and called Bain. From listening to Edge's side of the conversation, she got that Bain was ticked at Edge for waking him and no, he didn't have a clue where the freaking plant was. No one had stolen it while he was on duty.

After what seemed hours, Edge put his cell away. "Bain didn't—"

"Could Bain have stolen Vince?"

His smile turned patronizing. "Bain's more into stealing souls than plants. I'm sure Sparkle will—"

"Fuck Sparkle. Someone stole my damn plant and I want him back."

Edge's eyes widened. He couldn't have looked more surprised if a plant, well, bit him. "If clothes make the woman, then your clothes have made you into one tough lady." He grinned. "Not a bad thing."

"No one messes with my plants." Now how to back up the tough talk? "We have to start searching for him." What if whoever took him killed him? She choked back a sob.

Just then she felt the tiniest brush against her mind. Weak and trembling, it was still recognizable. Vince was alive and reaching out to her. "Mama is coming, baby." She yanked open the door.

"Where are you going?" Edge hadn't moved.

"I . . ." *I don't know.* She closed her eyes, took a deep calming breath, and then opened them. "Why don't you tell Sparkle what happened while I check on my other plants?" Then she remembered. "You have the keys to the greenhouse, don't you?"

Edge pulled them out of his pocket to show her. "While you're checking on your plants, I'll spread the word." He pulled out his cell phone again. "I'd tap directly into everyone's mind, but with so many shields to break through I'd sap all of my power." His expression turned grim. "And I'll never let anyone catch me at less than full power."

Something in his expression hinted at a past experience, and at another time she would've been interested, but not now. "You know the castle. Where do you think I should start looking?"

He shrugged. "Your guess is as good as mine." Edge followed her out the door.

All the way down to the greenhouse she prayed that by some miracle she'd find Vince there among her other plants. A brief glance around, though, dashed her hopes. She could feel her whole body slumping. Who could've done this? Her subconscious supplied a name. *Airmid.*

Feeling as though she were sleepwalking, Cinn wandered the aisles. She stopped briefly beside Eva, her miniature rosebush. Eva was finally blooming. Cinn touched one tiny bloom. This was her newest strain of sexual energy plants. She wasn't sure yet exactly how powerful Eva would be, but right now she didn't really care.

Edge had waited outside the greenhouse, and when she finally emerged he was just putting his cell phone away. "Everything okay in there?"

She just nodded.

"Sparkle is spreading the word. She's sending someone down to guard the greenhouse when you aren't here. As soon as he arrives, we can start searching." His expression hinted that he didn't hold out much hope, though. "What exactly makes this Vince so important to you?" He left unsaid that it was just a plant, after all.

"I put a little of myself into every plant." More than she'd ever admit to anyone. That was her secret. "It's like giving birth. They're my babies."

She could tell he didn't believe her. Probably thought she was just nuts. But before he could come up with a reply, the new guard showed up.

Tall, with brown hair and eyes, along with a wide grin, he was a welcome touch of normalcy. He pulled off a cap that had some kind of fish on it. "Hi there. I'm Wade." He stuck out his hand and engulfed hers in a hearty shake. "Sorry to hear about your loss. Just go on and do what you have to do. I'll make sure no one gets to your other plants."

"You don't have any idea how much I appreciate this." Cinn thanked God for the kindness of ordinary people.

"Don't you worry, little lady. Everything will be fine. I was down this way for a big boat show and thought I'd stop by for some R & R. Stayed here before when I was doing a fishing tournament. Nice homey place."

Cinn didn't think she'd go that far.

"So when Sparkle asked me to do this, I didn't have to even think about it. I've got lots of free time."

Edge handed Wade the key to the greenhouse. "No one not connected to the castle gets in here."

"Got it." Wade stepped inside and pulled up a folding chair. He pulled out a copy of *Texas Fish and Game Magazine*. "You just go on now. Sparkle knows your plants will be safe with me."

Cinn couldn't help it; she reached out and clasped his hand in both of hers. "I owe you, Wade."

For just a moment, something strange seemed to move in Wade's eyes. He shook his head. "Felt a little funny there for a moment." He grinned. "But I'll be fine."

She turned and followed Edge into the kitchen. As they wound their way around an annoyed chef, Cinn was a little more optimistic. "I like Wade. He looks like the kind of man you can depend on."

Edge shrugged. "Yeah, he's okay for a demon."

# Chapter Six

Dacian dragged himself up through the layers of nothingness that held him captive each day. Even as the layers thinned and he drew nearer to the surface, he sensed it was still daylight. The force of the sun battered him.

Why was he waking up? He tried to force himself back into the soft cocoon of sleep, but something wouldn't allow him.

He lay quietly, trying to analyze even as his mind still clung to the safety of the darkness. There. It came again. A light brush against his mind. And then a whisper, so soft he strained to hear it.

*"Help. Cold. Box."* The voice was thin and reedy, weak. And it had a shiver to it. Vince's voice.

Vince. Cinn. *Cinn*. In a moment he was fully awake. Had something happened to her? Something must have happened, because she'd never leave the plant unprotected.

Sitting up, he rubbed a hand across his face. Damn, whenever he rose before sunset he felt like someone had slugged him with a baseball bat. Over and over and over.

He was in complete darkness. Ganymede had given him one of the vampire rooms. It was next to the dungeon—handy if he needed to be restrained fast—and had no windows. But he could still feel the sun even if he couldn't see it.

No help for that now. He had to know what had happened. He turned on the bedside light, picked up the phone, and called Sparkle. "What's happened to Cinn?"

A few minutes later he put down the phone, grabbed his clothes, and dragged himself into the shower. He didn't want to waste time on a shower, but he needed the driving water flowing over him to make him functional until the sun set.

Once dressed, he glanced at his watch. Only an hour until dark. He could do this. Bracing himself, he pulled open the door and headed upstairs.

He tracked Cinn down in a corner of the great hall where she was busy arguing with Holgarth as castle employees scurried around them, getting ready for the night's fantasies.

"I will help you search for your plant, madam, *after* I interview my last wizard." Holgarth sniffed his contempt of anyone who could get so upset over something so trivial. "And no, you may not borrow any of the castle employees in the search."

Cinn was practically vibrating with tension. "You don't understand. Sparkle, Ganymede, Edge, and Bain have helped me search, but we haven't found anything. We need more people."

Holgarth turned what he probably thought was his kind expression on her, but he just looked patronizing. "I always prefer honesty, no matter how painful. Probably someone came in to clean your room, accidentally knocked over your plant, and hid the remains so they wouldn't get in trouble."

"But I was sleeping in the bed. No one came in to clean the room. Besides, there was a guard outside my door."

"Every minute?"

She hesitated.

Holgarth pounced. "See? Your guard probably went off for a few minutes, you were sleeping soundly, and someone took your precious plant. Although God knows why anyone would want it."

Cinn's expression turned mutinous. "So you're telling me that a demon on duty wasn't enough to stop the plant thief? Great security you have here."

"Hmm. Perhaps Bain felt the need for a salad before he hunted up his main course. Demons don't always have discriminating palates." His lips twitched. Either a crappy attempt at a smile or a nervous tic.

"Glad you think it's funny, wizard. I wonder how much of a giggle it would be if someone stole your staff, or wand, or whatever kind of damn stick you use." She crossed her arms and prepared to wait the wizard out.

"No one would *dare*. And I'd hardly call a wizard's staff a *stick*." Offended, Holgarth turned away and climbed onto the dais. He seated himself at the head of the banquet table. Another man sat at the foot.

Holgarth harrumphed. "You, Clarence, are the last of those who would take my place here. All the others have failed miserably. Are you prepared to show me your skills?"

Dacian noticed there were numbers on the backs of the chairs. "Holy hell, Holgarth. How many wizards did you interview today?"

"A mere ten. All spectacular failures. Now only one is left." He speared the wizard wannabe with a stare guaranteed to curdle the poor guy's blood. "I might suggest that you begin your career by changing your name. The name Clarence will not engender confidence in the untutored masses. Perhaps something more dramatic might help." He studied Clarence. "Or not."

Cinn turned to see Dacian for the first time. She

didn't smile, but pleasure flooded her eyes before the worry returned.

That momentary expression warmed him, no matter how much he tried to deny it. He started to put a comforting hand on her shoulder but stopped before he made physical contact. Because of what he was, vampire, his reactions were stronger than a human's. He wanted her. She didn't need to see him showing fang as a demonstration of his affection.

"Sparkle told me about Vince." He still didn't feel right telling her that Vince had chosen to speak to him rather than her. "Any clues to who took him or where he is?"

She shook her head. "I think he's still alive, though. But I need to get to him in time. Almost everyone's been really helpful." Cinn aimed a pointed stare at Holgarth.

Holgarth ignored her in favor of watching his last victim. The guy carried a staff that looked too big for him. He almost tripped and fell as he stepped off the dais.

"Gracefulness and agility are both parts of a wizard's mystique, Clarence. And I'd advise that you find a smaller staff." Holgarth's expression said that only wizards such as himself deserved a big staff.

Completely cowed, Clarence nodded and then raised the staff as he launched into a chant. Dacian had his doubts about this whole thing. There were too many people around. Anything could happen when an inexperienced wizard got going.

"You know, Holgarth, things could get out of control fast. Maybe you should take a few precautions so that—"

Holgarth turned and hit him with an imperious glare. "Don't tell me how to conduct my business, vampire. And you are certainly not the one to speak of control." He offered his trademark sniff of contempt.

Dacian could learn to hate this guy. But he was right. Every time Dacian lost control, he also lost a little of his self-confidence. The one mystery was why he could resist Stephan's demand that he return to him but not the rage. Until he solved the whole puzzle, he couldn't stay around people long. *Around people like Cinn.*

He stopped thinking about his own problems as Clarence's chant reached a shrill conclusion. Suddenly, everyone in the great hall disappeared except for Holgarth, Clarence, and him. But Dacian didn't care about the other people. "Where the hell is Cinn?" Before he could stop himself, he grabbed Clarence by the back of his scrawny neck, lifted him into the air, and shook him.

Holgarth coughed. "Umm, perhaps they haven't quite left the hall yet." There was something strange about the wizard's voice.

Still holding Clarence suspended, Dacian looked around. Nothing. He looked down. Nothing. He looked up. *Oh, hell.*

Bats, lots of bats, clung to the ceiling or darted frantically in every direction.

"Not very creative, Clarence." Holgarth didn't seem overly concerned. "Perhaps if you'd turned them into colorful balloons I might have deemed you more worthy. It's always more difficult to turn the living into inert matter. Here, let me demonstrate."

Dacian didn't know about that. He figured he could change a wizard into inert matter without working up a sweat. He dropped Clarence, who immediately scuttled out of reach, and bore down on Holgarth. The wizard hadn't allowed for his vampire speed, and had barely begun his chant when Dacian reached him. Dacian clasped the old man's shoulder and squeezed, just enough to remind Holgarth what he could do in a matter of seconds. Then he leaned close to the wizard.

"You're the high muckety-muck wizard. Change them back."

"Perhaps if you stop trying to crush my shoulder I might actually be able to do that. I don't function well while in pain."

Dacian shoved closed the door in his mind that demanded lots of violence and released Holgarth. But before Holgarth could do anything other than rub his shoulder, Clarence spoke up.

"I can fix it, I can fix it." Picking up the staff he'd dropped, he launched into a frantic chant that even to Dacian's ears didn't sound right.

With a horrified, "Stop, for God's sake stop!" Holgarth launched himself at the fledgling wizard.

Dacian didn't have a clue why Holgarth was so upset, but from the sound of Holgarth's voice he knew he'd better stop Clarence. He put his speed to good use. Dacian took Clarence in a flying tackle that effectively ended his chant.

Holgarth stood over them, breathing hard and looking pale. He waved his hand in a vague shooing motion toward Clarence. "Begone. Perhaps in a few hundred years you'll have your power under control, but right now you're what the common people would call a loose cannon."

Clarence didn't take Holgarth's criticism well. His expression turned ugly, all of his naive-young-wizard persona gone. "You're not a master wizard, old man. You don't have the guts to handle power the way it should be handled. You let stupid scruples get in the way of greatness. I won't make that mistake. I'll be a hundred times more powerful than you." With that pronouncement, he once again retrieved his fallen staff and left the great hall.

Dacian didn't have time to worry about the guy's bruised ego. The bats were growing more agitated. It was almost dark outside. All it would take was one person throwing open the huge doors leading to the castle courtyard to release them. After that, who knew where they'd go? "Do it now, wizard."

Holgarth didn't know that his long life hung by a very thin thread.

He cast Dacian a dark glance. Maybe he did.

Instead of answering, Holgarth flung his arms into the air and shouted a few words in a language Dacian didn't recognize.

And suddenly everything was back the way it had been. Castle employees continued doing what they'd been doing before their foray into the bat world, completely oblivious. Amazing. But most amazing of all was that Cinn was once again at his side.

No amount of warning shouts from his mind could stop him. He pulled her to him and kissed her. Not a relieved peck on the cheek. This was a deep exploration of her soft lips along with everything hot and sweet that went with them. For a moment she stood frozen, not reacting to the assault on her mouth. Then she opened to him and he took full advantage. Who knew where it would've gone if not for Holgarth?

"This is hardly an appropriate spectacle for the employees to witness." He was in full sarcastic mode. "And even though I'm sure you find it pleasurable, it will in no way help to locate Ms. Airmid's missing plant."

Yeah, Dacian could definitely hate Holgarth.

Reluctantly, he released Cinn. She had a glazed look in her eyes, but that wasn't all he saw in her eyes. Heat. And something unnamed, which excited his vampire senses way too much. He forced himself to think of totally gross things to keep his cock and his fangs in check. Imagining Holgarth naked did the trick.

"What happened?" Cinn had finally found her voice.

Holgarth brushed a piece of lint from his robe. "The last master-wizard failure turned you into a bat. And then he compounded the horror by almost losing you completely."

Dacian narrowed his gaze. "Explain the losing-her-completely part."

Holgarth was in his element. "If we hadn't stopped him . . ."

Dacian seemed to remember only one of them stopping him.

"He would've finished his garbled spell and every bat in our proverbial belfry would've become nothing, their molecules separating and mixing with all the other molecules in the universe. Even I, with my immense power, could never have pulled them back to their original bodies."

Dacian knew his emotions mirrored Cinn's expression. He wanted to hunt Clarence down and rip out his useless throat. He clamped down on his need to kill, but it was tough.

"I hope Clarence doesn't try something like that again." Holgarth looked really concerned. "I'm sure what happened was an honest mistake made by someone who could never take my place." Everything always came back to Holgarth's superiority.

"I do have to thank you, though, vampire. I'm getting old, and I'm not as quick as I used to be. Your instant reaction was immensely helpful."

Dacian was amazed Holgarth had deigned to even recognize his part in the whole thing.

"Now that the last tryout is done, can you help search for Vince?" Cinn might have been a little shaken, but she hadn't taken her eye off her ultimate goal.

Holgarth's sigh was long and dramatic. "I suppose if I must." He glanced at Dacian in what was supposed to be a male-bonding moment. "Women tend to be too emotional over things that really aren't that important."

Dacian could almost feel Cinn's steam build up. Any minute it would come shooting out of her ears.

"Women also have great intuition." She turned and started to walk away. "They know a pointy-headed jerk when they see one."

Dacian followed her as she flung open the great hall door and stomped out into the courtyard. A quick glance skyward assured him that he was safe from the sun.

All Cinn's bravado seemed to desert her once she was away from Holgarth. She raked her fingers through her hair before turning to him. "I've searched all afternoon. Where can he be?" She flung her hands into the air. "I don't even know where to look. I've hit everywhere I could think of in the castle. Sparkle made an excuse to go into all of the guest rooms, but he wasn't in any of them."

*Help. Cold. Box.* Dacian struggled with his decision. If he told her now that Vince had spoken to him, she'd be pissed off that he hadn't told her sooner. Besides, she'd feel hurt that her plant hadn't spoken to her first. The alternative was continuing to keep his mouth shut. But to optimize their chances of finding Vince, everyone had to know his last message. Someone else might be able to figure out where he was from those words.

Cinn was standing staring up at the darkening sky, her hair lifting in the light breeze. She'd come out without her coat, and even though it wasn't freezing in Galveston, it was cold enough. She'd clasped her arms around herself, but she was still shivering.

Without analyzing the right or wrong of it, Dacian made his decision. "Let's go down to my room and talk about it."

She looked puzzled. "What's to talk about?" But she let him guide her back into the castle.

Once in his room, she glanced around. "No windows. Doesn't this place give you claustrophobia?"

He laughed. And if it was a little bitter, so be it. "You have no idea what claustrophobic feels like."

Her interest in finding out shone in her eyes, but now wasn't the time to talk about him. "Vince sent me a message after he was taken."

That bombshell sat between them for a full five seconds before exploding.

"A message? What do you mean? Why didn't you tell me? What did he say?" With each question, her anger level rose.

Dacian held up his hands. "If you'll be quiet, I'll tell you what I know."

Her silence sizzled with impatience and fury.

"The first time I met Vince, I talked to him. You heard me. When we were on our way out of the greenhouse, he answered me." He tapped his head. "Up here. He only said two words, but it was an answer."

Cinn couldn't contain herself. "Why didn't you say anything?"

He exhaled deeply. "Exactly because of the expression I see in your eyes now. He should've spoken to you, not me. I didn't want you to feel bad, so I decided to keep it to myself. It didn't really mean anything. He didn't say anything important." He shrugged. "Probably just felt more at ease talking to a male first. Someone like him." That sounded lame even to Dacian.

"Like him?" Her expression said she was trying to decide what class of plants Dacian belonged in. Most likely something in the turnip family.

"I figured he'd eventually talk with you, too. By that time I'd be gone, and you'd never have to know he spoke with me first."

She narrowed her eyes. "You'd be gone. Are you planning on leaving soon?"

*Oh, shit.* He searched for an explanation that would appease her. "Who knows? But you won't be here long. Sparkle said you only planned to stay two weeks."

Cinn looked uncertain and then nodded. "I'm ticked at you for not telling me this before, but my anger isn't important now. What did Vince say after he was kidnapped?"

Dacian didn't know if it was healthy to assign terms like "kidnapped" to a plant. But then he thought about Vince's words and decided that yes, the plant was a sentient being. No way around it.

"His vocabulary's limited, but he said three words: help, cold, and box. That's it. I don't have a clue what it means."

"*Help* shows that he wasn't taken by anyone he considered a friend. *Cold* could mean he's in a fridge or freezer or somewhere outside. *Box* must mean that he's not sitting out in a field somewhere. Vince doesn't have many experiences to draw from, so any container with a lid would be a box to him." She seemed to have forgotten to be mad at him as she tried to figure out Vince's message.

Dacian stood. "Okay, we start by checking out fridges and freezers."

Cinn was glad to be *doing* something instead of sitting around talking. Action kept her from feeling just a little betrayed because Vince had chosen to say his first words to someone else. Action also kept thoughts of Dacian at a minimum. Right now she was floating across the emotional pool that was her response to him and that *kiss*. But given time to think and analyze, she could find herself sinking into deep water.

When they pushed into the hustle and bustle of dinner preparation in the castle restaurant, the chef was *not* a happy man.

"You will remove yourselves from my kitchen. Immediately." He wasn't a tall man, but he imbued his words with all the authority of an emperor.

"We just need to take a quick look in your fridge and freezers." Cinn fought to keep her tone calm and reasonable. Going ballistic wouldn't get her what she wanted.

"Absolutely not. No one enters my kitchen and disturbs dinner preparations." He planted himself firmly in front of them. "I told Sparkle that I'd allow you to pass through the kitchen to get to your greenhouse, but that's all."

Cinn had opened her mouth to launch a verbal blast that would blow his chef's hat right off his self-important head, when Dacian put his finger over her lips.

The shock of his touch kept her quiet for just a moment.

Dacian caught the chef's gaze and held it. "Tell me your name."

The man blinked and then stared into Dacian's eyes. "Chef Phil."

Dacian's smile was warm and encouraging. "We think you have some tainted food in your kitchen, Chef Phil. We're going to check the fridges and freezer."

Chef Phil nodded, still never looking away from Dacian's eyes.

"Good. You'll stand right here to make sure no one interrupts us."

"I'll stand right here."

As Cinn slipped past the chef, she stared at Dacian. "You said you couldn't glamour people."

"I lied."

"What else have you lied about?"

Dacian shrugged and then pulled open the door to the walk-in freezer. "Think of it as a continuing road of discovery." He waved her away from the door. "Don't come in. It's too cold. The cold won't bother me."

"I'm coming in." Left unsaid, but she was sure he understood, was the fact that she didn't trust him.

His expression said he was okay with that.

A short time later, they were on their way out of the kitchen. No Vince. Dacian stopped in front of the chef. "You'll only remember that you willingly gave us permission to look around your kitchen because of reports of contaminated food. We found nothing wrong. You're relieved."

"Relieved." He nodded.

Once outside the restaurant, they stopped to discuss their next move.

Dacian injected the voice of reason. "Before we go running off in another direction, we need to tell Sparkle and Ganymede what Vince said. With their powers, they may have skills to help find Vince that we don't."

Cinn felt stupid for not thinking about that sooner. "Where do you think Sparkle is? I don't have her cell number."

"I don't need her number."

He looked grim as he grew still, that scary quiet that screamed, "Hey, not human here."

"What are you doing?"

"Tapping into her thoughts."

"You didn't say you could do that."

"Everything's on a need-to-know basis, sweetheart."

*Sweetheart?* Who'd given him permission to call her *sweetheart?* That was a word she didn't use lightly. She'd never call him sweetheart unless she meant it. And he'd be long in the fang before she threw anything that loving his way.

She kept quiet for the short time it evidently took him to fill Sparkle in on the latest news. When he looked as though he was finished, she continued her train of thought. "So I assume you don't really need a phone at all."

"I use a cell all the time. A human mind is an easy-enter, but getting into a nonhuman mind is hard work. It drains my power. And a vampire with no power is a dead vampire. Permanently dead."

*"What's happened? Everyone's running around. I've been out all afternoon. Did I miss something?"*

Asima's voice in her head drew Cinn's gaze down. The blue-point Siamese gazed up at her with those spectacular blue eyes. If you could get past her annoyance factor, she was really a beautiful animal.

*"Thank you for the compliment, but I'm only borrowing a cat's form. As I should, since I'm the messenger of the goddess of all cats. And I have no idea why you'd think I was annoying."*

Okay, this had to stop right now. "Get out of my head, cat. No one gave you permission to root around in my thoughts." She cast Dacian a meaningful glare so he'd realize this was aimed at him, too.

Asima managed to put a puzzled expression on her cat face. *"Why would I need permission? You wouldn't even know I was there if I didn't tell you."* She paused to think things through. *"Although over time you'll learn to feel the light brush of my mind against yours. It's very subtle though, because I'm so powerful."*

Cinn was shocked. "You mean you're still going to read my mind?"

Asima blinked. *"Of course. How else will I find out what I want to know?"*

"Heard this before." Cinn knew that talking to herself didn't bode well for her mental health, but Asima had that effect on her.

Dacian stepped into the breach as Cinn tried to think of a way to reason with a being that didn't think in a human way. A good thing, too, because she was almost at the point of abandoning reason and resorting to throwing things.

"Someone stole a plant from Cinn's room. The plant is very important to her. We're trying to find him while there's still a chance that he's alive."

Asima looked fascinated. *"You called the plant a he. Why?"*

Cinn decided now wasn't the time to keep secrets. If there was a chance Asima could help in the hunt, she had to know what was at stake. "I enhance plants, Asima. I make them more than they otherwise would be. Vince is sentient. He feels emotions, and—" she glanced at Dacian—"can evidently talk. He's alive. And I don't want him to die cold and alone." Oh, boy. She blinked madly. *Not going to cry, not going to cry.* A tear slipped down her cheek. *Damn.*

Asima's eyes grew wide. *"Alive? Like you and me?"* She sounded horrified.

Dacian took up the explanation, giving Cinn a chance to pull her emotions together. Maybe that would count on the plus side when she finally added up all the minuses he'd racked up tonight.

"I'd say he's at the child stage. He feels emotions and reacts to them, and he's gaining a basic vocabulary. But yeah, he's aware like you and me."

"*Oh.*" Asima seemed more shocked than the explanation seemed to warrant. "*I . . .*"

Cinn would never know what Asima would have said because Sparkle and Ganymede joined them. Ganymede had cookie crumbs in his whiskers, and he didn't look too thrilled to be part of the search party. He must've seen her staring at the crumbs.

"*Searching for this plant is tough work. I have to keep my strength up. Besides, Sparkle baked cookies today. The real thing. No packaged crap. Maybe this depth and character thing isn't so bad after all.*"

From Sparkle's expression, Cinn hoped Ganymede wasn't counting on another batch of cookies any time soon. And Sparkle was wearing what must be her version of roughing-it clothes: designer jeans with rhinestones, clingy top that shouted expensive, a short leather jacket, and boots that Sparkle would never find in a discount store.

Sparkle wasn't smiling. "I ruined three nails on those cookies. Not that I notice my nails anymore," she hurried to assure everyone. "But the store stuff is just as good. Open the package, put the precut cookies on the pan, bake for ten minutes. Works for me."

And before Cinn could even think about saying anything, Sparkle turned on her. "Yes, these are my old clothes. I couldn't go searching for your plant naked, could I?"

Ganymede perked right up. "*Wouldn't bother me, cuddle-bunny.*"

Sparkle ignored him. "Edge and Bain are on their way. Everyone will help search until it's time for the fantasies to start. Then they'll have to take care of our customers."

Fair enough. Cinn appreciated any help she could get.

*"I'll help, too."* Asima's words said one thing, but her tone said she wasn't too excited about the whole thing.

Cinn wouldn't blame her if she backed out of the search party. Since Dacian and she had looked into everything in the castle that would qualify as cold and a box, the next step was to search outside. Cinn didn't figure Asima for a cold-weather cat.

Once Edge, Bain, and even Holgarth showed up, Dacian filled them in on Vince's three last words. Even with all her worry, Cinn got some satisfaction from their shocked expressions. A plant could communicate. Let Holgarth call *that* unimportant.

They worked out a search plan and then separated. Dacian and Cinn stayed together and Asima tagged along with them.

After searching all the garbage bins on the park grounds and not hearing any encouraging words from the rest of the searchers, Cinn was almost ready to give up. If they didn't find him soon it might be too late because the trash collectors would empty the bins in the morning and cart everything to the dump. And if she were honest, she'd have to admit that most likely he was already gone. Dacian hadn't heard his voice again, and she hadn't felt him brushing against her mind.

Asima had remained strangely silent. Not that Cinn didn't appreciate the quiet, but it gave her too much time to think. About Vince, about Dacian, and about how her life seemed to be spiraling out of control. She was in the middle of wondering how she'd react if Dacian reverted to his vampire nature—whatever that was—when Asima finally spoke.

*"What will happen to your plant if he's out in the cold?"*

"He'll die." Not exactly true. Vince could survive the cold, but if a lie would energize the search, then she'd lie her butt off.

Asima was silent for a little longer. *"Umm, maybe we should check some of the trash cans outside the park."*

Distracted, Cinn didn't pay much attention to her answer. "Where would we start? I bet there are a hundred trash cans outside the park walls. Besides, if someone was going to throw Vince in the trash, why not just heave him in one closer to the castle?"

*"Because this person knew that no one would bother checking outside the park?"*

Something in Asima's voice caught Cinn's attention. Squatting down, she peered into the cat's eyes. "Do you know something, Asima?"

Asima's gaze slid away from Cinn's. *"Maybe."*

Out of the corner of her eye, Cinn saw Dacian getting ready to yell at Asima. She held up her hand to stop him. Asima was a powerful being, and Cinn didn't think she could be bullied.

"Anything you know, you need to tell me now while we can still save him." Okay, she'd pull out all the stops. "He's just a baby, out in the cold, frightened and alone."

Emotion glistened in Asima's eyes. *"I'm not crying. Messengers of Bast are cold, analytical, and never ever cry."*

"I understand how strong you are, but are you strong enough to tell us the truth?" She held her breath. Everything depended on Asima now.

*"Well, there might be a trash can across the street from the park. On the seawall. Next to a bench. And that trash can might have a plant in it."* She blinked rapidly.

Cinn was already up and running. As she glanced at Dacian, she could tell from his expression that he was passing the info on to the other searchers. Asima kept ahead of them, covering the ground in long leaps. Lucky for Asima, there wasn't much late-night traffic on Sea-wall Boulevard or else she'd have used up at least eight of her nine lives.

Everyone converged on the trash can together. No one moved as Cinn reached into the can . . . and closed her fingers around Vince's pot. When she pulled the pot from the can, everyone cheered. Vince looked limp, definitely not in good shape, but at least no one had yanked him out of the pot. He could be saved. She gently rolled up his vine and tucked his pot under her coat.

She didn't stop to question Asima as she ran back to the greenhouse. Dacian stayed with her. Asima and the others didn't follow.

Panting, she stopped at the greenhouse door, and when Wade swung it open she hurried inside.

"Well, hello, beautiful lady. Did anyone ever tell you that you're as lovely as a rainbow trout?"

"Not now, Wade. I have to save Vince." Somewhere in the back of her mind she made note of Wade's strange compliment, but then pushed it aside.

Dacian remained silent as she worked over Vince. Finally, she straightened. "He'll survive. I'm leaving him here because of the controlled temperature and humidity. *I'll* guard the greenhouse tonight." And God help the person who tried to stop her.

"At least come back into the castle long enough to grab something to eat. Besides, everyone's meeting so Asima can tell her story. You'll want to be there." Dacian looked anxious to be gone.

Cinn stared at Wade. He stared back at her with adoration shining in his demon's eyes. She sucked in her breath. That was right, Wade was a demon. And he'd seemed so normal. If *he* could be nonhuman, then anyone could. But at least he'd have the power to defend her greenhouse.

"Fine." She looked at Wade. "I appreciate you giving up so much of your time today. I owe you."

"No problem, ma'am. You know, I'd trade my favorite Shimano CTE 200 DC reel with the computer chip in it for a night out with you."

Oh, boy. Cinn glanced at Dacian. Dacian didn't look amused. Well, she thought Wade was sweet. Strange, but sweet.

Once inside, Dacian and Cinn followed Sparkle into the meeting room attached to the restaurant. Asima perched on her own chair. She looked elegant and unflustered.

Ganymede didn't bother with a chair. He'd plunked his ample bottom on the table next to Sparkle's chair. Holgarth sat at the head of the table, probably his self-appointed spot. He was that kind of guy.

"Now that everyone is here." His glance at Cinn and Dacian suggested that they'd kept everyone waiting for hours. "We'll begin the investigation into how the plant, Vince, ended up in the trash can."

Asima turned calm eyes on Holgarth. *"You are such a blowhard, wizard. There doesn't have to be an investigation. I threw the plant into the trash can."*

Humans might have gasped. Nonhumans just stared. Well, Cinn was a human, and she gasped loud enough to cause everyone to glance her way.

*"I materialized in Cinn's room while she was sleeping. Bain was asleep on her couch. He sleeps very soundly for a demon."*

"You slept on my couch without my permission?" Cinn couldn't keep the horror out of her voice. A *demon* had slept with her.

Everyone stared at Bain. He shrugged. "I don't do floors."

As one, everyone's gaze swung back to Asima.

*"I took the plant. I was supposed to destroy it, but I felt bad about that. It's such a pretty plant. So instead of throwing it into the Gulf, I threw it in the trash can. I thought someone might pass by and find it."*

"And why did you do this dastardly deed?" Holgarth was at his pretentious best.

"The goddess Airmid told me to."

# Chapter Seven

Silence filled the room. Even Cinn didn't gasp this time. Dacian figured she'd used up all her air on her first gasp. He knew Holgarth was supposed to be asking the questions, but he couldn't wait for the wizard to spit the next one out. "Why would you do what Airmid told you to do?"

Holgarth's gaze was cold enough to freeze Dacian's eyeballs. "I believe that I'm in charge of asking questions, vampire."

Dacian wasn't intimidated. "Yeah, well, then ask them faster."

Holgarth turned to Asima. "Exactly why would you do what Airmid told you to do?"

Asima settled in. She looked like she was primed for a long explanation. *"I work for Bast, greatest of all goddesses, protector of cats everywhere, queen of—"*

"Yes, yes, we know. Get on with it." Holgarth tapped his finger impatiently on the table.

Asima speared him with an enigmatic cat stare that could mean anything from, "I think you're an amazing person," to "You're a wizened old fart."

Dacian suspected the latter.

*"Bast and Airmid have been best friends for thousands of years. So when Airmid needed someone to help her achieve her goals, she contacted Bast."* Asima offered a cat shrug. *"And Bast ordered me to help Airmid. I must obey my goddess."*

Holgarth leaned forward. "Why did Airmid want to destroy the plant?"

Asima looked as though she thought the answer must be obvious. *"Because he's an abomination."*

"He absolutely is not. He's timid and shy and—"

"Be quiet, woman." Holgarth was at his most bombastic.

"Oh, stuff it, Holgarth." Cinn half rose from her chair.

Dacian was proud of her. He couldn't remember the last time he'd cared enough about anyone other than his brother to feel pride in them.

Asima turned her gaze on Cinn. *"I apologize for what I did to Vince, but you must understand that I couldn't defy my goddess."*

"Yet, in the end, you did." Cinn seemed to find that an incredible act.

Asima sighed. *"Bast will be displeased with me."*

Holgarth made an attempt to wrest control of the meeting back into his own hands. "What else did Airmid want you to do?"

*"She wanted me to destroy all the plants in the greenhouse and then take care of the plants that were already in guests' rooms."*

"The bitch."

If expressions were anything to go by, everyone shared the opinion Cinn had voiced.

Asima brightened. *"Of course, I can't do that now that you have a demon guarding the greenhouse. Airmid wants me to be discreet and not call attention to myself."*

*"Like that's ever going to happen."* Ganymede made his first contribution to the discussion. *"Did you bring the bag of jellybeans with you, babe?"* He glanced hopefully at Sparkle.

Sparkle pulled a bag of candy from her purse and put it on the table. Ganymede dove in. Didn't look like he'd be contributing anything else tonight.

Asima was evidently used to Ganymede's insults, because she rattled on. *"And I obviously won't be able to reach the plants in the guests' rooms if you move them all into the greenhouse, too. You should do that right away before I finish taking the nap I intend to take as soon as I get back to my room."*

"And you assume you'll have a room to go back to?" Sparkle sounded gleeful at the prospect of kicking Asima's furry butt out the door.

*"Of course. I'm your only connection to Airmid."*

Dacian was tired of all this back-and-forth. Edge and Bain were starting to look restless, too. "Where is Airmid now?"

*"In the castle somewhere."*

Well, hell. Dacian glanced at Cinn. Her hands were clenched into fists in her lap.

"So let's go find the bitch." Edge had the right idea. "What's she look like?"

*"I don't know."* Asima looked bored. *"She communicated mentally with me."* And then before anyone could ask another question, she disappeared.

"I hate when she does that." Holgarth looked ticked.

It must have been tough losing his star witness right in the middle of the interrogation. Dacian pushed back his chair and stood. Cinn did the same.

"We have to get all the plants out of the guests' rooms." Cinn's voice didn't quiver, but the strain had to be working on her.

"Asima didn't say what Airmid had planned for Cinn." And right now Cinn was more important to Dacian than a hundred of her plants. "I'll be with her at night, but from dawn till sunset there always has to be someone watching her." He cast Bain a pointed stare. "Someone who doesn't sleep on the job."

Bain glared before looking away.

"I'll be with her in the afternoon." Sparkle didn't sound happy about that. "Tomorrow I have to buy new outfits. Ordinary. Serviceable. Cheap." She said each word as though it burned her tongue. "I'll need support." She glanced at Cinn. "Would you go with me to the . . ." She closed her eyes, girding herself to say the words. ". . . big-box store?"

"What store did you have in mind?" There wasn't a lot of interest in Cinn's voice.

Sparkle shrugged. "I don't know. I've never been in one."

*Oh, crap.* Cinn was going to have a hell of a day with the queen of sex and sin. Well, Dacian might not be able to help her with Sparkle, but he could sure make the rest of the night more comfortable. "I think Cinn needs some rest now."

"I haven't adjourned the meeting yet." It seemed as if that really bothered Holgarth.

"Too bad." Dacian guided Cinn out of the room.

She said nothing until they walked into her room and he closed the door behind them. "Thanks for getting me out of there." Cinn glanced around and then froze.

He followed her gaze. On top of her pillow lay a sprig of some plant. "What is it?"

"Lavender. From Airmid. Who else would put it there?" Her expression turned bitter. "Just a friendly reminder that she can go anywhere she wants and there's nowhere I can hide."

Fury rose in him. He felt his fangs pushing against his lip and knew if she glanced at him now she'd see the black eyes he'd shown her in the dungeon. With a huge effort, he pushed back against his need for violence. "You don't have to hide. I'm here with you. And there are enough nonhumans in this castle to give even Airmid a fight. She's on our turf now."

Cinn turned weary eyes toward him. "Thanks for the support. Appreciate it." She looked around as though she didn't know where to start. "I'm just going to grab a few things. I'm sleeping in the greenhouse tonight."

He didn't try to argue with her. He figured it would be useless anyway. "Ganymede will already be collecting plants from the guests' rooms. He'll be able to do it without disturbing anyone. I'll have a cot brought down to the greenhouse while you're gathering your stuff together."

Pulling out his cell, he ordered the cot along with pillows and bedding while she pulled what she'd need from her closet and then went into the bathroom. Torture was listening to her shower run while resisting the need to climb in with her.

He was vampire. Which meant that not only did he have preternatural speed and enhanced senses, but also a sex drive that in the right situation could be obsessive. It was getting to that stage with Cinn.

Dacian wanted to slide his hands over her bared body, slick from the warm water sluicing over her smooth skin. Then he'd slowly lick a trail . . . He shook his head. *Stop it.* Somewhere along the way he'd almost forgotten about Taurin and the danger from Stephan.

His torture ended when she finally emerged from the shower. Her face was scrubbed clean and she wore baggy jeans and a bulky sweatshirt. She had fuzzy slippers. And still he thought she was the sexiest thing he'd seen in centuries.

She seemed to feel a need to fill up the silence. "I didn't want to leave the room in my nightgown, but I have to be comfortable when I sleep.

He allowed his gaze to drop to those slippers again. They fascinated him. He knew he was smiling.

"They say sleep to me, okay?" She sounded defensive.

He held up his hands. "Hey, I don't care what you wear on your feet."

She wasn't appeased. "I can't get to sleep if I'm not wearing something I associate with bedtime. It's just a habit."

Dacian knew he shouldn't say it, but he did. "Do you have to wear something you associate with sex when you make love?"

If he'd expected her to flush and get all embarrassed, he would've been disappointed.

Cinn met his gaze directly. "That would be tough to do. I don't wear *anything* when I make love. How about you?" She looked as though she expected an answer.

"You're right. It's best with nothing at all." The mental image almost tipped him over the edge of his personal control.

She looked away from him then, as she headed for the door. He caught up with her and they took the elevator down to the hotel lobby in silence.

As the door opened and they started to walk out, another woman stepped in. She slammed into Dacian.

The woman's eyes widened as she stared at him. Slowly, she backed out of the elevator, never taking her gaze from him. "Dacian." That one word was whispered on a soft sigh of emotion.

He stepped from the elevator. "Kyla." Dacian remembered her after all the centuries. Their relationship had been a mistake, one of many in his life.

She put her hand over her mouth, her eyes wide. Beside him, he felt Cinn tense. *Hell.*

"Cinn, this is Kyla Mackenzie. A friend from a long time ago." He returned his gaze to Kyla. "Kyla, this is Cinn Airmid. We're working on a . . . project together."

"You're really alive." She'd removed her hand from her mouth, and now she just stared.

"Vampire?" Cinn got right to the point.

He nodded.

Kyla didn't even glance at her. "Everyone thought you were dead."

"An understandable conclusion." And if he sounded a little stiff, that was also understandable. "Why are you here?"

"I need to sit down." Kyla motioned toward a nearby grouping of leather chairs.

He steered a strangely quiet Cinn toward the chairs. When they were all seated, he waited for Kyla to explain, while he tried not to remember how they'd parted.

"Yesterday Eric got a call from someone named Edge. The guy said you were here. Eric called everyone he could reach who'd been there when the fire . . ." Her voice faded away as she looked down at her hands. Finally, she looked up again. "Anyway, Eric said he was flying in, and I said I'd be here, too."

"Is anyone else coming?" He didn't need any more Mackenzies complicating things.

She shook her head. "Wow, this is incredible. I mean, I know that Eric said you were alive, but to really see you . . ." Kyla trailed off again.

This could get uncomfortable. "Maybe we can get together for a few drinks before you leave. Catch up on each others' lives." That wasn't going to happen, if he could help it.

"Sure, sure." She waved him away. "I know you have things to do. Have you seen Taurin yet?"

"No." He knew his answer was clipped, but he couldn't help it. Taurin was the only person he loved in the world, and facing him would be one of the toughest things he ever did.

Dacian stood, and Cinn stood with him. No use prolonging this meeting. But maybe before he left he'd stop to say good-bye to her. After all, Kyla had obviously flown in just for him. He wished she hadn't. He didn't like to feel obligated.

By the time they got to the greenhouse, Dacian was mentally ducking the questions he could sense zinging silently his way from Cinn. He got a brief reprieve from Wade.

The demon met them at the door. He didn't even look at Dacian. He stared at Cinn. His gaze was a slurpy lick the length of a melting ice-cream cone. Dacian growled low in his throat. He didn't bother to analyze his reaction.

"I just wanted you to know I bought a new Pathfinder. I'm naming her Cinn. Maybe you'll let me take you out on her someday."

Dacian couldn't figure out how a demon's eyes could look like a lovesick puppy's.

"Wow, thank you, Wade." Her expression said she didn't have a clue what a Pathfinder was. "Umm, you can go get some rest now. Dacian and I will be here until dawn."

Wade's eyes narrowed on Dacian. But then Wade dismissed him to return his attention to Cinn. "I could protect you during the day. I wouldn't let you out of my sight."

The slight flaring of Cinn's eyes said she was getting

a mental image of the demon dogging her footsteps for an entire day. "I truly appreciate the offer, but I'll be going out with Sparkle tomorrow."

"Then I'll guard your plants." Wade's tone said that was settled.

Dacian had his doubts about that plan. For whatever reason, Wade believed he was in love with Cinn. Strange. Demons weren't usually an emotional lot. What worried Dacian was the demon's reaction when Cinn eventually had to tell him she didn't return his love. Dacian didn't know how powerful Wade was, but any demon could make a destructive scorned lover.

"Thanks."

From her expression, Dacian could see Cinn was coming to the same conclusion.

They watched Wade trudge reluctantly away, and then went into the greenhouse. Cinn's cot was ready for her. He'd sit in the chair. *And watch her sleep.* He'd enjoy the rest of the night.

But she wasn't quite ready for sleep. After checking to see how Vince was coming along, she sat on the edge of the cot. "So you and Kyla had a relationship?"

He was glad he'd long ago given up facial expressions. "What makes you think that?"

"Umm, maybe the weepy, soulful looks she threw your way? Those weren't the eyes of someone who'd just been a friend." She turned thoughtful. "And they weren't the eyes of someone who was over you."

He didn't try to hold back his laughter. "Where did that conclusion come from?"

"Did you guys have a relationship?"

"Yes."

"Did *you* break it off?"

"Yeah. But that was centuries ago, and believe me,

she's over it." Cinn didn't have to know about the threats Kyla had flung at him as he left.

She shrugged. "Maybe. Women understand other women. There's something still there."

He was just about to comment on her theory when Stephan stepped into his mind.

*"You know the routine, Dacian. Come back to me. You'll fight by my side. All my other children are here. We're waiting for you. Do I have to repeat the threat?"*

Not now! Not with Cinn so close. Dacian had never been so scared in his life. He had to stall his maker while Cinn escaped.

*"I've been thinking about it, Stephan. The whole punishment thing is getting old."*

He reached for Cinn and gave her a hard shove toward the door. "Run!"

Dacian heard Stephan's sigh whisper through his mind. *"You have someone there who you don't want to get hurt, so you're trying to stall me. Can I assume your answer is the usual?"*

Dacian didn't answer. Instead, he sent a mental warning aimed at Ganymede. He was the most powerful entity in the castle, and he'd handled Dacian before. Dacian's last coherent thought was a hope that he wouldn't kill anyone this time.

Cinn ran. She could hardly drag enough air into her lungs as she breathed in panting gasps while her heart pounded out a rhythm of terror.

But she wasn't running away from Dacian. She was running toward help. She had to reach someone who could stop what was happening to him. Anyone. She wouldn't be picky.

Cinn knew she'd never forget the moment when she

had looked into Dacian's eyes and saw true terror there. She'd somehow thought this was a man who feared nothing. Well, she'd been wrong. She didn't have to be a rocket scientist to figure out that Stephan was on the phone.

And as she'd bolted for the door, she'd glanced back. His fangs were fully extended and there was nobody home in those black eyes.

She sobbed as she ran. *Someone, please, someone, help him.*

She slammed into a big body and sat down hard on the ground of the courtyard. Cinn stared up at the man she'd run into. He was only a huge black shadow in the darkness. But before she could climb to her feet and start to run again, he lifted her up.

"What's wrong? Who do you want me to help?"

He'd read her mind. Nonhuman? She didn't care what he was. A troll or ghoul was fine with her, as long as he could help Dacian.

Fear made her breathless. She pointed toward the greenhouse. "Dacian. Vampire. Needs help."

She didn't get the last word out before he was off and running. At the same time, Ganymede came bounding out of the castle, followed closely by Sparkle, Edge, and Bain. Even Holgarth trailed the pack.

Suddenly, the adrenaline drained from her. She sat back down in the middle of the courtyard and put her head in her hands. Roars and shouts filled the air.

Then she realized someone stood over her. She looked up to see Holgarth peering down at her. While she watched, he straightened his hat. Then he smiled at her. Okay, so it was a creaky smile, but it must still be a great effort for the wizard to stretch his lips into that shape. She offered him a weak smile back.

"You did the correct thing. Between all of them, they'll get him back into the dungeon."

She slowly climbed to her feet. "What about all the noise? Won't some human call the police?" The words gave her a strange feeling, almost as if for this moment she wasn't lining up on the side of humanity. "And how do you explain hauling a vampire complete with fangs and scary black eyes through the middle of the great hall?"

Holgarth's smile was rusty, but he was trying. "My dear, this is the Castle of Dark Dreams, where fantastical things happen on a nightly basis. What else would you expect in a park called Live the Fantasy? Our customers love the drama. They think it's part of the fantasy."

While Cinn watched, horrified, Edge, Bain, and the stranger dragged Dacian from the greenhouse. He was smeared with blood, but from the looks of the men wrestling with him, most of it was theirs. She could see nothing human about the vampire they were trying to control. She didn't bother to wipe away the tear that slid down her face.

Ganymede and Sparkle led the parade toward the great hall. They stopped when they reached the place where she stood.

*"I could get him into the dungeon a little faster, but there's just so much fantasy the paying public will accept."* Ganymede looked up at Sparkle. *"Do we have any ice cream left? I need something to give me strength after that tussle."*

Sparkle just stared at him. "You didn't lift a finger to help. You can't be tired."

*"Couldn't help. No opposable thumbs, sweetie. And we didn't need my immense supernatural power this time."* He gazed up at her with a fair imitation of a big-eyed kitty.

"*But too much stress makes me tired. The weight of keeping the park running like a well-oiled machine takes a lot out of me.*"

"Hmm. I could swear that Holgarth, Edge, and Bain keep it running. And the only oil in your life is what you get in your daily doughnuts. You use your cat form as an excuse to be lazy, Mede." Sparkle threw up her hands. "Oh, what's the use?"

Ganymede moved off to lead everyone into the great hall. "*Holgarth went ahead to lay the lie on the humans. This'll just be a great fantasy to them. The dangerous and violent vampire finally captured and about to be locked up in the dungeon. Humans love that kind of stuff.*" He paused. "*Guess I'm just one of the common folk, because I like it, too. Breaks up the monotony.*"

Cinn clenched her hands into fists so hard her nails dug into her palms. She welcomed the pain. She hated how they were treating Dacian, even as she understood why it was necessary. It was what he would've wanted. But there had to be a way to help him.

"*You* could probably help him, you know."

Sparkle seemed to have a knack for striking at her weakest moment.

"How? I guess I could talk to him, but—"

"Cinn, Cinn, listen to your good friend, Sparkle Stardust."

Cinn didn't trust the sly gleam in her "good friend's" eyes.

"Sex is a powerful motivator for men. And the promise of sex would probably bring Dacian out of his episode just like that." Sparkle snapped her fingers.

"I guess so." It might not snow in Galveston, but Cinn decided she was getting her own personal snow job from Sparkle.

"Trust me. I know men." Sparkle looped her arm around Cinn's and led her toward the great hall.

Cinn looked over her shoulder. "My plants." She was torn. She wanted to be with Dacian, but she was afraid to leave her plants alone. When exactly had Dacian gained equal footing with her beloved plants?

"Wade is already there." She smiled. "You're really a big hit with him."

"But he has to be tired. He was there all day."

Sparkle shrugged. "Demons don't need a lot of sleep. And he's really motivated to help you. Which is strange. Wade has stayed here before, but he never looked twice at any woman. He was into his boat and fishing. Nothing else."

Cinn knew there was something important in Sparkle's comment, but she was too distracted right now to think about it.

As they walked down the steps leading to the dungeon, it seemed way too quiet. Sparkle knocked on the door and Edge opened it.

Edge looked like hell. He had cuts and bruises covering every exposed surface of his skin. His eyes blazed with his need for more violence. "When this bloodsucker is back in his right mind, I'm going to rip his freaking head off. I thought the night feeders were the weak sisters of the vampire world. What happened to this one?"

If Edge was expecting an answer from Cinn, he was in for a long wait.

Inside, Cinn only had eyes for Dacian. Once again he was chained spread-eagled against the wall. At least this time he'd kept all his clothes, even if they'd probably have to be tossed once he was sane again. Come to think of it, he didn't have any clothes of his own, so he must have borrowed these from Edge or Bain.

Almost without realizing it, she moved closer. His black eyes focused on her throat and he bared his fangs at her. She took a deep breath. Should she talk to him? What could she say?

And no, she wouldn't take Sparkle's advice. Sparkle might be fine with using the promise of sex as a surgeon's scalpel to cut away his rage and violence. But Cinn didn't want to use sex as a weapon.

Dacian hissed at her. He licked his lower lip, a strangely erotic gesture without any erotic intent. Cinn had a feeling he was only anticipating dinner.

His vampire nature terrified her on a primal level, just as it had the first time. But this time she knew the man, knew that this wasn't the real person. *But what if it is? What if the person he's shown you is a fake?* No, she wouldn't allow herself to believe that.

Someone touched her arm, and she uttered a startled squeak. She turned to see Bain by her side.

"I wouldn't go any closer if I were you." He might be warning her away, but pure joy and excitement gleamed in his blue eyes. "He's one of the most physically powerful vampires I've ever met. Good thing he's crazy right now, because I bet he has some serious supernatural powers when he's in his right mind." The demon shook his head in admiration.

"Will someone tell me what the hell is going on?" The stranger who'd bumped into Cinn in the courtyard stepped out of the shadows.

Gorgeous, with brilliant blue eyes and long dark hair, he was obviously angry. He was also obviously another vampire, because he was showing fang. At least his eyes were still blue. Cinn decided Dacian's black eyes scared her even more than his dental display.

"We're not sure." Sparkle shrugged as she studied her nails. She frowned at the three broken ones before remembering that she was building character. She focused her attention on the new vampire. "When Ganymede brought him in he was like this. Then he snapped out of it. Now we're back where we started. It's something his maker, Stephan, is doing to him. He can't control it, and we sure can't either."

Ganymede had taken a seat on top of the iron maiden. "*I say we leave him here and let him come out of it on his own.*"

Cinn's head was spinning with the seemingly constant stream of violence. Where had her simple life of working with her plants veered off track?

Edge started for the door. "Sparkle's right. Nothing we can do now until he comes out of it. Leave the guy alone. We don't need to make a circus out of it."

Cinn watched as Edge, followed closely by Bain, left. Holgarth had stayed up in the great hall to handle business.

Ganymede leaped from the iron maiden and padded to the door. "*Coming, sugar-bucket? Exercise always makes me hungry. I think some of your cookies are still left.*"

Sparkle sighed. "You can stay if you want, Cinn. Make sure Holgarth knows when you leave so he can lock the door. Try to get some rest, and we'll shop in the afternoon." She scowled. "Giant whoop."

As Sparkle closed the dungeon door behind her, Cinn realized she was alone with two vampires. Too bad she couldn't work up the energy to panic.

Dacian had stopped struggling against his bonds, but his eyes still held no awareness. It hurt her to look at him, so she looked at the strange vampire.

"Who are you?"

"Eric Mackenzie."

Okay, that told her exactly nothing.

"Why are you here?"

"For him." He nodded at Dacian.

"And you have a reason for being here for him?" Her temper was fraying, a victim of too much stimulus.

Eric smiled. Beautiful and threatening at the same time. "Yeah. I want to welcome him back to the land of the living, and then I want to knock him through that wall."

"Gee, I bet he'll be glad to have an old friend around." She returned Eric's smile. "Try to hurt him and I'll do my best to send you to that great blood bank in the sky." Cinn was too tired to worry about how Eric might take her threat.

Eric took a moment to study her and then nodded. "Fair enough. Now after you tell me who you are, tell me all you know about what Dacian's been doing for the last two hundred years."

# Chapter Eight

Dacian had the sense that he hadn't been out of it too long this time. And there wasn't as much disorientation. Both good things. He had the feeling Cinn had something to do with that. Because as he fought free of the rage and the memory loss that went with it, all he could think about was getting back to her.

As usual, along with his returning awareness came caution. He didn't say anything, didn't give a hint he was now back in his mind. He looked and listened.

What he saw and heard shocked him. He was back in the dungeon and in chains. All expected. It meant he probably hadn't killed anyone. But the sight of Cinn and Eric talking to each other was a kick in the gut. What was she telling Eric about him? What was Eric telling her about him? Of the two, what Eric was saying worried him the most. Eric knew what he'd done during the first few years of his rampages, before he'd decided to fake his own death and cut himself off from everyone and everything he'd ever cared about. Cinn already thought of him as a monster; she didn't need proof that her conclusion was right.

Eric glanced at him from where he sat beside Cinn on the dungeon's examining table. Dacian couldn't help his sudden stab of jealousy. He didn't want Eric anywhere near Cinn. And telling himself that he had no right to such feelings didn't mean a thing to his primal instincts.

Eric's casual glance sharpened. "Welcome back, Dacian. If you weren't in chains, I'd tear your freaking head off. I'll save that treat until you can fight back."

Cinn turned wide eyes his way. Then she smiled. He thought he'd fight his way out of the fires of hell just to see her smile at him that way.

"Are you okay? You were only out for about an hour this time. That has to be a good sign." She hopped off the table and came toward him.

Eric followed her and put his hand on her arm. Dacian hissed. He wanted to rip the other vampire's arm off.

Eric looked surprised, and then he smiled knowingly. "I see." He turned his attention back to Cinn. "Don't get too close until we're sure he's completely back."

"I'll never be more back, asshole." Not the best way to greet an old friend, especially one who was already pissed at you. But Dacian didn't seem to have any common sense when Cinn was involved.

Cinn glanced up at Eric, and Dacian hated that she looked to the other vampire for guidance. At least this time he was able to keep his mouth shut.

Eric nodded. "I think it's okay to let him loose." He concentrated on Dacian's chains, and they fell away.

Show-off. Dacian hated the awed expression on Cinn's face.

Eric must've sensed what Dacian was feeling, because he moved away from Cinn and leaned against the iron maiden. "I brought my wife with me. After I beat your ass, maybe I'll introduce you."

Dacian dropped his gaze as he made a big production of rubbing his chafed wrists. He shouldn't feel so relieved.

He took a quick survey of himself. Ripped and bloody

clothes, but at least he still had them. Then he raised his gaze to the man he'd once called friend. "I need a shower and change. So do you. What room are you in?"

"The one next to yours." Eric stilled as if sensing something no one else could. "Dawn isn't far away. You'll have to talk fast." Then he held open the dungeon door as they all left.

Holgarth met them outside the door. "The fantasies are finished, and the hotel guests are all happily asleep, so I thought I'd check to see if our resident bloodthirsty vampire had regained his sanity." He treated Dacian to a dismissive sniff. "I see he has."

Eric laughed. "Still the same old fun guy, Holgarth. God, how I missed your sarcasm and biting insults."

Holgarth almost smiled. Almost. "Ah, yes. I still remember fondly those wonderful moments of joyful mayhem you brought to the castle."

Dacian left Eric laughing as he pulled Cinn into his room. She collapsed onto a chair.

"Why don't you take a nap on my bed while I work things out with Eric? I'm meeting him in his room. You don't have to be there." He didn't *want* her to be there. He didn't want her to hear his transgressions paraded past her in living bloody color.

"I'm coming with you." She looked adamant. "I'll sleep after you go down for the count. I don't have to meet Sparkle until noon."

Dacian didn't try to change her mind. He needed all his remaining energy to face the man he'd once called friend. He didn't linger in the bathroom. A short time later he emerged to find Cinn fast asleep in the chair. He thought maybe he could sneak past her, but she woke just as he touched the doorknob.

"I sleep lightly, vampire. I'm tuned in to you, so don't think you can leave without me."

Her smile was sleepy and so sexy he wanted to forget about Eric and drag her into his bed. Dacian tried to push aside images of her riding his cock until time stopped. He was only partially successful.

Eric answered on the first knock. He swung the door open and allowed Dacian and Cinn to enter the room ahead of him. A woman waited to greet them. She had blonde shoulder-length hair and big brown eyes. Eric always had attracted beautiful women. Dacian's senses told him she hadn't been vampire for long.

Eric closed the door and went to stand by the woman. He put his arm around her waist and pulled her against his side. Dacian wished he had the right to do that with Cinn, but he didn't. He tried to strengthen the wall around his heart. Probably never would have the right. But that was okay. He'd been alone for a long time. You got used to it.

"This is my wife, Donna. We met here at the castle. She was doing a talk show. Still is. She's the hostess of *Donna till Dawn*." Eric didn't try to hide his pride in his wife.

"Donna, this is Dacian. He's the cause of all the trouble Taurin gave us." The glance he threw Dacian wasn't friendly. "And this is Cinn. Nice lady. Way too good for Dacian."

Donna made a big deal about wincing, and then smiled. She offered her hand to Cinn and then to Dacian.

Dacian didn't miss the searching glance she sent his way. "Since dawn is only about a half hour away, maybe we'd better get things moving."

Eric sat on the couch with Donna. Dacian and Cinn sat in chairs opposite each other.

"You guys can get to know me anytime. I think it's important that Eric and Dacian work things out first." Cinn leaned back and prepared to listen.

"Yeah, let's hear your story, pal." Eric heaved the ball directly into his lap. *Crap.* Dacian thought about making up some convoluted tale, but in the end he decided everyone needed to know the truth. He didn't want to stare into Eric's eyes while he confessed everything, so he looked at Cinn. And surprisingly, he realized it was most important to him that she understand and possibly forgive what he'd done.

She met his gaze, no judgment in her eyes. She'd listen with an open mind. A gift he wouldn't waste.

"You guys know bits and pieces of the story. I'll make this short." He spoke to everyone, but his attention stayed fixed on Cinn. "Six hundred years ago, Stephan made me. No, he didn't ask my permission. And no, it wasn't to save my life. A woman I thought I loved lured me into an alley where Stephan was waiting. After draining me, he thought it'd be fun to make a new vampire who'd worship at his undead feet. So I was born. He wasn't much older than me. I was his first creation, and his most powerful."

Eric interrupted. "What's this Stephan's last name?"

Dacian shrugged. "He's always had a god complex. Gods don't need last names. Anyway, two hundred years ago he decided he was powerful enough to pull all of the night feeders together under one banner. His. Alone, night feeders aren't much of a threat to other nonhumans, but an army of them could do some damage. Stephan is the only night feeder to survive this long, and he's ruthless. That gives him street cred with all the others. I'm almost as old as Stephan, and for two hundred years he's built his army at the same time he's tried to call me home. He says he needs my power by his side."

"And you won't go." Eric looked thoughtful. "Cinn told me what happened when you refused him."

"Yeah." Dacian raked his fingers through his hair. "At first I didn't know what was happening. Literally. And then I found out I killed people while my mind was out to lunch."

"Including some of the Mackenzies." Eric didn't sound mad about that.

"The Mackenzies had always been enemies of the night feeders, so my instinct was to kill them. I didn't recognize friend or foe." Dacian remembered Sean Mackenzie. If not a friend, at least someone he had known as a good man. Once again, he revisited his agony from when he'd found out he'd killed Sean.

"So you used our own plan against us." Eric shook his head in self-disgust.

"You and your friends had captured Taurin and stashed him in the warehouse as bait to draw me in." He shrugged. "I found out and decided it was a great opportunity to fake my death so I could go somewhere where no one would ever be in danger from me again. I can control fire, so I went in and set the warehouse ablaze. As far as you were concerned, I never came out."

"But you made sure Taurin and I got out." Eric had one more question. "How'd you escape?"

"The Mackenzies never thought a night feeder could gain much power. Your mistake. I can dematerialize, as long as I'm not in one of my rages."

"I can't believe I was that stupid. So why'd you decide to come out of hiding now?"

"My informant said that Stephan knew Taurin's location and was going to kill him to punish me."

Eric nodded. "I guess there's only one thing left to do."

He stood, and before anyone could move, he reached Dacian, dragged him to his feet, and punched him in the stomach. "That's for being a dumbass for two hundred years and not trusting your brother and me to find a way to help you."

Dacian was doubled over clutching his stomach, so he didn't see the exact moment Cinn brought the lamp down on Eric's head.

Eric turned to stare at her. He would've worn the same expression if a rabbit had hopped up and bitten his nose. "Ouch?"

Donna covered her mouth in an attempt to stifle her laughter.

Cinn glared at Eric. "I warned you."

Dacian's stomach had recovered from the blow, but now he was doubled over, laughing. How many centuries had it been since he'd felt like laughing? He couldn't remember.

Eric was still rubbing his head as he glanced toward the ceiling, toward the sky he couldn't see. "Dawn. We'll discuss this when we rise."

Dacian nodded. "I have to get Cinn to her room."

Cinn didn't want to be gotten to her room. She wanted to stay with him. An amazing development after seeing him in full vampire mode.

They'd only reached the top of the steps when Bain met them. "Hey, I've been given a chance to redeem myself. Lucky me. I get to guard you and your plants for the day. No sleeping on the job this time." His narrowed eyes said he wasn't feeling as lighthearted as he sounded.

Dacian handed her over to Bain without comment and headed back down the stairs. Cinn thought it would've been nice if he'd said a little something about how he was going to miss her. But of course, he wouldn't. He'd be . . . sleeping. She preferred that word rather than the oh-so-scary *dead*.

When Bain and Cinn reached her door, she didn't invite him in. "I'll only be a few minutes." And she made sure she kept her promise. No way did she want to step out of her bathroom or turn around while she wore only her bra and panties to find that Bain had beamed himself in because he'd gotten tired of waiting.

Once she left her room, they went out to the greenhouse. Wade waited for her.

Cinn was horrified. "You haven't been guarding the plants all this time, have you?"

Wade's gaze never left her. He didn't bother answering her question. "I can't think of anything but you. I tried looking over the *Bass Pro Shop Catalogue* and all I could see was you on every page."

She ignored Bain's snort. Okay, this was getting too weird. She didn't know how demons' minds worked, but a male mind was a male mind. And she'd never attracted this kind of mindless adoration. Didn't *want* to attract it. "You don't even know me, Wade."

Wade looked outraged. "Sure I know you. I know you're the sweetest, and most loving, and most beautiful, and—"

"No. I'm not any of those things." She racked her mind for an explanation. "When did you first realize how you felt about me?"

"I fell in love over that pretty little rosebush. You put your hand on mine, and it was like a hundred-pound catfish hitting the end of my line."

Cinn thought back. She'd touched the rose bloom, then she'd touched Wade's hand. *No.* She drew in a horrified breath. *Oh no, no, no.* She tried to keep what she was feeling from her voice. "Well, if you really care for me, you'll make me feel good by going and getting some sleep."

Wade looked as though he didn't know how to argue

with her reasoning. "Okay, but don't tell me *he's* going to guard you." He glared at Bain.

Uh-oh. She hoped her smile looked reassuring. "He'll keep me and the plants safe. Don't worry. Go get some sleep." *Please, please, please don't give me a hard time.*

Suddenly, the good-old-boy demon was gone. Wade's eyes changed. Was that red creeping into them? "Let me give you a little lesson in demons, Miss Cinn. I'm a Eudemon. We're a pretty laid-back lot. We don't go around causing trouble as long as we're having fun. Only time we give humans problems is when we're bored. A bored demon is not a good thing for mankind." He paused to let that sink in.

"Then there're the Cacodemons. They're the ones humans have to worry about. They go around looking for trouble to cause. They're the ones humans have named evil and spawn of the devil." He nodded toward Bain. "He's one of those kind. You won't be safe with him."

Wade's words made Cinn feel kind of creepy. She slid a sideways glance at Bain. He winked at her.

She sighed. "Look, Wade, I'm tired. I'm glad you told me about the two classes of demons, but right now I need sleep. No matter what you think Bain is, I don't believe Sparkle or Ganymede would allow him to stay here if he were that evil." She looked at Bain for confirmation. "You're not evil, are you?"

"I'm very evil." He grinned at her, as gorgeous a smile as a man could produce.

"Not the right answer," she muttered through clenched teeth.

"But since I know Ganymede will kick my ass if I indulge myself, I suppose you're safe for now." His tone said not to count out any time in the future.

"Thank you." *I think.*

Wade looked torn, but finally he moved away from

the door. He offered Bain one more glare before finally walking toward the courtyard.

Cinn waited until Wade was out of sight before turning on Bain. "You weren't much help."

He shrugged. "You wanted the truth."

"Do you think you can guard the greenhouse from outside?" Exhaustion was making her sway on her feet.

"Nope. I can handle some direct sunlight, but I burn easily." He put a hand over his heart, thought a minute, and then moved the hand to the other side of his chest. "Demon physiology is a little different from a human's."

Cinn didn't have the energy to fight with him. She'd just have to believe that no harm would come to her in the few hours she had to sleep. When she woke she'd have to think about Wade. And what would she do with Eva, her pretty little rosebush with the passionate punch? Cinn staggered into the greenhouse and fell onto the cot.

She woke to someone clasping her shoulder and shaking her.

"Time to go shopping. And don't think you can escape by pretending to be asleep." Sparkle sounded nothing if not determined. "I refuse to suffer alone. Drat. I broke another nail trying to wake you up. Luckily for you I'm not the same shallow person I once was or I might be really upset."

Cinn groaned. She had a feeling that putting her hands over her ears wouldn't do any good. She opened her eyes and blinked.

Sparkle leaned over her. When she saw Cinn open her eyes, she smiled. "Good. Get up, run up to your room, and change. I brought coffee you can drink on the way."

"Why do I have to change?" If she hadn't still been half asleep, she wouldn't have asked that question.

"Even if we *are* going to a big-box store"—Sparkle seemed to be suggesting that they were traveling into the bowels of the earth, where they'd encounter prehistoric creatures with exotic names like tyranno-cheap-flats, or bronto-made-in-China-purses—"I refuse to be seen with someone wearing fuzzy slippers."

Cinn looked down. *Oh, yeah.*

With Sparkle urging her on, Cinn finally got dressed and stuffed herself into the car.

Sparkle sat clenching the steering wheel with determined ferocity. "Fine, now where's a discount store?"

Cinn gaped at her. "How would I know? I don't know anything about Galveston."

"Well, I've never been to a discount store. Where do you think we'll find one?"

Cinn swallowed all the sarcastic comments that came to mind. "Seawall Boulevard seems to be a busy road. Maybe if we start driving we'll run into one. If that fails, we'll stop and ask."

Sparkle nodded and they started driving. They finally spotted the big store—huge sign, best-known chain in the country—and Sparkle looked surprised. "I never knew this was here. It looks . . . ordinary."

Cinn was so ready for this to be over. "That's because it has *ordinary* things in it that *ordinary* people buy."

Sparkle blinked. "Oh. That's why I've never been here." She glanced down at her designer everything and made a moue of disappointment. "And I thought I'd dressed down for this shopping trip."

If she hadn't been so exasperated, Cinn would've laughed. "Umm, no."

And so it began, the shopping afternoon from hell. Sparkle complained up one aisle and down another.

Things were too cheap, too ordinary, too this, too that, until Cinn wanted to wrap one of the pairs of too unsexy panties around Sparkle's elitist neck and strangle her.

Cinn had given up trying to cajole Sparkle out of her bad mood in favor of looking at a few things she might buy herself. She didn't realize she'd gotten separated from the reformed queen of all things stylish until she tripped. She would've gone splat in the undies aisle if someone hadn't caught her.

Cinn looked down to see what had tripped her. Then she leaned over to get a closer look. A tree branch? Growing out of the floor? Uh-oh. She slowly straightened and turned to look at the person who'd kept her from falling.

The woman smiled at her. "You're very hard to catch alone."

"Oh, shit."

"Actually, it's very good fertilizer. Growing things waste nothing." Airmid was tall and slender, with long flowing pale hair and an otherworldly beauty that even shoppers in a big-box store must be able to see.

Cinn glanced around. Of course, if there were no shoppers in this aisle, then no one would see anything. She swallowed hard. Where the hell was Sparkle?

"Relax, Cinn. I'm not here to rain hoes and sod down on your head. Yet. I thought we could have a little chat. Perhaps then you'd understand why I'm upset with you." Her smile was lovely, but it didn't hide the anger beneath it.

*Okay, trying to relax here.* "I don't understand why you're so upset. My plants don't hurt anyone."

"One of them bit the vampire."

"Oh, you know about that." *How* had Airmid found out about that?

"I know many things."

If Cinn were really lucky, the goddess *wouldn't* know about Wade. Suddenly, she remembered what almost happened to Vince. Now *she* was the one who was mad. "Why did you tell Asima to destroy Vince?"

Airmid raised a brow in surprise. "Because plants don't think. Plants don't feel. And plants *never* talk."

"Why not? Other species have evolved."

"Because *I* say so." Suddenly she was no longer the pleasant woman of a moment ago. Her pale green eyes darkened and her hair whipped around her face as a mini tornado circled her head.

Cinn gulped and stepped back. Time to keep her mouth shut.

Airmid's expression cleared and her hair once again lay in shining waves across her shoulders. "You're special, Cinn. Your family has always honored me. They've nurtured plants throughout the centuries. But no one in your family has ever had any of my power."

"Your *power*? I don't understand." Where was Sparkle? The longer she stood chatting with the goddess, the greater the chance she'd say something really dumb.

"I have no control over who in your family receives the gift. If it were up to me, I would have chosen your sister Ginger. But now that you realize how special you are, you have to abandon these disgraceful experiments and destroy the mutations you've already created."

"No." The word popped out of her mouth before she could stop it. It hung there in the air between the goddess and her. Cinn wished she could pluck it back and swallow it. Too late.

"You *will* do as I say." The eyes and wind thing started up again. "I am the Celtic goddess of the growing green. I am the herbal healer to the Tuatha De Danann. How *dare* you say no to me?"

The healer to whom? What?

Suddenly Sparkle was there. She clutched a bunch of bags, so she must've already paid for her stuff. She took one look at the pissed-off goddess and yelled, "Run!"

Cinn didn't need to be told twice. Wind roared down the aisles, panties and bras sailed past her, and she could hear display cases crashing to the floor. Screams filled the store as customers fled.

She and Sparkle were caught in the crush and carried out of the store on a wave of terrified customers. Even the greeters were hitting the exits. Once free of the mob, Cinn didn't stop running until she reached Sparkle's car. Sparkle was already inside with the engine running. Just as they peeled out of the parking lot and back out onto Seawall Boulevard, the roof of the store caved in.

Cinn was horrified. "What if there were people still in there? If anyone's hurt, it's my fault." In the distance she could hear sirens.

"It is *not* your fault. It's the fault of the ditzy goddess with anger issues." Sparkle relaxed a little as they got closer to the castle. "It's really too bad about the store. I suppose I won't be able to buy any more cheap and serviceable clothes there for a while." She didn't seem overly upset by the thought.

Cinn was still thinking about the people in the store. "I should've let her think she'd won."

Sparkle pulled into the employee parking lot near the hotel's side entrance. She parked and then dragged all her bags out to lug them into the castle. It was only when they were in the elevator that Sparkle hit her with the questions. "What did she want from you? What did you say that made her so mad? Did she tell you who does her hair?"

Cinn couldn't discuss any of it while she was frantic

about the people caught in the store collapse. She had to know if anyone had died or been seriously hurt. "I'll explain later."

Sparkle nodded, but she didn't look happy about having to wait for all the juicy details.

Cinn followed Sparkle into her suite. Ganymede sprawled on the couch, watching a movie. The only thing different from the last time Cinn had visited was this time he had an open cookie box by his side.

"Can I change the channel for a minute, Ganymede?" Something about the store would have to be on the news.

The cat looked as though she'd tried to steal his cookies. *"Can't do. I'm taping this. Don't want to mess with the old DVR."*

*Self-involved, piggy fur-ball.* Cinn glared at him. He ignored her.

*"See you did lots of shopping, babe. Glad you bought a bunch of clothes. Thought I'd help you while I was just hanging, so I called up some charity. They came by and took all your old stuff away. Now you won't be tempted by those fancy shoes and sexy outfits."* He paused, waiting for a show of gratitude.

Sparkle dropped all the bags on the floor.

Cinn waited for her eyes to darken and her hair to do the supernatural wind thing. Sparkle was a little more prosaic than Airmid, though. She jerked a mirror from the wall and heaved it at him.

Cinn wasn't about to get caught up in this seven-years-of-bad-luck event, so she ducked out of the room and hurried to . . . Where? She didn't want to go to her room. She didn't want to be alone. Airmid had been waiting to catch her alone.

Almost dark, and only one person she wanted to be

with. Without thinking things to death, she ran all the way down the winding stairs to the floor where Dacian slept. She pounded on his door. *Please, please, be awake.*

And when he finally opened his door, she flung herself into his arms. He caught her and held her close. At last she felt safe.

He pulled her inside and closed the door. Only now did she notice that all he wore was a towel around his waist. "Sorry. I got you at the wrong time."

His smile was a sensual slide of invitation. "No, you got me at exactly the right time."

# Chapter Nine

He'd lied. Dacian knew this was definitely *not* the best time for Cinn to show up. She was in danger. On many different levels.

He'd risen about fifteen minutes ago and immediately jumped into the shower so he could be ready as soon as the sun set to find Cinn and guard her through the night.

Yeah, okay, so he had other things he wanted to do with her through the night. Guarding her was only one in a long list. And that was where the danger came in.

Her hair was tousled and her face flushed from running down those stairs. Dacian knew she'd run because he'd heard her coming. His enhanced hearing was a blessing and a curse. Right now he could hear the pounding of her heart and the rush of blood through her body. Her blood sang to him, a siren's song. It would be sweet and . . . He felt the slide of his fangs and cut off all thoughts of her blood.

Dacian concentrated on the outer package. Too bad her clothes got in the way of his full appreciation. Her skin would be smooth and soft as he slid his fingers the length of her body. She'd be warm and moist as he pushed her legs apart and put his mouth . . . His fangs made a return appearance.

And as much as he wanted to drag her to the floor, rip her clothes from her body, and bury himself deep inside her, he knew those fangs were going to be a problem.

He wanted her too much, and his vampire nature was part and parcel of his whole sexual experience. Maybe if it hadn't been so long, or his lust weren't so overwhelming, he could make love to her without a show of fang. But he didn't think his control was good enough right now.

"Airmid destroyed the store."

He blinked, finally realizing how upset she was. "Airmid? Are you okay?" The hell with the store. He led her to the couch. Damned if he was going to let her isolate herself in a chair. Dacian drew her down beside him. "Tell me the whole story."

She didn't object when he tucked her against his side. He indulged himself in an almost-forgotten human reflex. He held the breath he no longer had while praying she wouldn't suddenly remember what she was cozying up to and jerk away. Who knew he actually had a sensitive bone in his undead body?

"Sparkle and I went shopping. She wanted to buy some clothes that proved she wasn't shallow. We got separated, and Airmid ambushed me. She wanted me to destroy my plants, I said no, and she lost it."

Dacian closed his eyes. Cinn was such an innocent. She had no idea how dangerous a pissed-off goddess could be. He wanted to rage against his inability to guard her 24-7. He opened his eyes. "Next time, take Bain or Edge with you. They're more reliable than Sparkle." From what he'd seen, anyone would be more reliable than Sparkle. Yeah, so he was letting her name sway his opinion. He just couldn't see a Sparkle Stardust as a dangerous, competent bodyguard.

"Everyone rushed to get out of the store, but I'm so afraid someone was hurt or killed. And it's all my fault. If I'd stopped to think, I could've stalled her, said I'd think about it."

He heard the guilt in her voice and wanted to find Airmid so he could stuff a few of Cinn's plants down her throat. "Don't blame yourself. You're not the one who destroyed the store. Airmid could've chosen a different way to act out her temper tantrum." He thought about calling Holgarth and asking him to check the news, but Cinn wouldn't want him to shield her from the truth. "Look, I'll turn on the TV and see if we can find out anything." As he reached for the remote, he hoped no one had died. But if they had, he'd be there to help her through it.

The first local station he hit had a video of the wreckage. Wow, Airmid didn't hold back when she got ticked. He glanced at Cinn to see her reaction. Her face looked calm, but she'd clenched her hands in her lap.

The reporter said the one thing Cinn needed to hear. "It was a miracle everyone got out. Officials reported only a few people with cuts and bruises. Amazingly, one part of the store remained untouched."

The camera panned past the rest of the destroyed store to focus on the garden section. All of the plants stood in perfect rows surrounded by pots, rakes, plant food, and other stuff connected to them.

"Airmid takes care of her own." Cinn sounded exhausted but relieved.

"Why don't you rest for a while?" *You can rest on my bed if you want.* No, bad idea. He'd never survive, knowing she was in his bed, never get the sensual scent of her out of his head. She'd haunt his bed forever.

She shook her head. "I have to go to my plants. Bain is guarding them, but I want to be there if Airmid tries anything. Besides, I need to check on Vince."

Dacian clenched his jaw, forcing his words back. He didn't give a flip about the plants. Okay, so maybe he cared a little about Vince. But she'd angered a goddess. Didn't she realize how much danger she was in? Hadn't she learned anything from her little shopping trip?

She glanced at him and then smiled. "I can't read minds, but I can sure read your expression. That vampire mask is slipping. Yes, I'm worried about me. I'd be stupid not to. But right now I don't know what to do to change Airmid's mind. The one thing she wants, I won't do. I won't kill my plants."

He nodded. "From what you've said, it seems like Airmid didn't want to involve Sparkle or the rest of us. She waited until she could get you alone. So you'll make sure you're never alone again until things get settled."

"You're a bossy man, did you know that?" Her smile took the sting out of her comment.

But all Dacian heard was the word "man." She couldn't be thinking of him as a bloodsucking horror and call him a man, could she?

Her smile faded as she continued, "Don't forget that you have your own problems. I haven't forgotten."

His good feeling faded along with her smile. She was right. He might pose as much of a danger to her as Airmid. And what if Airmid struck at the same time Stephan launched one of his attacks? Fat lot of good he'd do her then. He pushed the nightmare away. He'd deal with the here and now for as long as he could.

He nodded. "Wait while I get some clothes on, and we'll go to your greenhouse."

She watched him as he grabbed some clothes from his closet and headed for the bathroom. The towel rode low on his hips and with every stride her breaths came a little faster. *Drop the damn towel.* It was like reading a book with the best pages missing. His wide shoulders tapered down to a strong smooth back and then . . .

missing pages. Moving along, she could see the lower part of muscular thighs, and then his strong legs. But she couldn't get past the missing pages. She could only imagine his firm round butt. And if he turned around . . . Well, she'd save that for a later time.

While he dressed, she pushed her thoughts past his delicious body and what she'd like to do with it to concentrate on Airmid. How could anyone fight a goddess?

But Cinn didn't have a chance to come up with any solutions before Dacian emerged from the bathroom. Even wearing just jeans and a T-shirt, he was breathtaking.

At what point had his vampire status ceased to stand in the way of her full appreciation of him as a spectacular man? She didn't know, but it had.

He took her hand as they left his room and climbed the stairs to the great hall, where Eric stood with Holgarth and Kyla. Cinn figured there was no way to avoid talking to them.

And yes, she saw Kyla as a threat, though she wasn't sure why. Sure, Cinn wanted to make love with Dacian. For heaven's sake, look at the guy. Any woman with a normal hormone level would feel the same way. But she didn't for a minute think she had ownership rights. Didn't want any. Talk about grabbing a tiger by its tail. That was what getting emotionally involved with Dacian would be like. How would you let go and survive?

As they joined the group, Cinn offered the other woman a wide smile. Hey, she could be a hypocrite with the best of them.

"Ah, our princess of perverted plants and the demented vampire have joined us. How absolutely thrilling."

Cinn wanted to knock Holgarth's stupid wizard's hat

off his head and stuff it into his sarcastic mouth. She offered him her most poisonous smile. "It's nice to see you again, too. Interview any promising replacements today?"

The wizard pursed his thin lips as he studied her. "No one can *replace* me, Ms. Airmid. I promise you that. The best I can hope for is a pale reflection of my incomparable powers. The whole interview process is exhausting."

Eric laughed out loud. Nothing subtle about him. "The only incomparable part of you is your ego. It could swallow a midsize American city. But Cinn and Dacian don't know you like I do. Underneath all that obnoxious snideness beats a kind and generous heart."

"Kind and generous?" Holgarth looked horrified. "I can't believe you hate me so much, Eric. What did I ever do to you? Fine, so I did do a few things that might be construed as spiteful. But why would you feel the need to lash out with such awful accusations?" He managed a hurt expression. "I'm devastated." He turned and walked away, his robe whipping behind him.

Eric smiled at Cinn. "Remember this when he's starting to get to you. He hates anyone to think he has a heart."

"Got it." She was talking to Eric, but her attention was on Kyla and Dacian. She couldn't read anything into their expressions.

But jealousy was a master painter. In her mind's eye, Kyla gazed up at Dacian with those big blue eyes that were the same shade as Eric's. Must be a Mackenzie thing. Then Dacian ran his fingers through Kyla's long dark hair before lowering his head to . . . Cinn took a deep breath. Okay, so the other woman was tall and beautiful. So what? Since she was making up her own scenario, she'd inject herself into it. She'd be the one kicking Kyla's perfect butt out the castle door.

Dacian wasn't even looking at the other woman. His attention was all for Eric. "Airmid lost her temper when Cinn refused to destroy her plants. She brought down the store. Everyone will have to keep their eyes open for the goddess."

"What's she look like?" Kyla spoke for the first time.

Cinn could answer that. "Beautiful. Tall, slender, long pale hair. I'm not sure of the color. Maybe a mixture of blonde and red. Light green eyes. She was wearing a long flowing gown, pale gold. The kind that would float in the breeze." She thought for a moment. "Funny how everything about her was pale except for her temper. That was red-hot."

Eric nodded. "I'll pass the description on, although she might not take the same form next time." He frowned. "I've been thinking about this Stephan. If he wants you to fight by his side, why the hell does he keep on punishing you? He has to know that will just piss you off. Even if he forces you to help him, he could never trust you."

Dacian looked grim. "Stephan believes the only way to be a strong ruler is through fear. He . . ." He shook his head. "Never mind."

"Since we're into descriptions, they need to know what Stephan looks like." Cinn wanted to know what Dacian had been about to say. Why had he decided not to tell them? She realized she felt a driving need to know everything about him. *Danger: emotional minefield ahead.*

Dacian shrugged. "About five foot ten. Long blond hair. But that was centuries ago. Maybe it's short now. Blue eyes. Sort of thin. He always thought brains trumped brawn every time. Probably right. Oh, and he had a mustache. He was proud of that damn mustache, so maybe he still has it."

"That description could fit almost anyone." Kyla stated the obvious. She glanced at her watch. "Gotta go. I'm taking in a movie. See you later. Oh, and we'll have to set up a date to talk over old times, Dacian."

Some unidentifiable emotion flashed in her eyes for a moment and then was gone. Cinn tried not to build that emotion into something big, like an undying devotion to Dacian. She was only partially successful.

Kyla waved as she headed toward the door.

Eric didn't even glance her way as she left. He seemed deep in thought. "There's something fishy about this Stephan deal. Think about it. An informant tells your guy that Stephan knows where Taurin is and plans to kill him. What does your maker gain by that? Nothing. You'll still never join him and—"

"I'd find someone who could destroy him." Dacian's hands were curved into claws at his side.

"Right. So doesn't it make more sense to capture Taurin and threaten to kill him if you don't fight by Stephan's side? That's what I'd do." Eric frowned. "And if he's so hot to kill Taurin, why isn't he here already? A smart vampire doesn't take a chance on the enemy beating him to the prize."

Everyone was quiet for a moment. Then Dacian nodded. "You have a point. I don't have a clue what Stephan's thinking."

Cinn put in her two cents. "Do you think he knew Taurin was away from the castle?"

Dacian shrugged. "Who knows? I'll just have to make sure I'm ready for Stephan if he shows up."

Eric nodded. "I'll fill Ganymede in on what's happening. He probably doesn't know where Taurin is right now, but he can be ready to warn Taurin if he contacts anyone at the castle before he gets here."

Dacian looked uncomfortable. "Thanks for coming, Eric. And double thanks for staying." He didn't wait for Eric's response as he turned and strode toward the kitchen.

Cinn had to run to keep up. She drew even with him as they entered the kitchen. When they reached the greenhouse, he didn't bother to knock, but simply used his key. As they entered, Cinn could see Bain standing at the open door leading into the courtyard. He was talking to a bunch of people.

"Thanks for dropping by, folks. Spread the word about Cinn Airmid's amazing plants. We're open for tours from ten till seven every day."

*Tours?* Damn. Cinn had forgotten all about what Sparkle had said.

A woman in the back of the crowd shouted out, "You sure she's not selling any of these plants? I could use that dieffenbachia in my bedroom. Perk up my old man's sex drive."

*Sex drive?* The first tendrils of suspicion touched Cinn.

Bain shook his head as he laughed. "Sorry. These are all experimental plants. Maybe sometime in the future."

Bain watched the crowd wander away before closing the door and turning to face Cinn and Dacian. "Wow, that was pretty cool. I thought this plant-guarding would be boring, but the crowds kept me busy."

"Crowds?" Why would crowds be coming to see her plants?

"Yeah." He shrugged into his coat. "I told them all about your plants. How they give off pheromones that drive anyone near them into a fit of uncontrolled lust. And how being around them makes you skinny."

"Skinny?" She was only capable of one-word questions.

"I explained how their magnetic energy absorbs a person's fat. All you have to do is spend an hour a day with the plants and you'll be thin in no time. No dieting."

"You didn't!"

"I did." His eyes gleamed with wicked glee. "The best one was when I told them your Venus flytrap was better than any sex toy. All those cups are like mouths and they can—"

"No, no, no! Don't tell me. I don't want to know." She clapped her hands over her ears. "Hummmm. Hummmm. Not hearing you." Not a mature response, but it worked.

When she finally saw his mouth stop moving, she dropped her hands. She took a second to glare at Dacian. He seemed to think the whole thing was a hoot. Then she turned her fury on Bain.

"Who the hell gave you the right to lie about my plants?" Anger was the buzzing of a thousand enraged hornets in her head.

Bain looked puzzled. "I'm a demon, love. It's what I do. I lie." Then he smiled, that wonderful smile that should make her forget what he'd done. "But just think about it. I've made your little greenhouse one of the biggest attractions in the park."

"Get out. Just get out." She looked around for a weapon.

Bain opened the door and stepped out. Then he poked his head back in. "Oh, you might want to guard the bushy plant with the yellow buds. I said that eating just one bud would make anyone look twenty again. Lots of seniors seemed interested in that one."

She glanced at Dacian. "Hand me a weapon. Something long and pointy."

Bain closed the door behind him, and she could hear his laughter fading into the distance. Then she slumped onto the cot and dropped her head into her hands. "Oh. My. God. I can't believe he said all those things. Why didn't anyone warn me not to leave a demon in charge?" Suddenly, she looked up. "Is it seven yet?"

Dacian had wisely stopped smiling. He shook his head. "Don't worry, though. I'll take care of it." He flipped off the lights inside the greenhouse, made sure both doors were locked, and then he stood concentrating.

She didn't interrupt him.

Finally, he dropped down beside her on the cot and put his arms around her. "You and your plants will have at least an hour of peace now. I've surrounded the greenhouse with the suggestion that no one come here because it's closed."

Cinn leaned into him, allowing herself to relax for the first time all day. "I've never asked about your powers. Probably shouldn't. There are some things I don't need to know." She was thinking specifically about Bain and the Venus flytrap. "But back in the great hall you started to say something and then stopped." She left it up to him whether he'd tell her or not.

His expression said he didn't want to discuss it, so she was surprised when he responded.

"After Stephan killed me, he dumped me in a box and tossed me into a grave. Then he covered me up. I was out of it for three days. When I woke, I was in that box. I knew what it was, and I knew I was buried. I could hear Stephan laughing in my mind as I tore my fingers bloody trying to free myself. About the tenth day, when I was crazy with bloodlust and scared shitless, he told me he was the only one who could save me and to always remember who was in charge." Dacian's eyes were filled with self-disgust. "Then he told me to beg." His laughter had nothing to do with humor. "And I begged. Loud and long." He shrugged. "Finally, he let me go."

"And you've hated him ever since." Cinn knew *she* hated Stephan.

"Yeah." He invested all the centuries of loathing into that one word.

Cinn needed something to drive the image of what Dacian had endured from her mind, something life-affirming. She had no doubts about what she wanted that to be. Not on the cot, though. Too narrow. She glanced around.

Without speaking, she stood and walked over to the large table in the middle of the greenhouse. Her worktable. Well, there was work and there was *work*. She carefully moved several plants to one side.

Then she turned back to Dacian. She didn't say anything. She didn't need to.

He joined her beside the table. "I want to make love with you." His smile told her he was stating the obvious. "But I don't want you to feel . . ." For a moment, he looked as though he were searching for the right words. "Okay, I know I have scars inside and out, but I don't want them to have anything to do with why you make love with me. I want this to be about desire, not pity."

She put her finger over his lips. "Have you looked in a mirror lately?" Cinn rethought that question. "Okay, maybe not. So let me explain. Any woman would want you. Of course, *they* would be lusting after your body."

"And you don't lust after my body?" His laughter had an edge of uncertainty to it.

"Definitely not." She let her gaze slide the length of his body. Her interest snagged on the proof of *his* growing interest. "It's all about your mind. You have a *great* mind. It's long, and hard, and—"

"My mind is up here." He tapped his forehead.

"Oh." She looked up at him and smiled.

He knew it was going to happen. Here. Now. In this greenhouse, in the dark, surrounded by plants that were wiser than plants should ever be. And he didn't give a damn. He reached for her.

"Wait."

While he watched, puzzled, she grabbed a bunch of burlap sacks from a pile and then methodically pulled them over the nearby plants. Then she returned to him.

"Why?"

"I don't think they've evolved far enough to see, but I'm just making sure." She wrapped her arms around him and buried her face in his chest. He gently tugged on her hair, forcing her to meet his gaze.

"It's been a long time. I might not be patient, or creative, or even kind."

"How about quick? I'd like quick. Because I want you so much I just might . . ." Her imagination evidently failed her because her voice faded away.

He pulled her top over her head with hands that refused to remain steady, while she ripped at his T-shirt with frenzied intensity. Dacian finally paused long enough to yank it over his head. Then he returned to finishing the job of getting her naked.

He kissed a path along the side of her jaw while he

reached behind her to unclasp her bra. When her breasts fell free, he transferred his mouth to one of her ripe nipples. She shuddered beneath his lips.

"Take your jeans off and anything else you have cluttering up that gorgeous body." Her demand was a husky murmur.

Reluctantly, he abandoned her nipple to drag his shoes and jeans off. He'd been in too much of a hurry to bother with shorts. She hummed her appreciation.

Then he molded his palms over her round little butt and lifted her onto the table. Lifted her slowly, sliding her over his body, pressing her against his cock, and biting his lip to keep from moaning as her nipples scraped across his chest. God, he wanted to drive into her right now, with her bent back over the damn table. *Slow down, slow down.*

Holding his gaze, she lay back on the table. Then she wiggled her way into a more comfortable position. And every damn wiggle was a jolt to his cock.

"Your hunger is showing, vampire." Her smile was sensual and more tempting than man or vampire could be expected to resist. "I see heat behind the hunger. That's good."

"My eyes?"

"Black." But her gaze didn't waver. "And you're flashing fang. Just enough fang to make you look all sexy-dangerous." She reached over to draw a line down the center of his chest with the tip of her finger. "Sparkle thinks dangerous men are sensual. I know one who definitely is." She patted the table beside her. "Do you think I'm a dangerous woman?" She grinned. "Humor me and say yes."

"You have no idea." He grimaced as he joined her on the table. "Not the best setting, but I want you so much

I'd make love to you on an ice floe with a flock of penguins cheering us on. I wish I had Eric's power."

"Eric? What does he have to do with anything?" She traced his lips with the tip of her finger.

He drew her finger into his mouth before answering her. He swirled his tongue around it, teasing as he gave her a preview of what he intended to do to other parts of her luscious body. And when he released her finger, he kissed the tip of it while watching her from beneath half-lowered lids. She stared at him from eyes darkened with passion. Now was one time he appreciated his enhanced sight. The darkness hid nothing from him.

"Eric has the power to create fantasies. Not like the role-playing people get in the park. Eric gives you the real deal. No matter how weird the fantasy is, it becomes real. I wish I could do that for you." He was about to return to her breasts, but she stopped him.

"Silly man, don't you know that *you* are the fantasy?" Then she covered his mouth with hers.

And it was all over for him. No more attempts at being a patient lover. Forget the hours of foreplay. Weren't going to happen. He wanted it all. *Now.*

He slid his tongue across her full lower lip, and she invited him in. His tongue tangled with hers as he explored every heated inch of her mouth. Lost in sensation, he forgot.

Her slight flinch grounded him immediately. His fangs had come out to play. Damn. He stilled, not drawing away. There'd be no going back. He waited for her to pull away from him, to reject what he was.

Then she carefully touched the tip of each with her tongue. "Mmm, so deliciously dangerous. My inner cavewoman approves. There's something dark, primal, and irresistible about the ultimate alpha male," she murmured against his cheek, her breath warm, her words softly suggestive. To emphasize her point, she slipped her hand over his stomach and cupped his balls before dancing her fingertips the length of his cock.

He clasped her wrist, holding her still as he whispered in her ear. "Be careful what you wish for, because you're about to see dark and primal like you've never seen it before."

"Mmm. Promises, promises." She ran the tip of her finger around each of his nipples and he couldn't control his groan. "No hairy caveman, though. I like a smooth-skinned, hard-muscled man." She pulled his head down to her and gently nipped his earlobe. "Like you."

She was playful. He wanted to be playful, too, but he didn't know how. Maybe she could teach him. *Maybe you're delusional*. He needed to do what he did best.

He dipped his head lower and drew her nipple into his mouth. She arched her back as he flicked the nipple with his tongue and then sucked.

"Wow. That's some power you have. I can feel it all the way to my toes. They're definitely curling." Her tone was still light, but it now had a breathless quality to it.

As he transferred his attention to her other nipple, she showed her appreciation by sliding her foot up his inner thigh. Then she stopped. He wanted that foot to move higher, to . . . he couldn't decide. The possibilities were endless.

He needed to explore lower on her body, but that would mean she couldn't reach vital spots with her toes. And he had high hopes for those toes. *Move your freaking foot*. He stopped short of transmitting his mental command. That would be too much like begging.

So instead, he buried his face in the hair at the base of her neck while her essence did amazing things to him. The man in him wanted to bottle the rich scent of warm woman and hot arousal so he could lather up with it when he showered and wear it all day. But the vampire in him had no days, only nights filled with the scent and taste of her blood, a scent he'd recognize even if he lived six more centuries. The taste would have to wait.

Finally. She moved her foot.

She rubbed her toes against his balls, kneading them like a contented cat. Then she worked her way up to his cock. And if she used a little more pressure in her excitement, it was all good to him. There was a fine line between pain and pleasure, but Cinn came down hard on the side of pleasure. And when she made little sounds of enjoyment, it ramped up his arousal to spontaneous combustion level.

"I'm not—" He kissed his way over her stomach, pausing to swirl his tongue in her navel.

She abandoned her lethal toe attack. Gasping, she arched her back and moaned.

"Going to last—" He slid his hands beneath her tight round bottom and lifted her.

She wrapped her legs around him and started offering suggestions between hard pants. "Therethere-there!"

"Much—" He lowered his head and put his mouth on her.

"*Yes*. Moremoremore."

Sliding his tongue across the nub of flesh that brought women such pleasure, he allowed himself to enjoy her cry through the blaze of his own need. The taste of her would be with him always, unique and a memory of the sensual woman she was. Now came the true test. He dipped his tongue into her, in and out, in and out, imitating the sexual dance. And each time he thrust his tongue into all her moist heat, he knew she felt the pressure of his fangs. There was no way she couldn't.

She didn't pull away; she didn't ask him to stop. She just gasped, "*Longer. Say it. You're not going to last much longer.*"

"Longer." Lowering her, he pressed the head of his cock between her spread legs.

"Good. Because I was ready at 'I'm not.'" She arched forward and grabbed his hair, dragging him over her body.

He moved his body back and forth, his senses reeling each time her nipples scraped across his flesh.

She stared up at him, her gaze fixed on his fangs. He couldn't make them go away. They were an inescapable expression of his sexual excitement.

Cinn didn't tell him not to use them.

But he knew he wouldn't. He drew his finger over her throat, over the spot where her blood pulsed hot and strong. And she'd never know how hard it was not to. "Not this time."

No relief shone in her gaze, and for that he thanked her.

"If you don't fill me right now, vampire, my sexual frustration will blow out the walls of this greenhouse. Then you'll have to pay Sparkle for it."

She'd called him vampire. Her gift touched him. She accepted him as vampire and still wanted him.

Nothing could stop him now. With a shout, he sheathed himself in her, feeling her muscles clench around his cock. And then he withdrew, only to plunge into her again. Deeper, harder, driven by her cries and the rake of her nails over his back.

Everything became a blur, a desperate drive to orgasm. At some level he knew he was taking her with him. With each thrust, she rose to meet him.

And when the moment came, when the massive spasm hit him, he fought his nature with every ounce of his strength. She lay writhing beneath him, her throat exposed. All he had to do was lean forward and drink from her. It was a part of his orgasm, never before denied. He'd never *wanted* to deny it. This time he did.

Then it was too late. His orgasm carried him beyond the moment and her cry assured him that she came with him. The pleasure shook him, made him weak with its power, and made him wonder how it could be so intense without the feeding. He decided not to think about it, just to let the overwhelming joy of the moment flood him. Right now, Stephan didn't matter; all Dacian's regrets over his long lifespan didn't matter. All that mattered was this moment and this woman.

Finally, it was over and he managed to roll to his side and tuck her into him. Making love on a table took practice.

There were things to talk about, but he enjoyed the silence right now. Too bad it didn't last long.

"Hey." The door of the greenhouse rattled under the force of Wade's blows. "I brought something for you, my little bass queen."

Dacian guessed Wade wasn't talking to him.

Cinn groaned as she moved away from Dacian and swung her feet to the floor. "I can't believe this. What happened to your suggestion that everyone stay away?"

"I guess it doesn't work with lovesick demons." He wanted to unscrew Wade's head like a lid from a jar.

He and Cinn needed some coming-back-to-earth time.

More pounding convinced Dacian that Wade wasn't about to give up. Resigned, he rose and pulled on his clothes. Once Cinn was dressed, he went to let the pain in the ass in.

# *Chapter Ten*

Cinn moved in slow motion while her brain broke all kinds of speed limits. Any minute now the brain police would pull her over and ticket her. At least that was how it felt. She watched Dacian open the door, but all she could think about was the sensation of him sliding into her, filling her, and driving her to a screaming climax. Wow. Just wow.

Wade stepped into the greenhouse. He carried something. She wasn't interested. All she wanted was to revisit the feel of Dacian's muscles flexing and bunching beneath her fingers, his mouth on her breasts, between her thighs.

"You won't believe what I brought for you, Cinn."

Unfortunately, she would. She tried to concentrate. "You need to stop doing things for me, Wade." She smiled, but she was sure it lacked a certain authenticity.

"Nothing's too good for my new favorite fishing buddy."

Cinn allowed herself a silent groan. A quick glance at Dacian showed him torn between a scowl and laughter.

"I'll get seasick before the boat even leaves the dock. And I've never fished in my life. I won't make much of a fishing buddy." Not that she thought her argument would discourage him.

"I'll teach you. It'll be fun."

Cinn had her doubts. She desperately tried to dive back into her most recent memories of Dacian's bare body sliding across hers, the way her nipples had grown so sensitive that his touch was almost a pleasure-pain thing. She'd never thought she'd enjoy that.

"Here, let me show you what I bought for you so you could get started."

No. She didn't want to look. But she didn't have it in her to be rude, so she moved closer to see what he had.

"This is a G. Loomis tackle box." He waited for her reaction.

She made appropriate noises of awe before trying to refuse his gift in a way that wouldn't hurt his feelings. "Look, I appreciate your thoughtfulness, Wade, but I really can't accept this. I mean, we just met, and I don't want you spending your money on stuff for me. We can be friends without you . . ." Her words died as she watched his expression change.

Eyes all red and glowing. Lips drawn back from surprisingly sharp teeth. Total effect? Seriously upset demon.

Cinn rethought her response and came down on the side of nonviolence. "But hey, if I ever want to go fishing, I'll need a tackle box." She hated herself for encouraging him, but it seemed the lesser of two evils. She didn't need someone else mad at her, especially if that someone was a demon.

Wade's expression cleared. He grinned at her. "And look what's inside." He opened the box and stepped back.

She peered inside. "Thanks a bunch, Wade. Umm, since I don't fish, a little info would help."

He reached inside. "This is a pair of titanium pliers to pull the hooks from your catch."

Ouch. Bet that hurt. "Titanium?"

"Yep, only the best. Cost about three hundred bucks."

Cinn looked at the pliers with new respect.

"And this is your bait."

"Fishing lures?" At least she knew that much.

"Most tournaments don't allow live bait." He pointed at a few of the lures. "Top Dog Jr., Catch 2000, and these are Bleeding Bait Hooks."

"They're red." She thought about that. "Oh, right. Red. Blood. Got it."

She knew Wade was waiting, so she sucked it in and tried to look enthusiastic. "I'm so excited. I never expected all this. I bet it'll be loads of fun." Heaving over the side of the boat, smelling of dead fish, embedding a fishhook somewhere in her body. Yep, she couldn't wait.

Wade seemed satisfied with her show of enthusiasm. "I'll just sit here and keep you company while you visit with your plants. I can tell you about some of the big ones I've caught."

"No." Dacian finally injected himself into the conversation. "I'm officially in charge of guarding Cinn at night."

Wade's expression turned hostile. "What if you go crazy again? What then?"

Cinn winced. Wade didn't do subtle.

"*Then* you can guard the greenhouse."

She noticed that Dacian didn't mention Wade guarding *her*.

"Well, I can still stick around." Wade didn't give up easily.

Time for her to end this. "I'd love to talk to you, Wade, but I've got a killer headache. I won't make good company."

Wade mulled that over. "Okay, I guess you need to rest. Make sure you take something for it." He frowned. "Demons don't get headaches, so I don't really know what they feel like."

"Trust me, they hurt." She controlled the urge to toss in a moan of pain.

Wade started to leave, but paused at the kitchen door. "I wanted to warn you about Bain while he wasn't around. He's not just any demon. He's a prince of hell."

"A what?" She did *not* want to talk about Bain. She was still furious at him for telling all those lies about her plants.

"An arch demon. If he's here, it's not to help manage the Castle of Dark Dreams. He's one of the really evil ones, a *Titanic* kind of bad. He's that powerful."

"The *Titanic* sank." Dacian looked amused.

Wade wasn't amused. He ignored Dacian and focused on Cinn. "Do some research. He might be playing an ordinary guy, but he'd rip out your soul and laugh while he did it." Wade stepped from the greenhouse, and dinner smells drifted through the open door. "But I guess he fits in here. Edge deals in death, too. Watch out for both of them." His pointed glance at Dacian included him in the triumvirate of death. "Always remember what they are." Then he was gone.

"Nice guy." Dacian sounded vicious. "Maybe I'll send him back to hell. I bet he can find a nice fishing hole there."

Cinn couldn't let that pass. "Are Bain and Edge really that bad?"

Dacian shrugged. "Probably." He stared at her. "I have a lot in common with them." He didn't say anything more.

He intended to allow her to decide whether friendship—okay, making love with him—was worth the risk. But she'd already decided that, hadn't she?

Cinn sighed. Time to change the subject. And there were plenty of subjects to explore. "Wade's obsession

with me came on right after I touched one of my miniature rosebush's flowers and then touched Wade's hand. I
have a theory."

Dacian groaned. "Don't tell me the rosebush made
him your love slave."

She frowned. "Well, that's sort of extreme. But, yeah,
that's what I think happened. I have to test my theory."

"I'd let you test it on me, but how would you know if
it worked? I could give Wade a run for his money right
now without any help from your plants." He smiled.

That smile, rare and something to be treasured, took
her breath away as it always did. And the thought of him
as her love slave triggered an instant response—heat
buildup along with a heavy feeling low in her belly.
Against her express orders, her mind shot off a whole
bunch of images, all involving Dacian naked and doing
things to her body with his hands and mouth that . . .
*Distraction alert.* Now wasn't the time. Maybe later while
she was drifting off to sleep she'd pull out those images
and enhance them a little.

"No, I'll need another test subject, someone who
owes me." She knew her smile was evil enough to put
her in the same class as Bain. "I think Asima would be
perfect. As far as I can see, she doesn't have anything
special to do. And Eva wouldn't affect *Asima*, just whoever the cat touched." Cinn turned the idea over in her
mind. "And I have the perfect recipient, someone who
deserves an obsession."

"Uh-huh. And who's the lucky guy?"

"Holgarth."

"Why?" He waved his question away. "Never mind. I
get it. Everyone in the castle will high-five your
choice."

"It won't really hurt him. In fact, a little bit of love

and lust will do him good. Make him more human. Maybe." She pulled out her cell and called Holgarth. After enduring his usual sarcastic comments, Cinn finally got the wizard to agree to tell Asima her presence was requested in the greenhouse.

"Now we wait." Cinn plopped back down onto the cot. "After I do my test, I'll have to get someone who isn't named Wade to guard the plants. I need to shower, eat, and bang my head against a wall for a while." She wasn't stupid enough to suggest that Dacian stay in the greenhouse while she ate and showered. No way was she going to let Airmid catch her alone again. And what *was* she going to do about the goddess and her righteous wrath?

*"I understand I'm needed here. I hope this is important. I was dining when Holgarth interrupted me to deliver your message. And dining well, I might add. Sparkle would like me to catch mice for my dinner, but sautéed mouse is too bland for my palate. Beluga caviar is much tastier."* Asima moved with the natural lithe grace of her species. She wrapped her body around Dacian's leg and pointedly ignored Cinn.

That was just fine with Cinn. "I need you to help me with an experiment."

*"What kind of experiment?"* Asima was no dummy. She sounded suspicious.

"Well, I know you want to redeem yourself after what almost happened to Vince." Cinn would try the sweet approach.

Asima blinked. *"Why would I want to do that? I was only following the orders of my goddess. That's what I'm supposed to do. In fact, Bast is furious with me for ruining Airmid's plans."*

Okay, sweet wasn't working. She'd appeal to Asima's

ego. "I need someone with a strong will, someone who won't allow herself to become distracted by another's obsession."

"*I never obsess over anything.*" The cat paused to consider her words. "*Although I do admit to being very fond of certain operas. I suppose that is a kind of obsession.*"

"Yes, well, I need someone who can touch one of my plants and remain unaffected by the touch."

"*And what is the expected reaction?*" Asima wasn't walking into anything blind.

Dacian had heard enough. "Let's stop beating around the bush." He grinned. "Literally. Cinn thinks that when someone touches her little rosebush and then touches someone else, the touchee becomes fixated on the toucher. Sort of like a love-slave type thing."

"*That is ridiculous.*"

Cinn could see the interest in her eyes, though.

"*But I'm willing to participate in the name of scientific advancement.*"

"In other words, you're curious." Cinn wasn't fooled.

Asima twitched her whiskers. "*Perhaps.*"

Cinn figured she'd better get this over with before the cat reconsidered. "Eva's over here." She led Asima to the rosebush. "Jump up on the counter. Put your paw or something on one of the open blooms. My theory is that Eva's pollen causes the reaction."

"*An intriguing theory but highly unlikely.*" Asima reached out with one elegant paw to bat at a flower and then switched paws for another bat at a different one. Finally, she stuck her nose into a flower.

"Easy. Don't knock off the blooms."

"*Now what?*"

"Go up to the great hall and touch Holgarth with whatever part of you still has some pollen on it. Make sure you touch skin. There *has* to be a pollen transfer."

"*Holgarth?*" Asima sounded surprised, but then a sly gleam appeared in her eyes. "*Holgarth. Yes, I could enjoy spurning his pitiful advances.*" She brightened. "*This will be fun.*"

Cinn didn't know if she trusted the cat's obvious glee. But it was too late now.

"*I'll go right now.*" Asima bounded along the counter, pausing for a moment to bat playfully at Vince's leaves.

"Jeez, be careful, Asima. You could knock off some leaves. Oh, and whatever you do, never go near those plants in the corner. Those are my weed warriors. They're off limits."

"Uh-oh." Dacian winced. "You said the wrong thing to Asima. A cat is curiosity with claws."

Cinn saw the cat's intention in her eyes a second before she acted.

With one leap Asima reached the off-limits plants. And before anyone could stop her, she batted at a prickly cactus.

Cinn's shouted warning came too late. "Nooo! Don't touch Teddy."

Asima forgot to be careful. As she turned away from the cactus, one of the spines hooked in her side. And that fast, the plant had her. A whole section of one arm broke off at a joint and stuck to her.

Asima didn't suffer in silence. She bounded away, the section of cactus clinging to her like a drunken rodeo rider. Her yowls filled the greenhouse and probably set off car alarms in the parking lot.

"Son of a bitch." Dacian snatched a heavy burlap sack from the table. Then he leaped at Asima and wrapped the sack around her. He wasn't taking any chances with a pollen transfer.

She squirmed and screeched as he grabbed the pliers Wade had left out. Holding the cat as still as he could, he used the pliers to yank out the spines. Finally silence filled the greenhouse.

"That went well." Dacian dropped the piece of cactus into the trash. "Explain."

Cinn cast a nervous look at Asima, who was handling the trauma by methodically grooming herself. The cat didn't return Cinn's gaze.

"Teddy is my cholla, commonly known as a jumping cactus. No, he can't actually jump, but he has all these cylindrical joints. So when someone touches one of his spines, the whole joint breaks off and sticks to the victim. His spines are amazing. They can penetrate the toughest hide and are barbed like fishhooks. He's quite a guy."

"*Hmmph. That was an unprovoked attack. He should be behind bars.*" Asima had found her voice.

"He didn't attack you. You brushed up against him and he stuck to you. It's what a cholla does." Cinn knew she sounded as weary as she felt.

"Why is he in the corner with your weed warriors?" Dacian looked as though he didn't believe she'd given them the whole story.

She hadn't.

"Umm, no real reason. I just didn't want anyone to touch him and get hurt." Cinn felt righteous indignation. This was all Asima's fault. But maybe she should apologize to the cat. She turned toward Asima . . . just in time to see her licking her paws. "No. You'll wash all the pollen off."

Asima cast her a slit-eyed, pissed-kitty stare. "*I quit. You didn't warn me that this could be hazardous employment. Do you have insurance? Perhaps I should sue. Is animal cruelty a felony?*"

Cinn huffed her frustration. "Oh, for God's sake. I'm sorry, okay?"

Asima didn't answer. Instead she stood frozen, staring into space.

"Now what?" Cinn was getting tired of all the drama.

Asima cast an awe-filled gaze her way. *"Vince spoke to me."*

Just peachy. Vince spoke to everyone but her.

*"He said he forgives me for tossing him in the trash, and he's sorry I was hurt."*

"Kind of him." Why wouldn't Vince speak to *her*?

Before Cinn could stop her, Asima leaped onto the counter and bounded over other plants to get to Vince.

"Don't touch him! Don't you dare touch him." Too late. Asima stuck her nose against one of Vince's leaves. Cinn groaned.

*"I told him I was truly sorry he had to spend time in the trash. I feel like I just went to confession. Of course, I'm not a Catholic, so I don't know exactly how that would feel. Besides, the priest might refuse to give absolution to a cat. The church has these silly rules that—"*

"Shut. Up." Cinn spoke through clenched teeth.

*"Why?"* Asima looked sincerely puzzled.

*Because you make me crazy.* "Vince can communicate, he has feelings, and he's sensitive. You're *not* sensitive. You'll hurt him."

*"Uh, excuse me? One of your plants attacked me with malicious intent, and you have the nerve to accuse me of insensitivity? Perhaps you need to explain your reasoning."* She made a contemptuous cat sound.

"I don't know, I don't know." Cinn rubbed at her eyes. God, she was tired. Too much had happened today. Her thoughts were getting muddied.

Dacian was ready for this whole scene to be over. "Maybe you should leave, Asima. And ask Holgarth to send someone to guard the plants while Cinn gets something to eat and takes a shower."

Asima wasn't listening. She gazed up at them from eyes bright with wonder. *"Vince says he loves me. He admires my elegant manner and thinks my eyes are more beautiful than the stars he can see through the glass."*

She leaped for the door. *"No one has ever loved me. Ever. I want him to hear some of my music. He'll love it."*

Cinn looked at Dacian. "Don't say it. I know I made a mess of this. Maybe Airmid is right." She sighed. "I don't know anymore."

Dacian didn't want to think it, but he couldn't stop his mind's buzzing. Did she see him as she saw her plants? An experiment with the unknown? God, he hoped not. "Okay, we know Vince reacted to Eva's pollen. What about Teddy?"

Cinn looked over at the cactus. "I don't know. He's not as evolved as Vince, so he might not be able to express his feelings." She shrugged. "It doesn't matter, because we know what Eva does. Now I have to figure out how to cure Wade and Vince."

Dacian cast another glance Teddy's way. He wouldn't count the cactus out. But maybe Cinn was right. Even if Teddy had some emotional response to Asima, what could he do? Poor slob.

Cinn and Dacian sat on the cot waiting for a replacement guard. Neither spoke. They didn't have to wait long. Suddenly, the kitchen door entrance swung open and Ganymede padded in. Several hotel employees tagged along behind him. One carried a flat-screen TV while another toted a small fridge. A third pushed aside several plants and put a cat bed on the counter. Ganymede leaped into the bed as one of the men strung two extension cords out the door and back into the kitchen. Cinn and Dacian could hear the chef's shouted opinion of this disruption of his cooking routine.

"I don't believe this." Cinn narrowed her gaze on the cat.

"*Believe it, babe.*" Ganymede began to wash his face. "*I'll watch your plants, but you have to do something for me while you're out.*"

Dacian knew this wouldn't be good.

"*Sparkle is a hot-tempered woman. I love that about her. But sometimes she loses it for no reason. She got pissed off when I told her I'd given her designer stuff to charity. I thought I'd done something good, helped her build character. Anyway, after she threw a bunch of stuff at me, she told me to find somewhere else to sleep. She kicked me out with only the fur on my back.*" Ganymede glanced around. "*This'll do until she gets over her mad.*"

"Of course it will." Cinn seemed dazed.

"*Here's what I want you to do. Go up to our suite and get Sparkle to let you bring some treats down to me. I want the ice cream, chips, and cookies. I'll leave her the candy.*" He looked reluctant to give anything up. "*I would've picked up a few things in the kitchen as I came through, but Chef Phil doesn't stock my faves.*"

"And what if she won't give the stuff to me?"

Dacian could see from Cinn's expression that the last thing she wanted to do was confront Sparkle over Ganymede's treats.

"*Hey, there's a store right down the street. I'll pay you back when my lady forgives me.*" He stopped washing his face to stare at Cinn. He worked his poor-pitiful-kitty look. She wasn't buying. "*Meanwhile, I'll guard your plants. No half-ass goddess sprouting leaves will get past me.*"

Dacian winced. He hoped for Ganymede's sake that Airmid wasn't listening. Cinn just nodded.

After handing Cinn her coat and purse just in case they had to leave the castle, Dacian walked out of the

greenhouse with her. If he had any say about it, he'd
make sure she didn't go back there until dawn. She
needed to rest in her room, away from this freaking circus. *And how does she escape you?* She couldn't, because
he'd stay glued to her side for every one of his waking
hours. She'd just have to deal.

Stephan eyed the women his second-in-command had
brought for him to choose from. Kevin had good taste.
They'd all done their best to impress him. The dumb
shits thought this was a casting call. Well, maybe it was
in a way. Hey, welcome to Hollywood, baby. He smiled.

"Not that one. Not that one. Not that one. *That* one."
He pointed. Stephan was in a blonde mood today.

The chosen woman squealed her joy. Stephan nodded at Kevin. Kevin would take her to Stephan's room
and a good time would be had by all. Fine, maybe not
exactly by all. But by him, and that was the important
part.

The ringing of his cell interrupted his thoughts of
sex and blood. He glanced at the caller ID before answering. His contact had better have some information.

"Is Dacian at the castle?" Stephan listened to the reply and smiled. Good. "Did you find out anything of
interest about my oldest child?"

As he listened, his smile widened. "It was kind of Dacian to pass on a description of me. I'll make sure I don't
resemble it in any way when I drop by. And he's with a
human woman. Perhaps his brother isn't his only weak-
ness." That would be an unexpected perk. Yes, he could
use her against Dacian.

"How about Taurin?" This reply didn't make him
smile. "When is he expected back?"

He listened to the answer. Okay, now he was pissed.

"Find out. And when you do, contact me. My army's in place." Stephan cut the connection right in the middle of his contact's apologies. Why was it so difficult to find competent underlings? He felt the push of his fangs. The woman in his room would pay for his bad temper.

"Everyone is safely settled at the castle, my lord." Kevin was back.

"We got lucky." Stephan tapped one perfectly manicured nail on the arm of his chair. "The Castle of Dark Dreams doesn't have a great number of rooms. I was able to book fifteen of them. We have three sharing a room—two fighters and their meal. Thirty vampires should be able to take over the whole park with no trouble."

Kevin smiled. "And of course you have your insurance policy tucked away in a sixteenth room."

Stephan was in an expansive mood, so he smiled back. "Yes. What a marvelous surprise for Dacian and the others at the castle. If he thinks a few nonhumans can protect him, he's sadly mistaken." Gloating felt so *good*.

Kevin's smile faltered. "Do we know anything about the other nonhumans? How powerful are they?"

Stephan waved his concerns away. "What could possibly be more powerful than our surprise package along with thirty vampires?" He didn't wait for Kevin's reply. "We'll strike right before dawn when the least number of humans will be there. If we leave no witnesses, we can continue on without the city knowing there was a regime change. The Castle of Dark Dreams will be our Texas base of operation. The first of many such bases." God, he was brilliant. And powerful. Brilliance without power was no fun at all.

"That was a great move you made, your lordship, getting everyone in without alerting anyone in the castle."

Stephan shook his head. "Kevin, Kevin, have you learned nothing about me? I plan for everything. Humans man the check-in desk at the hotel. Our fighters simply arrived, checked in, and went directly to their rooms. They won't come out until it's time for the attack. Which will be as soon as I arrive." Kevin nodded.

"And all this fell into place because I found Dacian's paid snoop." Actually, one of his spies had found him, but since his followers were merely an extension of him, Stephan felt perfectly justified in taking credit. "Too bad Jim only had a phone number and not a location. He was pitifully willing to pass my information on to Dacian. He didn't have a very high pain threshold." Stephan frowned. "You disposed of his body?"

"Of course."

"Good. You may leave."

Stephan sat thinking for a while after he dismissed Kevin and before he went for his evening's entertainment. Once Taurin returned to the castle, Stephan would have to make sure Dacian didn't convince his brother to leave immediately. They had to be in the castle when he attacked. He wouldn't lose Dacian again. A few more mindless rages would keep his oldest child chained in the dungeon. And if Stephan's timing were perfect, Dacian would be chained to the wall, waiting to be plucked when Stephan arrived. He'd work on making that happen.

# Chapter Eleven

Cinn would rather have faced ten Holgarths than one Sparkle Stardust right now. Because the wizard was predictable. He was always cranky and sarcastic. But Sparkle was manipulative and changeable. Cinn didn't know if she could deal with what Sparkle might bring.

"Thanks for coming with me." She glanced up at Dacian. Cinn never tired of looking at him. His beauty and the memory of their lovemaking pushed into the background her fear of his uncontrolled rages and the realization that, hey, he was a vampire.

"No thanks needed. I'll be with you every second I'm awake until we get this Airmid thing solved." He smiled at her.

His smiles came more easily now. She hoped a little of that was because of her.

Turning her attention back to Sparkle's door, she took a deep breath and then knocked. And prayed that maybe Sparkle was somewhere else.

Sparkle flung open the door. "What?" She wore a pair of brown polyester pants, a white cotton top, ordinary sneakers, and an angry scowl.

Cinn stood speechless. It was sort of like seeing the Statue of Liberty holding up a Pyrex bowl. It just didn't look right.

Dacian explained things to Sparkle: "Ganymede wants his treats. If you don't let us take them, we'll have to make a trip to the store. You wouldn't be punishing Ganymede."

"Huh." She stepped aside to let Cinn pass, but she stopped Dacian. "Do a favor for me. Find Edge and tell him I have a job for him."

Dacian narrowed his gaze on her. "No, you can't order Edge to kill Ganymede just because he gave away your clothes. Buy more."

She heaved an exaggerated sigh. "As tempting as the thought is, that's not why I want Edge."

"So call him on your cell."

Now she glared at him. "You're a gorgeous guy, but you don't take hints well, do you? Okay, let me spell it out. I want to talk to Cinn. Alone."

"I'm not leaving her alone."

"I'm as powerful as you. I can protect her."

"Like you did in the store?"

Her gaze slid away. "That was an aberration. Sorrow overcame me for all those poor people forced to shop at that unbelievably ordinary store on a regular basis. I cry bitter tears for them." She sighed. "And for me. Give me a break, beautiful vampire. I want to talk to Cinn woman to woman. No men allowed. You'd be bored stiff anyway."

"And if I refuse?"

"Then not one treat from this place goes to that loathsome creature cowering in the greenhouse." She tapped her foot.

"Go ahead, Dacian. I'll be fine with Sparkle." Cinn managed a confident smile for him. Who said there was no martyr blood in her veins?

Dacian finally nodded. "Okay, but talk fast, because as soon as I pass on the message to Edge, I'm coming back." He turned and walked away.

Sparkle closed the door and motioned Cinn to a chair. "I'd offer you a glass of wine, but I broke all the wine bottles throwing them at Mede. Can you believe it? He gave away all my gorgeous clothes and shoes."

Cinn was almost afraid to say it. "He thought he was doing the right thing."

Sparkle sank onto the couch, crossed her legs, and stared at one sneaker-clad foot. "I can't help it. I'm losing the battle against shallowness, and I'm afraid I'll lose Mede in the process." She didn't meet Cinn's gaze.

"I don't understand."

"The Big Boss is in charge of all cosmic troublemakers. I almost lost Mede because of him. He said I was shallow. He gave Mede a choice: give me up or give up being a cosmic troublemaker."

"And?" Cinn was riveted.

"Mede chose me. We were lucky, though. The Big Boss gave Mede credit for being willing to sacrifice what he loved most for me. He let Mede stay a cosmic troublemaker. This time."

Cinn didn't see a problem. "You're wrong, you know. Obviously he didn't give up the thing he loved most, because he chose you. No offense, but Ganymede seems pretty focused on what's best for him. If he chose you, it was because he wanted you the most. Be happy." There. Problem solved.

Sparkle waved her explanation away. "No, no. It's not that simple. I have to make sure the Big Boss can never use me against Mede again. That's why I can't be shallow. That's why I have to wear these freaking clothes." She stood and paced. "But I can't make myself go outside this room in them."

Oh, God, what to say? "Well, you know, some really deep people wear good clothes. You can make up for being clothes-obsessed by gaining depth in other areas."

Sparkle looked interested. "Really? I never thought

of it that way. So I could wear great clothes as long as I helped the stylishly challenged dress with sensual flair?"

Not exactly what Cinn had had in mind. "Yeah, I guess so. It's the intention that counts. As long as your intent is to help people rather than just embarrass them, it shows depth of character."

Sparkle clapped her hands. "I can do that. I'll start with you."

What had she unleashed? "Umm, I'm happy with my own clothes, if I could find where you put them."

"In the trash. Too late now." Sparkle seemed distracted. "I have to get my old clothes back."

Oh, crap. "I don't know . . ."

"It'll be easy. The charity that made off with all my beautiful things has a store in Galveston. We'll just go down there tomorrow."

Cinn was afraid of that.

"What about Airmid?"

"What about her? I don't think she shops in resale stores."

Sparkle was being purposely dense. Cinn didn't have to be a mind reader to figure that out. "I'll have to stick with you every moment we're there."

Sparkled nodded. "This is so great. I can dress like a goddess again." She paused to consider her words. "Of course, I haven't seen Airmid's clothes, so I might actually dress better than a goddess."

"Okay, we've had our talk. Can I get Ganymede's treats for him?"

"Absolutely not. I'm not finished with our chat."

Cinn figured Dacian wasn't the only one capable of insane rages. Her own temper had started to simmer.

"One of my greatest trials while trying to attain

depth of character has been denying my true purpose. For thousands of years I've brought sexual chaos to the universe. It's who I am, my reason for being. I've denied myself because being the queen of sex and sin is, well, probably shallow in the Big Boss's eyes." She turned sad eyes on Cinn.

Cinn knew what Sparkle wanted her to say. And since Cinn wanted to get out of here with Ganymede's treats sometime before dawn, she chucked honesty in favor of expediency.

"I think you can still mess with people's sex lives as long as you're doing it to bring happiness into their lives."

Sparkle widened her eyes. "But I always do that."

Cinn crossed her arms over her chest and waited.

"Fine, so maybe I get a teenie weenie kick out of matching up people who are wrong for each other. And maybe occasionally I find it amusing to wait until they've had incredible sex and are beginning to bond before I rip them apart forever." Sparkle nodded. "I suppose that happens once in a while."

"See, it's all about intent again." She hoped Sparkle bought this explanation, because she was fresh out of bullshit. "You can still bring couples together as long as you're doing it purely for their happiness."

"I can't tear them apart afterward?"

"No."

"Bummer." Then Sparkle smiled. "But that's better than nothing." Her smiled turned calculating. "I thought we'd take a few minutes to talk about Dacian."

Uh-oh. Cinn knew where this was going. She glanced at her watch. "I don't think we'll have time. Dacian will be back soon, and Ganymede will be waiting for his treats."

Sparkle wasn't fooled. "I suppose I can let our chat go until tomorrow. After I get all my clothes back, we'll stop somewhere for dinner and discuss sex and hot men."

"I suppose so." *Lord, please let something happen so I don't have to talk about Dacian with Sparkle.*

Whatever Sparkle intended to say next didn't get said because Dacian pounded on the door. Well, Cinn supposed it was Dacian. Who else would be that eager to enter Sparkle's lair?

Sparkle heaved a huge sigh, rose, and swayed over to the door.

Cinn wondered if Sparkle would teach her how to walk like that. Not that she wanted to turn into a Sparkle clone, but a sexy walk couldn't be construed as abandoning her principles.

As soon as Sparkle opened the door, Dacian stepped inside. He immediately looked for Cinn, and she could see the relief in his eyes when he found her. That made her feel good. She wasn't going to lie about it.

"Let's get those treats so we can give them to Ganymede and get you back to your room for a while." He sent a pointed stare Sparkle's way.

Sparkle didn't give in gracefully. "Will you tattle if I mix vinegar in with Mede's ice cream?" She smiled. "He won't realize those little crystals on top of his sugar cookies are salt, not sugar, until it's too late."

Cinn wanted out of there. "Yes, I'll definitely tell him. Now can we get the stuff and leave?"

A short time later, both Dacian and she walked into the greenhouse with arms loaded.

Just in time to see one of Teddy's lethal arms go whizzing across the room. It missed Vince and stuck in a wood panel behind him. Vince's vine reached out, wrapped around his nearest neighbor's pot, and proceeded to drag himself out of the line of fire.

She knew her mouth was hanging open. Dacian's sure was. Ganymede merely looked entertained.

*"Yo. You took long enough."* Ganymede stared at Cinn. *"You got yourself some cool plants. Don't think those two like each other. My money's on the cactus. The vine just keeps taking evasive action. Eventually the cactus will nail him."*

"Oh, shit." Dacian dropped Ganymede's treats on the counter and strode to where Vince now hid behind another plant.

Cinn couldn't believe her own eyes. Teddy was attacking Vince. There was clear intent to harm. This wasn't just a plant feeling an emotion. This was a reasoned response to said emotion. How had Teddy taken that step? And Vince was evolving so fast he frightened her. Not only was he thinking and talking; now he'd figured out a way to become mobile.

*"Hey, sweetie, would you put my ice cream in the fridge for me?"* Ganymede was using his I'm-just-a-helpless-kitty voice.

"If you're such a powerful guy, why don't you use your mind to do it?" But *her* mind wasn't on Ganymede. War in her greenhouse. This had never been in her plans. What had happened?

*"Sure I can do it myself, but it gives me a rush to get you to do it for me."*

Cinn couldn't be bothered to argue, so she did what he asked.

*"Oh, did my honey-bunny mention me?"* He clawed open the cookie box.

"I think the words 'loathsome creature' were uttered."

Ganymede's expression brightened. *"That's a step up from 'rotting roadkill.' My babe still loves me."*

"If you say so." Her mind was still on her plants. "We have to do something about Teddy and Vince."

Dacian had picked up Vince's pot and now stood with it in his hands. "What do you want to do with him? If we leave him here, the cactus will eventually get him." He kept an eye on Teddy as he spoke.

"Or Teddy will destroy himself trying." She had to find a way to counteract Eva's damage. Cinn had thought she was being so damn smart with her experimenting, but now she had a bunch of out-of-control plants.

"We have to make sure no one else touches Eva. And we'll have to take Vince with us." She raked her fingers through her hair. "I can't believe that Teddy's really jealous of Vince."

"Believe it." Dacian nodded toward the door. "Let's get out of here. You need some downtime in your own room away from the plants and everything else."

*"Enjoy yourself."* The TV was on and Ganymede was already into the cookies. *"No puny old plant goddess will get past me."* He curled up in his comfy bed.

Cinn had to take his word for it. She was too tired to be any good to her plants. She allowed Dacian to lead her through the kitchen. He stopped at an empty table in the restaurant.

"You need to eat first."

He pulled out a chair, and she collapsed onto it. Dacian was right. She needed food. Speaking of food . . . Cinn watched him set Vince on the table and then take the seat across from her before she asked her question. "How often do you have to feed?" *And please don't feel the need to go into graphic detail.*

"Usually about once every few weeks. I'm old enough

to go a long time between feedings. But Stephan's attacks take a lot out of me. I always have to feed after one of them."

She nodded. *Don't ask, don't ask, don't ask.* She asked. "Do you drain . . . ?" *Do you drain your victims dry? Do you kill them? Do I really want you to tell me?*

He leaned back in his chair, a small smile playing around his sexy lips. "I don't 'drain' anyone, Cinn. I take a little from a lot of people until I've had enough. All I leave them with is the thought that they must be coming down with the flu because they feel a little weak."

"Well, that's great. I—"

"Don't make me into something I'm not." He wouldn't let her think he was some kind of shining example of a 'good' vampire. "I take from a lot of different sources just like most vampires do nowadays. The discovery of a bunch of drained bodies would turn the spotlight directly on us. We can't have humans thinking vampires might be real."

"Oh."

"I've killed in my time: when I was a young vampire, when Stephan first attacked me and I didn't know what was happening, lots of times."

"Trying to convince me you're a murdering bastard?" Her expression was neutral.

"No, just wanted you to have a realistic view of what I am."

Cinn nodded, but didn't look particularly horrified. "Since I'm into personal questions, will you tell me about your scars? And yes, I want to know. And no, I don't really have the right to expect you to answer me." She shrugged. "Your choice whether you explain or not."

He had a few minutes to decide what to tell her while

the waitress took her order. In the end, he decided to tell her the truth.

"For a few years after Stephan began messing with my head, I didn't have a clue what I did when I was out of it. Then one day I ran into Kyla. We'd lived in the same area for a while. She told me I'd killed half the people in a nearby town. And that was just during one killing rage. There must have been other towns, other dead people."

"You can't blame yourself. The killings were on Stephan's head."

The anger he heard in her voice surprised him. "*I* killed."

She made a rude noise.

"The next time the rage hit, I came out of it with some personal damage. Guess my food fought back." He didn't try to hide his bitterness. "I wanted to make sure I never forgot what I was capable of doing during a rage, so I imposed my will on my body. I kept it from healing long enough for the scars to form."

Cinn looked away, and he got the feeling she was trying to control her reaction. Finally, she returned her gaze to him. "Kyla knew about your rages?"

"No, she knew about my killing. I didn't tell her about Stephan."

"She was there when the Mackenzies tried to trap you, wasn't she?"

"Yeah. I'd killed some of them, too." He didn't feel anger at Kyla's part in the plan. She was a Mackenzie, and clan was important to her.

He sat quietly while Cinn ate. Thinking. Things were getting complicated. He didn't just want to make love with Cinn until it was time for him to leave with Taurin. He wanted to break Stephan's hold on him so he didn't *have* to leave her. And that was one of the scariest revelations of his long life.

Then there was Airmid. How could he leave the castle while the goddess was still a danger to Cinn? Okay, that wasn't even an option. He couldn't. He'd have to find a way to protect his brother and Cinn. From two different dangers. No, three, counting himself.

She rubbed her hand across her eyes. "Now that I've stuffed myself, I feel as though I could sleep for a week."

Dacian paid for her meal and stood. He picked up Vince. "Then you need to sleep. In your own bed." He answered her unspoken question. "Alone."

"But the plants—"

"Will be fine." He guided her to the elevator. "Ganymede doesn't always come across as a supernatural heavyweight, but I have a feeling he could take both Airmid and Stephan down in a fight. Together. He owes you, so let him watch the greenhouse till dawn."

"And you?"

"I'll stay with you until Bain or Edge takes over." He grinned to lighten the moment. "Airmid isn't the only one they'll have to guard against. You'd better hope the effects of Eva's pollen wear off after a while. I think poor Wade's getting desperate. He'll probably try to give you his boat next."

She groaned as Dacian unlocked her door and they stepped inside. "I forgot about Wade. I feel so bad for him. I have to find a way to reverse the pollen's effect."

He hated to ask the hard questions, but there was one that needed asking. "What will you do with Eva?"

Cinn didn't answer for a moment. She busied herself gathering up her nightgown and slippers, but she finally paused before going into the bathroom. "I don't know.

God, I really don't know. It's not her fault. I bred her that way. Only I didn't know she'd be so powerful. I thought she'd be like Jessica and Sweetie Pie."

"Who?"

Her smile was a little ragged around the edges, but it was still a smile. "They were two of the original plants I supplied to Sparkle. They feed off of sexual energy. Sparkle got a kick out of putting them in guests' rooms. They're two of the plants we brought from the castle for safekeeping while Airmid's on her rampage."

"Any idea what went wrong?"

She shook her head. "Maybe I fiddled with her a little more. Who knows? But I have to make sure this doesn't happen again. I won't destroy her, so I either have to put on gloves and snip off her blooms or isolate her when she starts flowering."

He didn't say anything.

"Maybe some of what Airmid's ticked about is legit. And Eva will hate being isolated."

"Will she?"

Cinn nodded. "You're right. I don't know if she feels anything. But what will I do about Vince and Teddy? They *do* feel."

"Uh, Vince can hear you."

"Oh, God." She went into the bathroom and closed the door behind her.

Dacian set Vince down on the coffee table and then he relaxed onto the couch. "You and me, Vince. Both fuckups." He thought over what he'd just said. "Sorry I insulted you. I think you're pretty amazing. But we've got to find a match for you. Someone who isn't Asima. I bet Cinn has at least one more plant in that greenhouse who can communicate with you. We'll have to find it." He didn't really believe that. What were the chances?

But he didn't want Vince to feel as if he didn't belong anywhere. *Like I do.*

Enough of the self-pity. He occupied his mind with thoughts of Cinn's bare body stretched beneath him, her hands touching his cock, stroking him until . . .

Cinn came out of the bathroom. She hung up her clothes and then climbed into bed without saying anything, without meeting his gaze.

He didn't push her.

When she'd finally pulled the covers up to her chin, she looked at him. "I need to sleep tonight. And then tomorrow I have to think. In that order."

He nodded. "Do I have to do anything for Vince?"

She smiled, and if her smile was a little sad, at least she was smiling. "Talk to him."

Cinn woke to the sound of opera. The aria rose and fell in full-throated splendor. And pulling the covers over her head didn't drown it out.

*"Are you awake yet?"* A weight on her chest shifted. *"Are you awake yet?"* The voice in her head was louder this time. *"Are you—"*

*Argh!* "Yes, I'm awake." She flung the covers off her head.

Asima sat on her chest, her blue almond-shaped eyes fixed on Cinn's face. *"Good. I've been waiting ever so long for you. I tried to be very quiet."*

"Your music isn't quiet."

*"Opera is meant to fill a room."*

"Yeah, well, I think it's overflowing the room and probably flooding the hall." She hated to wake up cranky, but Asima was a buzz-killer. "What are you doing here?"

Asima leaped from her chest and padded over to the

coffee table. She jumped up, lay down, and wrapped her long body around Vince's pot. She batted gently at one of his leaves. *"He adores me, you know."*

Just what Cinn needed. A reminder that she had some major problems in her small plant world. "Yes, but you don't have to encourage him."

The cat widened her eyes at Cinn. *"Why ever not? If someone worships the ground you walk on, then you have an obligation to make yourself available to him. Besides, I love being worshipped."* Her raspy purr filled the room.

Cinn hated to ask, because it only reminded her that Vince didn't talk to her, but she wanted to know. "Has Vince said anything about his feelings, and about Teddy's reaction?"

*"He's said many, many things."* Asima stretched her body and yawned. *"He longs for me to take him with me. Of course, that would be impossible. But I've promised to visit with him as much as possible each day. And he's very upset about Teddy. He feels that Teddy can't treat me in the manner I deserve. Teddy's rather a primitive little soul."* Asima took a moment to lick several of Vince's leaves. *"Grooming is so important. Anyway, Vince is afraid of Teddy. I don't think he wants you to put him back in the greenhouse."*

"Well, maybe he should deign to ask me directly." Okay, that was snarky, but yes, she was a little jealous of the people Vince *had* spoken to.

Asima didn't comment on the outburst, but her expression said clearly that perhaps Cinn wasn't a worthy recipient of Vince's confidences. Fine, so Asima's expression said no such thing because cats didn't have expressions. But Cinn knew that was what her royal kittiness was thinking.

Cinn gave up on Asima and turned her thoughts to someone much more interesting. "Was Dacian still here when you arrived?" She swung her feet to the floor and stood.

"No, but I was. To my everlasting regret."

The deep male voice froze her in the middle of a stretch. She swung toward the narrow castle window. Someone had pulled back the heavy drapery. Edge sat in a chair he'd dragged over to the window, so he could bathe in the sunlight pouring through the glass.

"I thought Bain was guarding me during the day. And why are you inside my room?"

Edge raised one tawny brow. "*Dacian* was in here. Besides, I don't wait outside any woman's door. Deal with it. And Bain had other things to do." His smile suggested that whatever Bain had to do didn't bode well for the world.

Cinn gripped her bottom lip between her teeth. He was right. She'd have to deal with it. Airmid would take any moment of aloneness as an invitation to visit with Cinn. And Cinn didn't really want to have another conversation with the goddess. "You're right."

She went to the closet and pulled out an outfit without even looking at it. They were all the same—sexy with designer labels.

"Sparkle came in and took some of those clothes." Edge sounded unconcerned.

She turned to look at him. "Did everyone in the castle tramp through my room while I slept?"

He shrugged. "She said something about not going outside the castle wearing the big-box horrors she'd bought."

Cinn nodded. "I'm getting dressed, going down to eat breakfast"—she looked at the clock on her night table—"or maybe I should say lunch, and then I'm going to take care of my plants."

"Sure." He got up and turned off Asima's music. "There, that's better."

Cinn didn't wait to listen to the argument. Closing the bathroom door behind her, she pulled on her clothes as she thought about the coming afternoon, and more importantly, the coming night. Dacian would be with her from sunset to dawn if she had anything to say about it. Funny how just a few days ago all she could think about was escaping from here. Now she looked forward to spending the night with a vampire. A *bad* vampire. She smiled to herself. But a very *good* vampire in several important ways.

"I think it's disgraceful how they never give you any alone time. I was going to snatch you last night when you went into the bathroom, but I thought you'd be more rested today."

Cinn had only a second to recognize Airmid's voice, realize she'd made a basic mistake in closing the bathroom door, and shout for help.

Airmid grabbed Cinn a moment before the door crashed open and Edge stood looking around. Cinn yelled at him, but he just cursed and rushed from the room.

"Good try, but he can't hear or see you. I do have some useful powers."

Cinn fought to free herself from the lock the goddess had on her arm, but her wild swings and kicks somehow didn't connect with Airmid.

"Don't waste your energy. You can't touch me."

Then with seemingly no effort at all, she dragged Cinn out into the bedroom and over to where Vince sat helpless on the coffee table. Asima had evidently rushed from the room with Edge to look for Cinn.

"We'll take this little guy with us."

The goddess scooped up Vince and then suddenly they were all somewhere else.

Cinn looked around her. Damn. As far as she could see were plants and more plants. Not in rows, but scattered all the way to the horizon. Cinn had a problem with this scene, though. When she looked down, she saw . . . clouds. "Where are we?"

"In one of my newer gardens. I'll fill in the rest of the landscape later." Still clasping Cinn's arm and carrying Vince, she strolled off across the clouds.

*Dreaming, dreaming, dreaming this.* Cinn's mantra got more frantic with each minute. *We're in deep shit, Vince.*

"*I know.*"

The two words sucked Cinn's breath from her throat. *Vince?* He'd finally talked to her. Too bad she couldn't take time to enjoy the moment. "Where are we going?" *What are you going to do with us?*

"We're going to my home where we can relax and talk."

They might talk, but no way was she going to be able to relax. She glanced down. Whoa, the clouds beneath her feet had been replaced with a stone path leading up to . . .

Her gaze traced the path to a home covered in vines and surrounded by thick greenery. Sunlight created patterns of shadow and light as it shone through a canopy of ancient trees. Okay, this wasn't exactly Cinn's vision of Mount Olympus, but she supposed it was right for Airmid.

The goddess dragged her through the front door and into what looked like Cinn's Aunt Theresa's old house. Small rooms stuffed with dark furniture and littered with what must be antiques. Cinn wasn't an antiquey kind of person. She liked bright airy spaces filled with new things untouched by human hands.

Plants sat on every flat surface. The goddess set Vince down on a table next to a beautiful but uncomfortable-looking chair. Cinn's Aunt Theresa would've known what century the chair came from.

Airmid finally released her and pointed to another chair. "Sit."

Since Cinn had no idea how to get herself back to the Castle of Dark Dreams and was definitely not leaving without Vince anyway, she sat.

Airmid folded herself gracefully onto her chair and then smiled at Cinn. "Now, we'll discuss how you can get back into my good graces."

Okay, Cinn was confused. "You're a goddess. I've ticked you off. So why are you discussing it with me? Don't you have more violent ways to change my mind? I thought bringing down the store around my head was rather effective."

Airmid's laughter was a musical tinkle. "I lost my temper. I try not to do that very often. But I'm sure we can reach an agreement."

Cinn's common sense shouted, "Don't make her mad." She decided to give her common sense a listen-to this time. "What did you have in mind?"

"Good. You're willing to listen." The goddess rearranged her long flowing gown. "First, you have to abandon these ridiculous experiments. You're embarrassing me in front of the other immortals."

*Temper, temper.* "Perhaps we can compromise."

"Compromise?" Airmid looked as if the concept was beyond her understanding.

"Yes. I'll only experiment on healing plants in order to enhance their curative powers." Of course, Cinn would get to decide what curative powers needed to be enhanced.

Airmid stared at the fireplace mantel for a long time. "Hmm, that seems like something I could agree to."

Cinn kept her hands folded in her lap so the goddess wouldn't see how they were shaking. She didn't have any experience negotiating with goddesses. "Anything else?" She knew her smile was a total failure.

"You need to destroy the plants you've twisted into things they never should be." Airmid reached out to stroke one of Vince's leaves.

Oh, hell. "Umm, I don't think I can do that."

Airmid rose and paced to a window, where she pointed at the plants resting on the sill. "*These* are plants, Cinn. They use sunlight and water to grow, not sexual energy. They don't feel emotions, they don't think, they don't talk, and they certainly don't go into jealous rages with each other. They are simply here. And when I need a few leaves for my healing potions, I simply pluck them."

Ouch. Cinn winced.

With each word, Airmid's long hair lifted in that silent wind Cinn was beginning to associate with an incoming temper tempest.

Cinn tried to ease the tension building in the room. "How do you know your plants don't have emotions? Have you ever tuned in to them?"

"Why should I? I am the goddess of all healing plants. I have no need to 'tune in' to them. Of course they don't have feelings."

Cinn didn't like to do this, but she had to give the goddess a demonstration. "Threaten one of your plants in some way. Then try to feel the emotions of the plants around it."

Something in Airmid's expression caught at Cinn's throat. She leaped from her chair just as the goddess reached the table and plucked Vince up. "What a marvelous idea. I think I'll destroy this one and see if my plants care at all. I doubt they will."

Cinn rushed at Airmid even as the goddess lifted Vince's pot high above her head. *Too late!* She was going to be too late to save Vince.

# Chapter Twelve

Without warning, a flash of light blinded Cinn for a moment. Then everything happened in starburst blasts. Dacian appeared and grabbed her. Edge materialized beside Airmid and jerked Vince from her grasp. Then another flash of light and they were all back in her room at the Castle of Dark Dreams.

"What the hell happened?" Her legs were so weak she dropped onto a chair the moment Dacian released her. "And how can you be up when it's"—she glanced out the window—"already dark." Time was definitely misbehaving. What had seemed only a short time in Airmid's world had been hours here.

*"Yo, your furry caped crusader saved your butt."* Ganymede sat in regal splendor atop her bureau. *"Airmid the airhead is probably still trying to figure out what happened."* He chuckled. *"She'll be one pissed-off immortal."*

Dacian tried to translate for Cinn. "As soon as Edge saw you were gone, he sent a mental shout-out to Ganymede. The cat woke me up. We all met here, and eventually Ganymede was able to trace the path to Airmid's home." He held up his hand to ward off her question. "Don't ask. I don't have a clue how he did it. Then he sent us to where you were. We grabbed you, and Ganymede pulled us back here."

Cinn glanced at Ganymede with new respect. "Wow, I'm totally impressed. Thank you." Now, if only someone could stop Airmid from ambushing her every time she grew careless. And no, she refused to have a bathroom bodyguard.

*"No problem, babe. Had to do it, though. My sweetie would never forgive me if I lost you. Besides, I need you to keep me in snacks until Sparkle lets me move back in."*

Edge looked thoughtful. "One thing I don't understand. If Airmid is so pissed at Cinn, why didn't she just kill her when she had the chance?"

"I wondered about that, too. She sure doesn't have a problem with destroying my plants."

No one seemed to have an answer to why Cinn was still alive.

Speaking of plants . . . "Who's guarding the greenhouse?" Panic touched her. Airmid would be in a temper, and she might strike at Cinn's plants even with someone guarding them.

"Bain has it covered." Edge smiled. "No one messes with Bain, even a pissed-off goddess. The man has skills."

Cinn didn't think she wanted to know what those skills were. The new world she'd stepped into when she had arrived at the castle overwhelmed her. She needed some adjustment time.

There was only one person she wanted with her now. She looked up at Dacian. His expression convinced her she'd never take a shower alone again as long as Airmid was doing her thing. "Thank you." She gazed at everyone in the room. "Thank all of you."

Then her attention returned to Dacian. "I want to take Vince back to the greenhouse." She didn't think she'd mention that Vince had finally spoken to her. That was personal and could wait. "We'll somehow make him safe there."

"And then you can go with me to get back my clothes.

We're lucky. The store is open late tonight." Sparkle had slipped into the room. "Of course, I want my clothes back only so I can go forth and teach the masses the joyously ecstatic feeling that comes from looking sexy and stylish."

Everyone stared at her.

"What?"

Dacian answered. "Airmid kidnapped Cinn from her bathroom."

Cinn put in her two cents. "Ganymede was the hero. He sent Dacian and Edge to rescue me." She raised her gaze to the ceiling. "Just a suggestion, but a person with true depth of character would understand the power of forgiveness."

"They would?" Sparkle looked blank for a moment. Then she smiled. "They *would*." She turned to Ganymede. "Since I'll be getting my old clothes back tonight, I don't need to be mad at you anymore. Time to leave that moldy old greenhouse and come home, my very own golden god."

Golden god? Cinn took another look at Ganymede. All she saw was a chubby black-and-white cat. Talk about love being blind.

Ganymede leaped from the bureau and padded to the door. *"I'll get my things right now. And don't worry, I'll never again touch any of your clothes, no matter how shallow you get, my sweet strawberry."*

Sparkle blew him a kiss before offering a finger wave.

Cinn hummed in her mind until the Splenda moment was over. There was just so much artificial sweetness anyone could stand.

"I'll be with Cinn everyplace she goes as long as I'm awake." Dacian's stare dared anyone to argue with that. Even Sparkle stayed quiet.

Edge finally spoke up. "Be careful. Don't get caught somewhere we can't reach you quickly."

They all understood his implication. If Stephan attacked Dacian's mind at the wrong time, a lot of people would die.

*Including me.* Somehow the thought didn't horrify Cinn as it once had. That didn't mean she wouldn't be ready to run like hell if Dacian told her to.

Dacian nodded. "Sparkle will be with us tonight."

Cinn found his comment interesting. She didn't associate Sparkle with raw power. Sparkle did her sex thing and that was it. But Cinn had been wrong about Ganymede. So maybe she was underestimating Sparkle.

"Wow, I broke another nail. I'll have to think of a reason to get a manicure that isn't shallow."

Or maybe not.

As everyone except for Dacian left, Sparkle paused in the doorway. "I'll give you an hour for your plants. And don't forget we're doing dinner."

With that threat hanging over her head, Cinn clutched Vince to her as she followed Dacian down to the greenhouse. He didn't say anything, and that gave her time to think. Silence was her enemy. She didn't want to think right now.

They'd almost reached the greenhouse when Dacian broke his silence. "You know, I wanted to kill Edge when I found out he'd let you go into the bathroom alone. Then I remembered that I did the same thing last night. Someone's going to have to take care of Airmid."

Cinn didn't like the sound of that last sentence. "What did you have in mind?"

"Maybe Ganymede can put one of my insane rages to good use. I could distract the goddess while Ganymede took her out."

"No!" Her reaction was immediate and unequivocal. Dacian would die. Amazing. That thought filled her whole mind, her whole *heart*. There was no room left to worry about the ethics of destroying a goddess or even wondering if it could be done.

He slid her a sideways glance. "Yeah, you're probably right."

Translation: I'll do it when the time comes. Cinn fought down her panic. Things wouldn't come to that. She'd figure out something else. Then they were entering the greenhouse and she stopped thinking.

"Ohmigod." That was about all that came to mind. Asima was crouched beside Teddy with an open book in front of her. Teddy had suddenly sprouted colorful mittens at the ends of each of his prickly arms. And Asima's special brand of musical torture shook the glass walls of the greenhouse.

"Just. Kill. Me. Now." Bain lay on the cot, his hands pressed tightly against his ears. "If you don't do it right now, I'm going to murder a cat. I'd enjoy it. A lot." His eyes shone bright crimson.

Dacian must've believed him because he quickly pulled the plug on Asima's small but excruciatingly powerful stereo system.

Bain slowly lowered his hands. "Oh, God—and I don't use that term lightly—that feels so good. I was considering abandoning my post and taking a fun vacation in the fires of hell. My boss is missing a bet by not having that cat by his side."

Asima hissed her displeasure. *"You are all uncivilized cretins. You have no appreciation of the finer things in life. I was exposing Teddy to some good music."* She lowered her nose to the open book. *"And good literature, too. I'm reading one of Shakespeare's plays to him. No trashy romance novels for him."*

Cinn sighed. Words just wouldn't come. She looked at Dacian.

He nodded. "I'm putting Vince on the floor under this table. It'll shield him from anything Teddy can fling his way. Oh, and you might want to figure out how the cactus is managing to move his arms enough to actually throw a part of himself. Must take lots of concentration on his part. You'd better hope he doesn't figure out how to go mobile."

"If I knew how to stop this whole nightmare, I would." She knew she shouldn't snap at him. He was sacrificing a lot to help her. Lord knew he had his own troubles to worry about.

Then another revelation hit her. She would do whatever it took to protect Dacian from Stephan. *Whatever* it took. Other than her plants and her family, she'd never experienced that level of commitment.

Cinn walked over to Asima. "Look, I appreciate how you're trying to help Teddy, but you can't have the music. Not unless you use headphones. We need Bain to protect the plants."

*"I could protect them."*

Could she? Cinn didn't know. "But protecting them is Bain's job right now. He hates the music. So make sure he doesn't hear it."

Cinn could see the mutiny in Asima's eyes, but the cat finally nodded her head. *"I understand that you can't trust me because of what I did to Vince. But Bast hasn't asked me to hurt any of your plants again."* The thought seemed to cheer her.

A tough question. "What if Bast *does* ask again? What will you do?"

For a moment, Asima's gaze looked evasive, and then she seemed to make a decision. *"I wouldn't hurt Vince or*

*Teddy. I can't make any promises about your other plants, though.*"

"Fair enough." Cinn appreciated her honesty. "I understand your loyalty is to Bast, but you also have to understand why I don't want you to be alone with my plants."

Asima nodded, and Cinn turned to Bain. "Will you be okay as long as the music is off?"

"Yeah. But I hope you guys figure out something soon, because a greenhouse guard is not who I am. I destroy, I don't nurture. This whole gig is killing my street cred."

Cinn was a quivering ball of stress. "We're trying, and I really appreciate you giving up your usual wicked activities to help the cause."

Bain smiled at her, and she thought briefly that for evil incarnate he was a spectacularly beautiful package of temptation.

"I heard that." Dacian's growl trailed her out of the greenhouse.

"You wouldn't have heard it if you weren't in my mind. Where I definitely haven't given you permission to be." Cinn didn't know if it was possible, but she had to find a way to keep everyone from rooting through her thoughts. Especially Dacian, since so many of her thoughts centered around him.

"I try to stay out, but I saw the way you looked at the demon." He sounded outraged.

Cinn couldn't help it; she smiled. "What way? The same way I look at you? You're not a perceptive vampire. If you were, you'd notice that no matter how I looked at Bain, I didn't get the same feelings I get when I look at you." There. That was as much as she was willing to admit.

He blessed her with that slow sexy smile that tied her toes into big goofy bows.

She was still feeling the glow when they met Sparkle in the lobby of the hotel. Sparkle wore black silk pants, a bright red silk top, and stilettos with four-inch heels.

Sparkle laughed at her expression. "I know. Not appropriate for a trip to a resale shop. But it feels so good to look like me again that I couldn't help overdressing."

That was an understatement. "So what's the plan?" Cinn hoped this foray out into the real world ended better than the last one.

"It's dark. The plan is to get there before the place closes."

Sparkle waited until they all piled into her car before saying anything else. "This should be pretty straightforward. I simply go in and take my clothes back."

Cinn hesitated to bring this up. "What if they don't want to give them back?"

Sparkle looked unconcerned as she pulled into the parking lot of the store in question. "Of course they'll give them back. They're mine."

A few minutes later, Sparkle was leaning over the counter, glaring at a woman who refused to look intimidated. "You will tell me where my clothes are and return them to me right now." She emphasized the "right now" by punching a hole in the top of the counter with her fist.

The woman gasped as she reached for her cell phone.

Uh-oh. Cinn saw a 911 call in their immediate future. She touched Sparkle's arm.

"What?" Sparkle snarled the word as she turned on Cinn. Her amber eyes were glowing. Not a good sign.

Dacian just stood there grinning. Jerk.

"A person who wasn't shallow and had lots of character would understand that being charitable is a positive trait, definitely something that would impress, say, a Big Boss."

"Charitable?" Sparkle looked as though she needed to flip through a dictionary.

"Right. I'm sure the nice lady here"—who had just crossed herself—"would be perfectly happy to sell your clothes back to you."

"Sell?" The glow was fading from Sparkle's eyes.

"A charity needs money. If you pay to get your clothes back, everyone benefits. The charity gets money, and you get a positive check in the Big Boss's not-shallow column."

"You're right." She turned back to the woman. "Show me where my clothes are and then tell me how much I need to pay for them."

The woman's hand eased away from her cell phone. "We didn't have a chance to price the stuff that just came in, so it's all in the back."

And if the woman's voice was a little shaky and her steps a little meandering as she led them into the back, Cinn understood perfectly.

"Oh, here they are." Sparkle pounced on her stuff. "How much do you want for all of this?"

"Well, I really don't have that priced yet and—"

Sparkle dug into her purse and tossed a pile of bills onto the counter. "Will this cover it?"

As the woman counted the money, her eyes widened. Evidently the bills *would* cover it.

A short time later, with Sparkle's clothes safely packed into her car, they stopped at a restaurant on Seawall Boulevard. Soon they were settled at a table with a view of the Gulf of Mexico.

While Sparkle and Cinn ate, Dacian amused himself by studying his own personal menu. The woman three tables down had initiated eye contact. She was the type he'd usually feed from: pretty and someone who'd serve up a sexual side dish. Tonight he wasn't interested. Which didn't mean he wasn't hungry. He slanted a look at Cinn. Her return glance was a little desperate.

"I feel so fulfilled now that I'm helping my fellow man. Woman, in your case. My outfit looks wonderful on you. I called my stylist as soon as you explained that I can look good and still be a worthy person. I'll take you with me tomorrow. We'll do your hair, makeup, and nails. You'll emerge a new woman."

"Don't you have to make appointments way ahead to get all that stuff done?" Cinn looked hopeful.

Sparkle waved her away. "I make it worthwhile for every person in the shop to squeeze me in whenever I need to be squeezed in. They'll all come in early to take care of us." She looked at her own nails. "It's okay, babies, you'll look beautiful again tomorrow."

"Now . . ." Sparkle looked at Dacian and Cinn.

Dacian didn't know if he liked the tone of that "now."

"Have you two had sex yet?"

The man at the next table turned to look at them.

"Not your business, Sparkle." Dacian met her gaze directly.

"Of course it is. Cinn explained to me that my calling in life was perfectly praiseworthy as long as I was doing it to improve people's lives." She tried to look humble, but the slyness hung around in the depths of her eyes. "I want you guys to be happy, and I think having wild sex a few times a night will really lower your stress levels."

The man at the next table had evidently told his wife, because she cast a furtive glance their way.

Suddenly, Sparkle clapped. "I have a great idea. I'll create your own special castle fantasy." Her eyes glittered with excitement. "Eric was great when he was here. He was Eric the Evil. You can play the wicked vampire this time, Dacian. You've lived the part, so you shouldn't have any problem with the role-playing."

"Someone stop her." Cinn's mutter went unnoticed.

"Cinn, you'll be the intrepid vampire hunter. We'll fix you up with a cute little stake and everything. We'll get Edge and Bain to join in so it'll feel more authentic. Now here's the best part." She slid the tip of her tongue across her full lower lip.

Everyone at the next table leaned closer.

Dacian knew he should be as horrified as Cinn evidently was, but he couldn't help being intrigued. Whatever Sparkle came up with would end in sex, and if the sex was with Cinn, then he was game.

Sparkle tapped Cinn's hand to make sure she had her attention. "Your trusted partners, Edge the Immortal Death-bringer and Bain the Demon Hell-spawn, will help you to subdue the vampire. But he's so absolutely gorgeous you decide to have your wicked way with him before you stake him."

Cinn's gaze flickered around her, pausing when she noted the rapt attention of the couple at the next table. "Oh, God, this is so embarrassing."

Dacian figured that Sparkle and embarrassment didn't meet very often.

"This is soooo good. You and your helpers secure the vampire to the table in the dungeon. The one with all the neat restraints. Then when your helpers leave, you rip his clothes from that luscious body."

The man and woman at the next table stopped even pretending to eat.

"Then—"

It seemed like the whole restaurant stilled.

"Then you drive him to the brink of orgasm with your lips, tongue, teeth, and talented fingers. And just when he can't stand one more minute of the exquisite sexual sensations, you—"

"Go home." Cinn stood.

A small moan of disappointment whispered across the room.

Dacian sort of felt the same way. He was ready for the fantasy to happen right now. He wouldn't mind if it took place here on one of these tables. He was that hot for Cinn. But no restraints. That would remind him too much of his rages.

Cinn beckoned to a waiter. "Our bills and a doggie bag." Her stare told Sparkle in no uncertain terms who the doggie was in this group. "I really can't see any character-building aspects in this whole thing."

Sparkle looked surprised. "I don't see why not. You obviously need to loosen up. I was just helping with that." Her gaze slid to Dacian, and she smiled. "I think Dacian loosened up a lot." Her gaze drifted lower. "Or not."

Just as the waiter brought their bills, Sparkle made her point. "The old me would try to match people who were completely different in all ways except for sexual compatibility. That led to lots of conflicts outside the bedroom."

"Well, you're doing it again. Dacian and I have nothing in common." Cinn avoided Dacian's stare.

*Except for the incredible sex.* Dacian figured she was way into denial if she wouldn't even own up to that. But he was into his own denial. He didn't want to admit that her rejection hurt, because he'd survived this long by not caring whether or not anyone accepted him.

Sparkle narrowed her gaze on Cinn. "You're refusing to admit this in the same way you refuse to admit that what you do with your plants is beyond ordinary. Wake up and smell the truth, sister. Both you and Dacian are being threatened by a supernatural power. Both of you have lived in your own kind of isolation." She held up her hand to stop Cinn's denial. "Just because you're surrounded by family doesn't mean you're not alone. Each of you is misunderstood by the ones closest to you."

Okay, he took exception to that. He glanced around, noted the other diners' avid interest, and lowered his voice. "Taurin understands me just fine." Dacian didn't care if he sounded defensive. "I chose to abandon him. I walked away and for two hundred years didn't contact him. He has no brother, not in the true sense of the word."

"Crap." Sparkle could be succinct when she wanted to be. "You've defied Stephan for two hundred years to keep Taurin safe. The same way Cinn is defying Airmid to protect her plants." She plunked her money down on the table and turned to leave the restaurant, but she threw a last shot over her shoulder. "My character rating is soaring. I've brought together two lonely but caring people who truly need each other." She glanced skyward. "Put that on your spreadsheet, O Big Boss."

Cinn avoided looking at Dacian, which just made him mad. So they had nothing in common, huh? More like she didn't *want* to have anything in common with a vampire. How about what had happened on the greenhouse table? She'd seemed pretty involved with that. But maybe it was just about the sex. He immediately felt outraged.

And as much as his mind told him he was overreacting, his emotions stayed in upset mode. But now wasn't

the time for a confrontation. So he remained silent all
the way back to the castle while Cinn stared out at the
dark gulf waters.

By the time they headed through the great hall toward her greenhouse, he'd managed to build a wall
around his anger. The nightly fantasies were in full
swing, and he spotted Eric leaning against a far wall,
watching the costumed castle employees spin fantasies
for the customers.

As he wound his way toward the other vampire,
Cinn finally spoke. "If you want to talk to Eric, why
don't I ask Holgarth to walk to the greenhouse with
me?"

She couldn't wait to be rid of him. "Sure. I'll be there
as soon as I'm done here."

He watched her join Holgarth, who was standing by
the door, probably intimidating every customer who
dared enter the castle. He was that kind of guy.

Eric grinned at him, but Dacian could see the caution in his eyes. Even Eric was leery of his unpredictable
rages. "What's happening?"

"I think we need to talk about Stephan."

Eric nodded.

Dacian appreciated that Eric didn't waste time with
useless talk. "I'm not the only one who should be worried about him. He's gathering his army, and as soon as
he feels secure in his power he'll try to take out any
other vampires who might stand in his way."

"That would be the Mackenzies?"

"The Mackenzies are the dominant vampire clan.
He'll have to destroy you if he wants to rule the vampire
world."

"What's your point?"

"I can't destroy my maker, but someone will have to,

and soon. My original plans were to grab Taurin and run, try to find a place to hide him where Stephan wouldn't find him. My plans have changed."

"Because of Cinn." Eric didn't make it a question.

"Yeah. A little. But if Stephan thinks Taurin is here, why hasn't he already taken him?"

"Maybe he knows your brother isn't in the castle right now."

"And how would he know that?"

Eric nodded. "Yeah. Someone here would have to tell him."

"If Stephan has a spy in the castle, then he knows I'm here."

Eric looked thoughtful. "You think he just used Taurin to flush you out into the open, that he fed that info to your guy on purpose?"

"It worked once before."

They were both silent, remembering the fire and its consequences.

"So what do you think will happen?" Eric's eyes glittered with excitement.

"I'm not sure. If he just wanted me, he could have tried to take me as soon as I arrived. And I don't know why he'd wait until Taurin comes home to strike."

"If he wants you to fight on his side, then he'll still want Taurin as a hostage to ensure you don't run as soon as his back is turned."

Dacian didn't like that scenario, but it made sense. "This isn't a good place for him to wage a battle. Too many nonhumans."

"He could take you out of contention by doing what he's done before. You won't be much help to anyone chained to the dungeon wall."

"There's that." Dacian hated feeling so helpless.

What he hated even more was the thought that he wouldn't be able to protect either Taurin or Cinn.

"Who do you think the mole is?" The expression in Eric's eyes didn't bode well for whoever was passing info to Stephan.

Dacian shrugged. "Could be anyone, even a human." He'd started this talk with Eric to enlist the Mackenzies' help in destroying Stephan, but now he was rethinking things. "If Stephan comes here, people will die. Human and nonhuman. I don't need more deaths on my conscience."

Eric shook his head. "You're wrong. The castle is the best place for a confrontation. It can be defended. And Sparkle can close down the park for a while so no humans will be involved. She doesn't run the park for the money. It's here for her amusement."

"I guess you're right." The full scope of what might happen was finally unrolling in his mind. Not much could scare Dacian, but this did.

"I'll set up a meeting of every nonhuman who might be involved. And I'll put a call out for any Mackenzies who can make it here."

"Do I sense battle plans?" Holgarth had moved silently up to join the group. He waved away Dacian's unspoken question. "I deposited her in the greenhouse. Edge is guarding it tonight. Wade is there, too, along with Asima." His thin lips twitched, which for Holgarth must be a rolling-on-the-floor belly laugh. "The plant lady is safe for the moment."

*For the moment* was the operative phrase. As angry as he was with her, Dacian couldn't stop worrying, couldn't stop *caring*.

Eric changed the subject. "Something important has come up, wizard. We need to call a castle meeting."

Surprisingly, Holgarth didn't pepper Eric with questions. He simply nodded. "I left my post by the door where I spend agonizing hours trying to explain the intricacies of our fantasies to clueless humans because I have a message for you, vampire."

Both Eric and Dacian looked expectantly at him.

Holgarth made an impatient sound. "The message is for the rabidly insane vampire of the group." He took a moment to straighten his pointed hat and smooth a few nonexistent wrinkles from his robe.

Dacian ground his teeth and barely controlled the slide of his fangs. The old fart was delaying on purpose.

The wizard met his gaze. "You have no idea how many of those less talented than me have used that term of disparagement."

"Yeah, so you've proved you can slip into my mind. And if the shoe fits—" Dacian shrugged. "So what's the message?"

"Taurin contacted me. He and his wife will be home tomorrow night."

# *Chapter Thirteen*

Cinn gazed helplessly around her greenhouse. Even here with her plants, where she'd always felt secure, everything was out of control. Asima whispered sweet nothings in Vince's ear, er, leaf, while Teddy waved his mittened arms at them. Wade tramped down the aisle, his eyes bright as he carried his newest offering to her. And Edge sat, muscular arms crossed over his chest, scowling as he glanced at his watch.

She didn't want to deal with any of this, and that was just wrong. How to save her plants and herself from Airmid should be occupying her every waking moment. It wasn't. Instead, she thought about Dacian.

She'd made him mad. She'd felt his anger on the way home. He probably thought her silence meant she was still denying what Sparkle had said. Little did he know she'd stayed quiet because she was busy trying to find the right string to pull that would untangle the huge ball of confusion bouncing around in her head.

Paranormal entities didn't exist. Hah!

She'd helped her plants evolve simply by hard work and her scientific knowledge of plants. Had to finally admit she was wrong about that.

Everything she'd done had improved her plants' existence. Right. She'd turned Eva from a pretty flowering plant into a danger to society. Teddy was so much better off spending his days feeling frustrated jealousy. And Vince would be thrilled to realize he was the only one of his kind. No companions in his future, no hope of living an independent life.

*Way to go, Cinn. Major screwups. You've managed to make everyone miserable. Yourself included.*

But with her personal weather forecast predicting storms and more storms, she clung to one shining ray of hope. Dacian. He'd lodged in her heart and brought light, warmth, and an emotion too new, too deep, to accept right away. It was there, though. It was definitely there.

See, she'd finally found the right string to pull.

Cinn wanted to make love with him again, and again, into infinity. In order to have any chance of doing that, she had to save him from Stephan. Cinn wasn't a violent person, but she would cheerfully plant a big fat stake in Stephan's heart if it would free Dacian.

Wait. What had Sparkle said that first night in the dungeon? Something about Cinn using her healing power to help Dacian. She'd dismissed it just as she'd dismissed almost everything that didn't line up with her narrow view of reality. Maybe she could—

*"I'm so happy you're finally opening yourself up to your inner power. Although I wouldn't give Sparkle any credit for your transformation."* Asima sniffed her opinion of Sparkle.

"What?" Cinn hadn't noticed that Asima had left Vince's side. The cat now sat on the counter next to her.

*"Haven't you wondered why Airmid hasn't knocked you in the head and dumped your body into an unmarked grave?"*

"Well, maybe, a little."

*"Hmmph. It's because she can't."*

"And how do you know this?"

*"I serve a goddess. I know these things. You obviously share some of her power or else you never would have been able to*

*create such amazing plants. Airmid can't just erase someone who is basically part of her. Huge congratulations, you're a demigoddess."*

"Okay, head ready to explode here. That doesn't make much sense to me." Then what *had* made sense lately?

*"Fine, I'll reword it in language you can understand. Airmid can't kill you without destroying a little of herself. Most goddesses aren't into self-sacrifice."* Asima seemed to feel she'd said everything that needed saying, because she began washing her face with one delicate paw.

Sparkle wasn't the only one experiencing rapid growth. Cinn's basic beliefs and understanding of reality were expanding and morphing at warp speed. Her character? Not so much. Considering her violent thoughts aimed at Stephan, she'd guess that her character had taken a major hit.

"But she can still kill my plants."

Asima paused in the washing process. *"Oh, yes, she can certainly do that."* The cat glanced over at Teddy. *"I have to visit Teddy now and read to him. It's truly difficult for one cat, no matter how beautiful and talented, to keep two plants happy. Of course, they're both male, so I have to be careful not to appeal to their baser instincts."*

"Uh-huh." Cinn didn't intend to go there. Ever.

She didn't notice when Asima wandered off because Wade had arrived.

"Sorry I took so long getting to you, but I stopped to talk to Edge."

Cinn glanced at Edge. He was grinning. Well, she was glad this awful situation amused Lord Death.

"Here. I got you this G. Loomis fishing rod. One of the best out there." Something elemental appeared in his eyes. Something she hadn't seen there before. "After we make love down in my cabin, we can come up on deck and fish while we look at the stars. You'll love it out on the boat at night."

That did it. She had to find a cure. *Now.* "It's beautiful, Wade. What a shame it's too cold to go out on a boat."

Wade looked glum for a moment and then brightened. "It never stays cold for long in Galveston. First warm spell, we'll take her out."

*Please don't let him suggest we go to his room.* She'd have to turn him down. And no matter how sweet he seemed at the moment, he was still a demon. Cinn didn't want to stir up any demonic rages.

But evidently Wade's imagination didn't run any further than the deck of his boat. He nodded happily.

"I'll always treasure this gift, Wade." Cinn felt like gagging on her own hypocrisy. As soon as Wade was back to normal, she'd return all his gifts.

Just as Cinn was wondering what to say next, Dacian arrived. She closed her eyes. *Thank you.*

"Hey, Wade, great-looking rod you gave Cinn. She'll get lots of use out of that." Dacian slapped Wade on the back.

Wade narrowed his eyes. He might be completely oblivious to Cinn's distress, but he understood perfectly that Dacian was a rival.

"With *me*. I'll teach her how to use it. Don't you have someone to bite somewhere?" When he wasn't casting puppy-dog looks Cinn's way, Wade could be pretty intimidating.

"I'm an employee of the castle. It's my job to protect Cinn for the night. So I won't be going anywhere." Left unsaid was, *"But you will."* Dacian held the demon's gaze. "And right now I'm throwing everyone out so Cinn can work in peace." He smiled as he said it, but the smile exposed some fang.

Edge was already on his way out the door, and Asima was reluctantly saying good-bye to Teddy. With a huff of frustration, Wade left.

"You might want to take the mittens off Teddy, Asima. They aren't good for his growth." Cinn hoped her smile didn't look as weary as it felt.

*"They're good for my paws, though."* But she pulled them off with her teeth and dropped them on the counter beside Teddy's pot. *"I'll be back in the morning, and I'll bring some new music and a new book."*

Cinn controlled her need to scream and scream and scream. Asima's presence was a good thing, actually. It would be tough on Teddy and Vince if the object of their adoration paid no attention to them.

She looked up at a frowning Dacian. "Thank you. I couldn't take much more."

He nodded stiffly. "I know you probably want to be alone, but after what happened in your bathroom, I have to stay here."

"And why would you think I want to be alone?" She had to tread carefully as she tiptoed around his hurt feelings.

He grew still in that way she was starting to recognize as uniquely vampire.

"It must be hard for you, being around supernatural entities you had no idea even existed a few days ago, accepting the presence of beings legends say are deadly and to be feared. I'd be surprised if you *didn't* prefer your own company." He sounded strangely stilted.

Amazing. The big bad vampire was uncomfortable with her. But no emotion showed behind the mask he'd slipped into place.

"Well, be surprised. I want to be around *you*."

He couldn't quite hide his shock, or his pleasure. "Why did you deny everything Sparkle said?"

She sighed and dropped onto the chair Edge had been using. "Because I was trying to deal with all the things you just named. Because I don't know what to do next. Because . . . I think maybe some of what Airmid said was true. I should've experimented more carefully, put in some fail-safes. But most of all, because I find I'm really attracted to a man who happens to be a vampire."

His smile was the slow sexy one she'd been missing. "And I'm really attracted to a woman with goddess connections, if what I heard Asima say is true."

"You were standing there all that time?"

"The conversation was entertaining." He thought about delving a little deeper into her feelings, but now wasn't the time or the place.

"The demigoddess thing is interesting, but I don't know how it's supposed to help me."

He sat on the cot. "It tells you that what you did with these plants stemmed directly from the power you got from Airmid, not something you learned in a university."

She threw her hands in the air in frustration. "So how do I make everything all right?"

"First you have to decide what all right is. Do you want to take Teddy's emotions and his ability to act on those feelings away from him? Do you want to take away Vince's ability to think and communicate?"

"Honestly? No. But I do want to take away Eva's power to do whatever she does. And I want to make sure I don't create any more weed warriors."

"So you're willing to agree to Airmid's terms at least as they pertain to dangerous experimenting?"

She nodded.

"But you're not willing to destroy what you've already created."

"Right."

"Then you negotiate."

"How?"

"We'll think of a way."

She leaned from her chair and slid her fingers along the side of his face. He clenched his jaw. The table was here and the temptation was, too. But not tonight.

"Thank you for taking the time to really listen and not just brush off my concerns. And thank you for making this a 'we' operation."

Something awoke in him, something new and unsettling, but also exciting, something . . .

"So anything new to report?"

His thoughts scattered, leaving the one thing he didn't want to discuss. But he couldn't keep it from her. "Holgarth said Taurin will be home tomorrow night."

"And you weren't going to mention this?" Her voice had a dangerous edge to it.

He shrugged. "If I told you, you'd want to talk about it. My brother is off limits right now." Because if he thought about Taurin, he'd release the hordes of chittering fears and questions held back only by his will. So, no, he wouldn't talk about his brother.

She merely nodded. "Got it. What did Eric have to say?"

"We think Stephan might be coming here to take Taurin and me once we're both in the castle. Eric believes we should make our stand here instead of running. The bottom line is that Stephan will eventually get around to attacking the Mackenzies, along with any other nonhumans who get in his way. It would be better if we stop him before he gains any more power."

If his news shook her, she didn't show it. She met his gaze. "And 'we' would be?"

"Any nonhuman who wants to help stop Stephan. Eric is putting out a call to the Mackenzies. I'm guessing that Ganymede, Sparkle, Edge, Bain, and Holgarth will join in."

"Asima?"

He shrugged. "Who knows?"

"Me?"

"No." Even the thought of her putting herself in that kind of danger made him want to rip out someone's throat.

"If I'm a demigoddess, then I'm not technically human."

"Close enough. The answer is still no. In fact, we need to find someplace secure for you and your plants where Airmid can't reach you. The battle would be the perfect time for her to attack."

Dacian watched her eyes darken and then narrow. She was mad. But he didn't care how pissed off she got; he'd make sure she wasn't anywhere near Stephan when the bad stuff went down. And if Stephan won?

That would mean he was dead. Permanently. Because no way would he allow Stephan to use him as his personal weapon. Dacian didn't want to think about that eventuality, but he'd have a plan in place to make sure Cinn was safe. Just in case.

He frowned. He didn't want to die. For the first time in centuries, he had a reason to not just exist, but to *live*. And that reason was Cinn Airmid. She made him want to throw on his red cape and go forth to slay rogue vampires and overbearing goddesses.

"We'll talk about this when I'm calmer." With that pronouncement, she rose, turned her back on him, and started working with her plants. He listened to her mur-

muring to them. God, he wanted her to use that tone of voice with him.

That led to other thoughts. No red cape to go with these musings. He wasn't human anymore, and no matter how well he could mimic human responses, sometimes he had to let the vampire out. That part of him grew more restless by the hour.

He was a sensual being, and Cinn triggered every sexual fantasy he'd ever had. And every one of them involved burying himself deep inside her at the same time he tasted the life force pulsing just beneath her smooth skin. He felt the slide of his fangs just imagining it.

But would she ever accept that part of him? For the first time in six hundred years, he wanted a woman enough to deny his need to feed during sex. He raked his fingers through his hair. Damn, this was getting serious.

After what seemed like hours, she finally finished with her plants and returned to him. "I've put Eva behind the weed warriors. No one will get past them to touch her."

She bit her lip in concentration and when she released it, the damp sheen almost made him groan. Then he realized she was still talking about her plants.

"I'll have to tell whoever's guarding the greenhouse when I'm not here to make sure no one goes near the weed warriors. I don't need the kind of publicity I'd get from someone claiming a pitcher plant chomped on them."

"What about tonight?"

She looked uncertain. "I want to sleep here, but what about you? What will you do, just sit around, watching me sleep?"

"I can think of worse ways to spend a night." *Spending the night on the cot with you would be even better.* Not a good idea. Too open. People who slept in glass houses shouldn't make love on a cot. *Or on a table in the middle of the freaking greenhouse, dumbass.* But at the time it'd seemed the right thing to do. He smiled.

"Then I think I'll lie down and get some sleep right now. When I wake up I'll have someone go with me while I take a shower and change clothes."

Jealousy rocked him. He hadn't seen it coming, and he didn't know what to do with it. Someone had to guard her, and he wouldn't be available. Then he remembered. "It'll probably be Sparkle. Didn't she say she'd made an early hair appointment for you guys?"

Cinn groaned and collapsed onto the cot. "No, no, no. I don't want to spend the morning getting stuff done to me. I have to figure out how to reverse whatever Eva did."

Now that Dacian knew it wouldn't be Bain or Edge guarding Cinn while she took her shower, he could joke about it. "Look on the bright side. At least Wade won't follow you there with another fishy gift."

"Uh-huh." Already her voice sounded groggy. And in a few minutes she'd fallen asleep.

It was a long night. Cinn didn't even stir to go to the bathroom. And as dawn neared, Sparkle appeared at the door. She wore leather pants, a hot black silk top, boots, and a long black leather coat. Dacian wondered how someone like Ganymede had ever ended up with her. Sparkle didn't look like the kind of woman who would love a guy whose idea of a good time involved the TV remote and never-ending snacks. Maybe the cat had some secret charm Dacian had missed.

Thank God Sparkle had arrived, though. He needed a break from the path his thoughts had trudged all night. A circle with no beginning and no good ending.

He recognized where his feelings for Cinn were

headed. Not a smart place to go. But no matter how easily he'd controlled his emotions in the past, they were partying hard now.

And what about Taurin? Dacian should have a great speech ready to help soften his brother's heart. After all, he'd had a long time to practice it. But as he left quietly and headed for his room, his mind was a blank. No fancy words could excuse walking away from Taurin for two hundred years.

Dacian rose an hour before sunset. It was a good thing vampires didn't dream, because his would've been leaning toward the horror side. His brother chasing him with a stake. Cinn running off with Bain while she left him to babysit Teddy and Vince.

Then he smiled. Or maybe he would have spent his resting hours dreaming about Cinn. Naked. And wanting. Him.

He spent a little more time than necessary showering and dressing. What time would Taurin arrive? And how had Cinn's trip to the hairdresser gone?

Finally disgusted at himself, he yanked open his door and headed for the stairs. He didn't have to hunt Cinn down in her greenhouse. She was watching as Holgarth humiliated another wizard wannabe. He walked over to stand beside her.

When she first turned to look at him, there was something in her eyes that made the coming night a success no matter what happened. He couldn't put a name to it, but it was definitely good.

He wasn't an observant person when it came to women's clothes and hair, but whatever they'd done to Cinn at that shop had been witchcraft. Dacian had always thought she was beautiful, but now? She was . . . His male mind didn't think in terms of breathtaking, but if he'd been able to breathe, she would've taken it away.

"Holgarth is a sadist. I've watched him destroy the confidence of three men who came in here thinking they were pretty good wizards. He's working on his fourth now."

Dacian dragged his gaze from Cinn to look at Holgarth's last victim of the day. The man met his gaze, almost as though he'd been waiting for Dacian to notice him.

This guy was different. Dacian had spent six hundred years observing people. All kinds. This one was dangerous. No evidence to back up his gut feeling, but he knew he was right.

Dacian glanced at Holgarth. The wizard frowned. But Dacian couldn't tell whether it was because he sensed the wrongness in his last applicant or because he was just being his usual obnoxious self.

"Those who came before you were woefully inadequate. I hope you've learned from their failures. And if perchance you also are doomed to fail, please don't waste any more of my time." Holgarth's gaze sharpened as he studied the man.

Middle aged. Not a kid. But kept in shape. Good quality suit and shoes. Didn't advertise that he was a wizard. Short neat haircut. Ordinary face. Asked to describe this man ten minutes after seeing him, most people wouldn't remember what he looked like.

"Perhaps you would care to demonstrate what you can do." Holgarth held up his hand to signal he wasn't finished. "A *controlled* demonstration, of course."

"Of course." The man smiled, but the smile didn't reach his eyes. Cold eyes.

He didn't whip out a staff or a wand. He didn't mutter incantations. He didn't move; he didn't speak. But suddenly the castle rose off its foundation and hovered in the air. Even if Dacian hadn't felt the liftoff, he couldn't miss the movement because Edge had just opened the door and stepped in from the courtyard. It wasn't fully dark yet, so Dacian could easily see the courtyard falling away.

Screams rent the air, and people scattered. Holgarth raised his staff and shouted in a language Dacian had never heard. Nothing happened.

Then the stranger simply nodded, and the castle settled back onto its foundation. And more amazing than that, the humans who'd just been screaming and running went calmly back to what they'd been doing.

"What the hell just happened?" Dacian knew he spoke for everyone. At least for the ones who still seemed to remember the castle lifting off. He glanced at Cinn. "You saw and felt it, didn't you?"

She nodded. Her eyes were wide in her pale face. "Holy hell, who is that guy?"

Dacian turned to look at the man. Only the wizard wasn't who he'd been a minute ago. In the ordinary, forgettable man's place stood someone quite different.

He stood about six five with wide shoulders. Beneath the long black coat he wore, Dacian could see a black T-shirt tight against a hard abdomen. Worn jeans and biker boots completed the outfit. Dacian didn't have a clue about the guy's face because he'd pulled the hood of his coat far enough forward on his head to put his features in shadow. Pale blue eyes gleamed out of those shadows, though.

"Who are you, and is this your real form?" For once Holgarth had shed his shitty attitude.

The man shrugged. "Name me as you will. It means nothing to me. And this is my real form." His soft laughter sent chills all the way to the bone. "For now. I'll be in my room if you decide I'm worthy to take your place." And then he calmly strode from the great hall.

"It'll be kind of tough to contact him in his room since he didn't give a name." Cinn looked more frustrated than afraid.

"Real or an illusion?" Dacian wasn't sure.

"Real." Holgarth joined them. "He's more powerful than I am." He sounded as though the admission was ripped from his soul.

Dacian didn't want to feel sorry for Holgarth, but the emotion crept past his defenses. "Yeah, but he had the element of surprise on his side. I bet if you'd had time to prepare, you could've done something just as spectacular."

"No, I couldn't." The three words were almost a whisper. "I tried to stop him, but my spell had no effect."

Dacian had no answer for that. Cinn remained quiet. Holgarth turned and walked away.

She sighed. "I shouldn't feel sorry for him, but I do." She looked at where the other wizard had disappeared. "Whoever he is, he's scary. I'll take Holgarth over him any day."

Dacian took her hand and walked with her from the great hall. "Where do you want to go?"

"I had a late lunch, so I'm not hungry yet. Let's relieve Bain at the greenhouse. I needed a break, and Sparkle volunteered him."

He didn't say anything until they'd walked through the kitchen and stood outside the closed greenhouse door. Dacian brushed at her softly curling hair, amazed at the texture and how it affected him. If he got this aroused just touching her hair, he'd better keep his hands off any other parts of her.

"You look beautiful tonight." Compliments didn't

come easily to him. It had been a long time since he'd felt like giving one.

"I guess Sparkle's little shop of hair horrors did a good job. Carl cut and styled. Then Gerty did my nails. And finally Linda did the makeup. I left a new woman." She glanced down at the sexy black dress that hugged every curve. "I have to hand it to Sparkle. Her dresses highlight the sensual in a woman."

Even though she was making light of it, Dacian could see the pleasure his compliment had given her.

Just then the door swung open. Bain beckoned them in. "Don't just stand there; get in here so I can get out. I have demon things to do before the fantasies start."

Dacian was curious. "What *do* you do when you're not working here?"

He expected a wiseass answer from the demon. Instead, he got none at all. Bain speared him with a hard stare and then shrugged. "This and that. Many creatures come out at night. What we do is our own business."

Dacian couldn't argue with that. He watched Bain leave and then turned back to Cinn.

She shook her head. "I don't know about Bain. Even saying the word *demon* gives me the chills, but sometimes I like him. But that's because he can be funny in a sarcastic way. Then he says something like that, and I wonder if the personality he shows is a cover for something a lot darker."

"Don't forget what Wade said about him. Take it from one dark creature that recognizes another like him. Never forget what he is." He got serious. "And that goes for me, too."

Cinn's good mood seemed to be evaporating with all the talk of dark creatures. He felt bad about that, so he attempted to cheer her up.

"Hey, look around. No Wade stalking you with gifts from the sea. No Asima playing loud music. We're alone."

"Not exactly."

The male voice spun him around. The man had slipped in through the door leading to the courtyard.

"Dacian. It's been a while." The man didn't smile.

Dacian stared at him, memories piling on memories, so many that they faded into the distant centuries.

"Hello, Taurin."

# Chapter Fourteen

Taurin's face was a calm mask—no narrowed eyes, no thinned lips. No welcoming smile either. Dacian's brother wore his vampire face.

So Dacian searched for hints in Taurin's body language. Clenched fists. That could mean he was trying to control his emotions, or more likely, he wanted to punch Dacian's face in.

Dacian understood his brother's reaction because he wore his own mask. But he was better at it than Taurin. He didn't clench his fists.

Tension snapped and crackled around the greenhouse. Dacian figured if he touched metal right now he'd shock his ass off.

He wanted to take the few strides separating him from his brother and wrap his arms around him.

He wanted to walk out of here lugging his shame behind him.

He did nothing. He waited.

"Guys, this is all crap. You haven't seen each other in two hundred years. Hug each other. Punch each other. *Talk* to each other." Cinn threw up her hands. "I'll wait outside. And no, I won't need a guard because there're plenty of people in the kitchen at this time of night. Oh, a warning: Wreck my greenhouse and you pay in blood." She slammed the door leading to the kitchen as she left.

Dacian sensed fear beneath Cinn's frustration with them. Fear they'd fight? He didn't think so. She probably shared his fear that they'd turn and walk away from each other.

Well, he wouldn't be the one walking. "Heard you got married."

Taurin nodded, but his mask didn't slip. "She'll give me hell for slipping away from her like this to meet you. She's afraid I'll try to kill you. The thought has merit."

*Why did you do it? Why did you let me think you were dead for two hundred years?* Taurin's unspoken accusation hung between them, poisoning the air and the closeness they'd once shared. Was forgiveness possible?

"Do you want to hear the story?" Dacian was losing his vampire cool. He clenched his hands into fists.

"Tell it." Taurin's voice gave nothing away.

Dacian kept it short. In clipped sentences he described what happened each time he turned Stephan down. He didn't spare himself as he described the slaughters for which he was responsible.

"And you didn't think I'd want to know about this? Didn't think I might be able to help you? Didn't trust me enough to share what you planned?" Taurin's smooth mask was slipping also. Anger, hurt, and a long sorrow shone in his eyes.

Even though Taurin didn't emphasize any of his words, Dacian knew which one his brother wanted to shout. *Trust.* He'd hurt Taurin, and knowing that tore at him.

"If I'd told you everything, would you have let me disappear for two hundred years without contacting me?"

For the first time, Taurin broke eye contact. "No."

Dacian remained silent. He'd made his point. It was Taurin's turn.

Dacian's brother met his gaze again. Anger had

pushed the other emotions into the background. "Did you know I spent two hundred years trying to kill Eric Mackenzie because I blamed him and the other Mackenzies for your death?"

Dacian winced.

"Yeah, and he almost killed me right back. I'd be dead if it weren't for his wife, Donna. She saved me after Eric left me in a field to meet the sun."

Son of a bitch. Dacian felt the slide of his fangs. He'd rip Eric apart, he'd . . . He forced back his unreasoning bloodlust. Eric had only been protecting himself from a perceived rogue vampire. *You caused the whole thing, almost got your brother killed.* If hate hadn't crazed him, Taurin would never have taken on any of the Mackenzies.

Dacian had to say the words. "I'm sorry."

They seemed to bounce right off Taurin. "So what brought you back from the dead?"

"All those centuries in Alaska, I kept contacts with the outside world. I had someone watching both you and Stephan. I got word that Stephan knew where you were and was going after you to get to me. I knew I had to reach here first and take you somewhere safe where Stephan couldn't find you."

"Fuck that." Taurin's anger exploded. "It's okay for you to watch over me, but I'm not allowed to try to save you. What kind of shit is that?"

Dacian only knew three words that would defuse all of Taurin's fury, tough words for someone like him to say, but they needed saying. "I love you."

Taurin visibly wilted. "That's playing dirty, big brother."

Dacian nodded.

"I'm not running, you know."

"Neither of us is running. I know I'm done with it. The main players in the castle are having a meeting later tonight to decide how to beat Stephan."

"You think he'll come himself and not just send some of his underlings?"

"Yeah, I think he'll come himself. And I think he wants both of us. If he just wanted me, he could've struck as soon as Ganymede brought me here. He wants something more."

"You think he figures if he holds me hostage you'll do what he wants?"

"Something like that." Beneath the conversation about their mutual enemy, Dacian could feel the dark river of their emotions still foaming, still at flood stage.

If Taurin wouldn't take the steps that would close the space between them, Dacian would have to. He didn't hurry as he walked to where his brother stood.

Taurin moved with the preternatural speed of his kind as he punched Dacian in the stomach.

"Bastard." Dacian spoke from his doubled-over position. "Eric got me in the same spot."

Taurin gave him no more time to complain, because he dragged Dacian upright and hugged him. "I never stopped looking for you once we realized you'd planned your disappearance. Don't ever do that to me again." Emotion clogged his voice. "Just don't ever."

Dacian wasn't up to speech right now; he could only nod. But then he didn't need to say anything. His brother couldn't help feeling all that emotion pouring off him.

Taurin dropped his arms and Dacian stepped back just as an angry voice came from outside the greenhouse.

"Where the hell are they? Are they killing each

other? Well, if Taurin isn't already dead he will be when I get through with him. We'd just gotten here, and I was talking to Eric when my husband slipped away. From me! I've helped him search for Dacian. I've shared all his hopes and fears for his brother. I should've been there when he saw him for the first time in two hundred years. Okay, so it's not just curiosity. I wanted to make sure the grand reunion didn't end in a bloodbath." Fierceness entered her voice. "And if Dacian was cruel to Taurin, he'll answer to me."

"Oh, shit." Taurin rubbed his hand across his face. "Prepare to meet my wife."

Dacian would have felt a little more worried if he hadn't heard the laughter in Taurin's voice.

Cinn stared bemused at Taurin's wife. Because that was the only person this woman could be. With long black hair and big blue eyes, she didn't look as though she should pose a threat to Dacian, but Cinn knew looks were deceiving. Who would guess that Cinn would even think of going one-on-one with Stephan? But for the right man all things were possible. And that admission really scared her.

Cinn glanced back at the greenhouse door. "I haven't heard any cries of agony or objects breaking." She smiled at the other woman. "By the way, I'm Cinn Airmid. My plants are inside the greenhouse, so I have a vested interest in this not turning violent." *My* man *is in there*. And no matter how loud her common sense shouted, "Take that back," Cinn knew the words were true. Lately her brain and heart hadn't been on the same page often.

The woman relaxed a little and returned Cinn's smile. "I'm Kristin Veris, Taurin's wife. All of this is a huge surprise. We'd barely walked in the door when Eric intercepted us. He just said, 'Dacian's here.' Eric always did know how to drop a bombshell."

"I guess that rocked Taurin." Cinn still didn't hear any worrisome sounds from inside the greenhouse.

"You wouldn't believe the look on his face. He grew completely still and just asked where. Eric said he wasn't sure. I thought we'd spend a few minutes finding out what was going on before hunting for Dacian. When I turned to look for him again, he was gone." Kristin stared at the door. "I can't take it anymore. I have to know they aren't both lying dead in there." And without another word, she opened the door.

Cinn squeezed in right behind Kristin. A quick glance assured her both brothers were standing and there was no blood. She turned her relieved gaze on Dacian. "Introductions?"

"Cinn, this is my brother, Taurin." He glanced at Taurin. "This is Cinn, my . . ." And his voice trailed off.

His *what*? She had to know.

*"Just his. He hasn't added the last word yet. But it looks very promising."*

Vince. Cinn felt the familiar shock. She guessed that would never go away. She stared over at the periwinkle. He looked just like an ordinary plant. How could he be sentient? Had she really done that? Where was his brain? How had he learned so much language in such a short time? How could he communicate mentally? And why was he talking to her now? Her head felt ready to explode from all her questions.

Vince's laughter was light but definitely male. *"I have no brain like yours. I think with every one of my leaves. I learned language by listening to many thoughts. And I did not communicate with you at first because I was in awe. You are my maker, my goddess.*" The voice in her mind faded to a whisper on the last word.

No, she wasn't anyone's goddess. She didn't want Vince thinking of her that way. But she had no time to digest the implication of Vince's words because Taurin was smiling at her. God, he looked so much like Dacian.

"Hi, Cinn. Looks like you've already met Kristin."

Cinn managed to smile past the unanswered questions ping-ponging around in her brain. What was she to Dacian? How could she deal with plants she didn't understand anymore? She forced herself to answer him. "Yes. We met outside the door. We both thought we'd be counting body parts when we finally got in here." But she saw now that it had been a needless worry. No one could miss the love the brothers felt for each other. It shone in their eyes.

If any of them thought they'd have time to talk over the bad old days, they were doomed to disappointment. Cinn heard the door swing open behind her and turned in time to see Ganymede pad into the room. Sparkle followed at a more leisurely pace.

It amazed Cinn that Sparkle had gotten there at all. Her leather pants were tighter than tight, and her clingy top was nothing but a second skin. There couldn't be much breathing going on in there. Her boots had skinny four-inch heels. It was a wonder she didn't get a nosebleed from the sudden change in elevation.

Sparkle offered Cinn a finger wave as she moved to her side. She leaned in to whisper, "This outfit is to arouse every male who sees it. And since I'm unattainable, they'll go home and have wild sex with their wives. See, I'm making the world a happier place."

Cinn wasn't sure she followed Sparkle's convoluted

reasoning, but if rationalization worked for her, Cinn was fine with it. "Why are you guys here?"

Ganymede answered her question. *"Nice to see everyone getting along."* Actually, his expression said he would've enjoyed a little bloodshed before the brotherly love kicked in. *"I've called a meeting in the greenhouse. Only nonhumans involved in the park get to attend. We need to talk about Stephan."*

"Stephan?" Kristin looked confused.

And while Taurin brought her up to speed, Dacian had his own question. "Why here?"

*"Easier to control who might be listening in. The greenhouse tours stop at seven, so there won't be a lot of hotel guests and tourists wandering around out here at night. I'll sense as soon as someone comes close."*

One by one, everyone arrived. Finally, Ganymede stared at the greenhouse door and there was the click of the lock. *"Okay, we're all here except for Donna."*

"What about Kyla? She's a Mackenzie, and she's in the castle. I put out a call for the Mackenzie clan to meet here anyway, so she'll be part of the battle." Eric shot a pointed stare at Bain. "She'd probably be more trustworthy than a demon."

Bain simply laughed.

Ganymede hissed at Eric. *"I decide who's here and who isn't. I don't know this Kyla. And I don't care who thinks she's trustworthy. Are you done?"*

Yay, Ganymede. Cinn grinned. Yeah, she knew she was being petty and sort of jealous, okay, a lot jealous, but she was glad Kyla wasn't at the meeting.

Eric subsided with a muttered complaint about mini-tyrants.

Cinn glanced around. Dacian, Taurin, Kristin, Bain, Edge, Eric, Holgarth, and Asima. Asima? Then she pushed aside her lingering doubts about the cat. Ganymede wouldn't have invited her if he didn't trust her. Asima padded over to Teddy and curled up next to him.

But before Ganymede could begin, someone knocked at the door. With an annoyed hiss, Ganymede sent the door crashing open. A woman slipped inside. Cinn only had time to note that the woman was gorgeous, with shoulder-length blonde hair.

She waved at everyone. "I'm Donna Mackenzie, Eric's wife. I did my show from a local affiliate and then drove like hell to get here. Did I miss anything?" But even as she asked, her gaze riveted on Dacian. "Where have you been for two hundred years?"

"*Hold the questions.*" Ganymede's tail whipped up a storm. "*Here's the deal. I filled all of you in on this dumbass vampire, Stephan. He's gathered an army of night feeders and now he thinks he's Napoleon. Well, we're about to give him his personal Waterloo.*" He glanced at his wizard. "*Fill them in on the details.*"

Holgarth still looked a little shaken. Cinn didn't blame him. The hooded wizard must've really rattled his confidence. Besides, it was scary knowing someone with that kind of power lurked somewhere in the castle.

She glanced around her. Okay, there were a bunch of people in the castle with scary power. But at least she knew they were on the side of the angels. She glanced at Bain. Or maybe not.

"We have no idea how many vampires Stephan will bring with him. Not that it matters." Holgarth sneered his contempt of all night feeders. "Even this Stephan, ancient though he is, won't have the power of the Mackenzies or any of us."

Uh-oh. Cinn watched Dacian's eyes narrow. Holgarth forged on, unaware or uncaring that in making light of Stephan's power, he'd also insulted Dacian.

Wait. He'd said "any of us." For whatever reason, Cinn had assumed that Kristin and Donna were human. "Umm, just checking something out. Am I the only human here?"

Holgarth huffed his displeasure at being interrupted. "I'll refrain from listing all your human frailties and simply give you the short answer. Yes. Now unless you have another inane question to ask, I'll get on with the really important things we have to discuss."

"You get off on making people mad, don't you?" If Cinn had the power, she'd activate Teddy and have him shoot a few dozen spines into someone's pompous butt.

Holgarth raised one supercilious brow. "Of course. And it's so pathetically easy to do."

Cinn glanced around the group. "How do you guys put up with him?"

Edge laughed. "The old guy has his moments. Ignore him."

And as angry as Cinn was with Holgarth, she felt a twinge of sympathy when he winced at the word "old." Maybe feeling vulnerable caused Holgarth to lash out at those he felt were weaker than he. Okay, cut the psychoanalysis. Maybe Holgarth was just naturally badtempered.

*"This is taking too long."* Ganymede paced the counter. *"I have a game to watch and a bowl of popcorn waiting for me. Here's what's going to happen."*

Cinn caught the humiliated expression in Holgarth's eyes before he quickly masked it. Ganymede shouldn't have done that.

*"Holgarth is going to activate the park's gargoyles. For anyone who doesn't know, they're our special defense system. Cool guys. They keep out whatever we tell them to. Once awake, they'll make sure no night feeders except for Taurin and Dacian get into the park. They won't bother humans."*

Cinn couldn't keep her mouth shut. "What if a few night feeders are already inside? And maybe Stephan hired some humans to infiltrate the castle."

Ganymede yawned, exposing sharp little feline teeth. *"No night feeders are in the castle. We would've sensed them. And humans don't have enough power to worry about."*

Ganymede, the equal opportunity insulter. Cinn decided not to argue with him. It would be a waste of time.

Ganymede glanced at his wizard. *"Will you need help?"*

Cinn sensed Holgarth's reluctance to admit he needed help with anything. Didn't anyone else see what Ganymede was doing to him? Maybe being nonhuman meant you didn't care too much about the feelings of others. Score one for the human side.

"Yes. I'll need Eric, Edge, and Bain. I can't use Dacian or Taurin. They're night feeders. They'd just confuse the gargoyles. Awakening the gargoyles takes immense power." He paused as if gathering himself to speak the next sentence. "It will take more than just my power."

Ganymede went on without seeming to notice Holgarth's distress. Of course, Ganymede evidently didn't know about the hooded wizard. Maybe Holgarth should have told him.

*"Good. Get it done right after the meeting."* Then Ganymede turned back to the others. *"Once the gargoyles are awakened, we'll have time to plan our defense. Stephan will probably hang around Galveston, figuring we'll have to come out of the park sometime. So once we have our plan in place, we'll shut down the park for major repairs and send the humans home. Then we'll invite him in."* And if a cat could smile, then Ganymede was smiling.

Cinn hated to interrupt his self-congratulation, but she had an important question. "What about Airmid? I don't know if she's here or not. We can't sense her. Can your gargoyles keep her out, too?"

Ganymede seemed to actually give her question some serious thought before shaking his head. *"Goddesses are too high in the paranormal hierarchy. The gargoyles can't touch them. But she's not a player in our battle with Stephan, so I don't think she'll interfere. We'll continue to keep a guard on the greenhouse. If things get tight—not that a bunch of puny-ass night feeders will be a problem—then you'll have to protect your plants the best way you can alone."*

A quick glance from Dacian assured her she wouldn't be alone if he could help it. She wouldn't be the one to remind him that Stephan would probably make sure he was chained up in the dungeon and out of the fight.

*"Now go forth and kick butt."* Ganymede leaped from the counter and padded to the door. It swung open. *"Coming up with me, sweetie?"* He glanced at Sparkle.

"Be there in a few, snuggle-bunny." Sparkle joined Cinn, Dacian, Kristin, and Taurin. "I apologize for what Mede said about the night feeders. I don't think he even thinks of you guys as night feeders, so he wouldn't realize he was insulting you."

Cinn was just thinking how thoughtful Sparkle was when she ruined it.

"I read somewhere that a sign of character depth is being sensitive to the feelings of others." She glanced toward the ceiling. "Put another check in that right column, Big Boss." Sparkle dropped her gaze. "Mmm, someone knows how to choose great clothes for you, Cinn. I think you should make time for sex tonight. Oh, and when you're finished with the rest of my clothes, just tell me and I'll send someone for them."

"I thought you gave them to me." Not that Cinn really wanted them. Okay, so she did. They made her feel sexy. And she wanted to look like a sensual woman for Dacian. And if that was shallow, she didn't care. No Big Boss would bring the hammer down on her.

Sparkle widened her eyes. Cinn guessed she thought it made her look innocent. "Now why would I do that? I simply loaned them to you out of the goodness of my heart. I'm a very generous person. But if you really like them, we can go shopping sometime and I'll help you choose your own sensual wardrobe."

Holgarth coughed loudly. "It pains me to interrupt what must be a fascinating conversation, but we have vampires to defeat and a castle to defend. So could I possibly have just a measly few minutes of your precious time? Then you can all have lewd sex until dawn."

Sparkle just laughed. "Try it sometime, wizard. If anyone needs it, you do." She turned toward the door. "I'll clear away all humans from the courtyard and the entrance to the great hall." And then she left.

Dacian tossed a disbelieving glare at the wizard before turning to Taurin. "Why hasn't anyone killed his ass before this?"

"Many have tried, my sporadically insane friend, but none have succeeded." Holgarth smiled, a creaky, insincere lifting of his lips. "That's not to say I don't have my admirers. Napoleon found my advice invaluable."

"He fired you." Edge didn't waste words.

"And immediately suffered a rather substantial loss at Waterloo." The wizard tried to twist his face into a sympathetic expression, but the muscles just wouldn't respond. Probably a Botox moment.

Cinn paused before following the others out the door that led into the courtyard. Asima was still by Teddy. No one had stayed behind to guard the plants.

Asima stared at her from those blue eyes. *"I'll keep them safe."*

"What if Airmid shows up? You know what Bast, Airmid's good buddy, would want you to do."

Something moved in Asima's eyes that Cinn had never seen before. Something dangerous. *"I will keep them safe. From everyone."*

Cinn believed her. God, she hoped she wasn't making a huge mistake. She nodded at Asima and followed Dacian into the night.

They all stopped in front of the great hall, where two massive gargoyles guarded each side of the doors. The gargoyles had huge bulging eyes and mouths open in silent screams. Ugh, grotesque. Cinn shuddered. Maybe Holgarth should go high-tech with his security system. She wasn't sure waking these guys was a terrific idea.

Holgarth held his staff in one hand while he beckoned to his helpers with the other. "Join hands. The end person holds my hand. During the ritual I'll call on your power to join with mine in waking these two protectors. They in turn will wake the others in the park."

"That won't be necessary." The rumbling male voice was all too familiar.

Cinn turned with the others. The hooded wizard stood behind them. He hadn't been there a moment ago.

"Where the hell did you come from?" Bain didn't sound intimidated.

"From inside the castle. Where else?"

Cinn didn't mistake the humor underlying the wizard's answer. Well, if it was a joke, he was the only one who got it.

"Tell me your name." Holgarth's voice sounded intense. He certainly wasn't amused.

Cinn agreed with Holgarth. Something wasn't right

with this guy. Dacian moved closer to her and pulled her hard against his side. She felt the tension in his body.

"If you know my name, I give you power. Now why would I want to do that, wizard?" He gestured at the gargoyles. "You want to awaken them. Why?"

"Butt out." Edge of the few words.

"Okay, you don't want to tell me why. How about if I awaken them and then leave? After I'm gone you can give them their orders."

Holgarth started to speak. "I don't think—"

The wizard exhaled in mock weariness. "Look, I came a long way to try out for this job. I've already given you one demonstration of my power. Let me do this." Then he paused as if considering something. "Unless you weren't serious about finding a replacement. If that's the case, then I think you need to refund me the money it took for me to come here."

There it was. The challenge. Holgarth would either have to give this new guy a chance or admit he really wasn't looking for someone to take over his job. Cinn thought Holgarth had figured he'd never find anyone suitable. Well, this wizard had called his bluff.

With a terse nod, Holgarth gave his permission. "You'll need the power of these others."

"No, I won't need any help."

How much power did this guy have? Cinn watched him. Suddenly, a staff appeared in his hand. Evidently this was tougher than lifting the castle off its foundation and then making everyone forget it had happened. But he didn't wave or pound the staff. He simply held it as he muttered some words.

A rumbling growl was the only warning. Then suddenly the gargoyles awoke. Their eyes glowed yellow as they stretched their mouths wide and roared. The roars were echoed from different areas of the park. Then the roars faded away, but the yellow eyes continued to glow.

The wizard turned to Holgarth. "It is done. I'll return to my room now. If you make a decision about your replacement, let me know."

"How can I let you know if I don't know your name or what room you're in?" Holgarth's voice lacked its usual bite. Right now he just sounded like a tired old man.

Cinn expected the kind of reply that Holgarth in his prime probably would have delivered. Something like, "You're the wizard. Figure it out." But surprisingly, the man simply walked back into the castle, leaving everyone staring silently after him. She felt Dacian relax.

"Let's give the gargoyles their orders and then get out of here." His smile was a flash of wickedness in the darkness. "Sometimes Sparkle comes up with good ideas."

Cinn knew she should be too worried about Airmid, her plants, and Stephan to think about making love. But when the making love involved Dacian, she could lose herself for a few hours.

Holgarth just nodded. He raised his staff and intoned, "Guardians, keep all night feeders other than Dacian and Taurin Veris out of Live the Fantasy."

Kristin looked troubled. "You know, I think Cinn was right. Maybe you should enlarge that a little. What if Stephan has picked up some mercenaries who aren't night feeders?"

"Who of power would waste their time joining a losing endeavor?" Ah, you couldn't keep the old Holgarth down. "But if you insist." He focused on the gargoyles. "Also keep away any who would harm those who rightfully dwell here." Even though Kristin and he were about the same height, he still managed to look down his nose at her. A wizard of many talents. "There. Is that sufficient?"

Cinn thought they should have worked on the wording before giving the command. Sure, Holgarth was a lawyer, but she had a feeling his mind wasn't completely on his job tonight. But she was a newbie in the group, so probably she should keep her mouth shut. She looked up at Dacian.

His smile was temptation dipped in chocolate. Sexy with addictive qualities. "We'll check on your plants and then . . . then we'll do something else."

Eric and Donna walked up beside Dacian. "Thought I'd give you a welcome-home present." Eric winked at Cinn as he slapped Dacian on the back. "Let's have a quick drink at Wicked Fantasy while I discuss it. And don't worry about your plants, Cinn. I just checked in mentally with Asima and everything's quiet." He nodded at Taurin and Kristin. "You guys come with us."

Taurin shook his head. "Thanks, but we're tired. We'll see everyone at sunset." He grinned at Dacian. "And make that two drinks, big brother. Eric's welcome-home presents take a lot out of you."

Cinn wanted to hug Eric and Taurin for treating Dacian like a friend and brother once again.

Eric rubbed his hands together. "I'm going to give Cinn and you one hell of a fantasy."

# *Chapter Fifteen*

Cinn sipped her drink as she watched Dacian over the top of her glass. Even though Stephan's threat still hung over him, he looked happier. No wonder. His brother and friend had forgiven him. She shared his happiness. But did she want to care this much? Her emotions could come back to kick her in the face. After all, she didn't know how he felt about her. He'd enjoyed making love with her, but making love didn't necessarily touch a man's heart. Too bad it was so close to hers.

Both men were drinking something from a bottle. Cinn didn't ask what it was.

Eric leaned back in his chair as he grinned at Dacian and her. "Okay, here's the deal. I have the power to create a fantasy you'll never forget—I just need to know what both of you want. Make sure you don't choose something the other one hates."

Donna added a whispered warning: "Be careful what you wish for. I ended up naked with Eric."

Cinn glanced at the gorgeous Eric. "That doesn't sound so bad."

"Floating in the clouds."

"Oh."

"I got to wave to the president as Air Force One flew past."

Cinn could only stare.

Then Donna grinned. "Eric takes the ordinary in extraordinary directions. He's amazing."

"I assume this fantasy involves us making love?" After listening to Donna, Cinn figured that was a given.

Eric looked puzzled. "Why else would I exert myself?"

"Look, I appreciate your offer, Eric, but lovemaking has to be spontaneous. It can't be planned like a dinner party or the plot of a book—the salad will be followed by the roast beef . . . the love scene will take place on page 310."

Dacian laughed. "You have no idea how good Eric is. He's one of the most powerful Mackenzies, and his fantasies are legend. From talking to people who've been lucky enough to experience one of them, I'd guess it'll feel damn spontaneous."

"Here's how it works." Eric set out to explain the unexplainable. "I make up a fantasy for you, and at exactly the right moment, it'll pull you in. I don't have to be there. You won't be aware of it happening; just suddenly you'll be someone else, somewhere else, with someone else's memories. And no matter how bizarre things get, you'll absolutely believe it's real."

She frowned. "I doubt it'll work on me. I can't be hypnotized, something about not responding to suggestion. So how do you do it?"

Eric shrugged. "I don't have a clue how it works. It just does."

Cinn thought Eric was a great guy, but his fantasy story was nuts.

Eric must've read her expression. "Humor me." He glanced at Dacian. "Tell me two things you want in your fantasy."

Dacian didn't hesitate. "Put me someplace warm in the sunlight." Then he held up his hand. "Wait. I thought of something else. I want junk food and a beer." He laughed. A real laugh. "Sparkle isn't the only shallow one in the castle."

Cinn felt a revelation coming on. "Those are all things ordinary people would take for granted. Being vampire has its downside."

Dacian looked as though her comment bothered him. "Guess you wouldn't want to be vampire then."

"It's not bad, Cinn." Donna reached across the table to pat her hand. "Sunlight and food are like dessert to us. They'd be fun to have, but we don't go around thinking about them all night. As long as we have our main course. The upside outweighs the downside, believe me." The look she threw Eric simmered and sizzled.

Something was going on that Cinn didn't understand. Everyone was too intense about the vampire thing.

Dacian shrugged. "It's no big deal." But his expression said it was.

Then it hit Cinn. Sex with a human wouldn't mean anything special to a vampire unless his feelings ran deeper than mere lust. Suppose, just suppose, a vampire wanted a more permanent relationship. A vampire who loved a human would be doomed to a long cold twilight as his mate grew old and finally died. Not a good outcome for either person.

Cinn didn't know what to say, where to go with her thoughts. Confusion *wasn't* leading to clarity. She wanted to pig out at the table with all the courses lined up in front of her—enjoy immortality with all its perks while still keeping her humanity. Why couldn't she have it all? *Whoa, halt, stop.* Dacian hadn't said one thing about wanting more than a sexual relationship.

"Nothing comes without sacrifice, even being human." Eric's stare made Cinn want to squirm. "What about you? What do you want in your fantasy?"

For a moment, Cinn considered not playing, but then she gave in. "Only one thing: no plants. Anywhere."

"Why not?" Eric looked intrigued.

She sighed. "I have to be honest. I don't really believe in your fantasies. And I know that even if they *are* real, the plants won't be *my* plants. But I'd still worry"— she felt her cheeks grow pink—"that they might be watching."

Eric first looked startled, and then he laughed. "Having them around really bothers you? You're lucky then that Sparkle didn't put any of the plants you supplied into your room. Jessica and Sweetie Pie have grown fat and sassy feeding off the sexual energy in guests' rooms."

Cinn glanced away. "I've never put myself on the receiving end of my plants' talents. Maybe if I had I wouldn't have done so much experimenting." Her voice became firm. "But they're here now, and they're my responsibility."

Eric already seemed to be thinking about the fantasy. "Got all the info I need. You'll get your fantasy when it's the right time." He glanced at Donna. "I think we have a few hours to explore our own fantasy before dawn." Donna and he pushed back their chairs.

"Wait." Cinn absolutely didn't believe in any of this, but just in case, she had to ask. "Why not postpone the fantasy until we can enjoy it? There'll be plenty of time after Airmid and Stephan are taken care of."

Eric shook his head. "Not a good idea. Live in the moment. It's the only time you're guaranteed." He looked dead serious as he rose and left with his wife.

She swallowed hard as she stared at her drink. Too bad Eric had interjected pesky thoughts of things like danger and death. Taking a gulp of her drink—no polite sips this time—she looked up at Dacian . . .

And shielded her eyes from the sun's glare. She

laughed out loud. Her hair blew in the light breeze as she climbed the last few feet to her goal. She wasn't supposed to be here, but knowing the right people at the stadium had made access possible. She'd get at least fifteen or twenty minutes of excitement before they hauled her down. Making sure her backpack hadn't slipped, she hauled herself over the edge of the locomotive cab's roof.

She wanted to shout her triumph. Everything was perfect. A warm May day at Minute Maid Park, a ball game between the Astros and the Yankees, and she had the best seat in the place, a perch atop the park's replica of a nineteenth-century locomotive.

She glanced down from the cab's roof at the track that ran along the top of the park's west wall. When she raised her gaze, she knew what she'd see—a panoramic view of the ballpark on one side and downtown Houston on the other.

She raised her gaze. She saw neither. What she saw was a naked man stretched out on the roof. *Her* roof.

But questions of ownership could wait while she caught her breath. Oh. My. God. Even with the threat of park security looming over them, she had to pause to do homage. She skimmed her gaze the length of that long strong body. Hard muscle. Smooth skin. And a thin sheen of sweat that made every inch of gorgeous male yumminess gleam in the warm afternoon sunlight. Dark hair framed a face that could make a grown woman cry, if she weren't already hyperventilating over his bare body.

*Pull yourself together.* She took a deep breath and went on the attack. "You're on my roof."

"*Our* roof."

His voice was dark, delicious, and definitely dangerous. And if she wanted to throw in another *d* just for the hell of it, she could attach "dumb" to her name for worrying about who owned the roof when he was *naked*.

"You're naked."

"You noticed." His lids were half closed as he tipped his face up to the sun and then drew one hand slowly across his bare stomach.

Her gaze dropped to a point a little below his stomach. Oh, boy. "Thousands of people can see you. The police will take you away." They'd make him put on his clothes. What a waste.

He turned his head to look at her. "No one can see me. I'm magic, sweetheart."

She could believe that. "Magic or not, I'm claiming half of this roof. I called in too many favors to let you have the whole thing."

"You're a risk taker or you wouldn't be up here." His dark eyes shone with growing interest flavored by sensual intent. "I like women who aren't afraid to take a chance." He smiled. "On many things."

*Do something. Right now.* That smile had the same kind of effect as staring directly at the sun. It could blind her to all the things she should remember. Like making love with a man on top of the Minute Maid Park locomotive could get her fired. Strange, though. She couldn't seem to remember what her job was. Not a very memorable job. So maybe losing it wouldn't be a bad thing.

"Mmm." She sat down, braced herself on the slightly sloped roof, removed her backpack, and opened it. She forced herself not to look at him. She'd watch the game, eat, and forget all about him. Easy. Not even a naked man could compete with a ballpark hot dog with relish, a beer, and a great game. *And you are such a liar.*

She gazed around the stadium. Funny, not one person was even glancing their way. She gave up and looked at him. "You're really magic?"

He only smiled. And that smile was a promise of sexual sorcery like none she'd ever experience again. *Don't miss it.*

"I'll trade you." His gaze shifted to her backpack. "A hot dog, beer, and chips if you have them." He sat up and leaned over to look inside. "Good. There's enough for two."

"And I get in return?"

"Whatever you want, sweetheart."

An irresistible deal. She pushed the backpack toward him and watched him eat while she worked on her own hot dog and beer. He ate slowly, savoring every bite, and as he slid his tongue across his full lower lip to get the last lingering taste, she imagined what those lips, that mouth, could do to her body.

He finished his last swig of beer and once again fixed his attention on her. "No ice cream? No cake? No chocolate?" His eyes softened, grew smoky with a banked fire behind them. "Then I'll have to find my dessert somewhere else."

Anyone who agreed to be his sweet treat would probably not survive, but melting in that beautiful mouth would be a great way to go. She shoved aside the possible pleasure to examine the practical. "And what happens if, right in the middle of dessert, the Astros hit a home run? This old engine will chug across that eight hundred feet of track, whistling, and smoking, and steaming, with bells ringing. You think no one will notice then? The security guys will be waiting to haul us off to jail."

His smile was a deadly lifting of his lips. "No one

will haul us off to jail. Besides, Fosen doesn't give up home runs. The Yankees don't have to worry about anything going over the wall when he's pitching."

She carefully put their trash in her backpack and just as carefully placed it on the ridge of the roof so it wouldn't slide off. Fine, so she was playing for time.

Who was she today? The woman who drove to work each day, came home and watched TV, and then went to bed? Or was she the woman who'd said to hell with it and climbed up here because she'd always wanted to do it? The first woman wouldn't even speak to a stranger; the second was planning to make love with one. It was no contest. The second woman drop-kicked the first off the roof and then brushed the monotony of her life from her hands forever.

She peered over the side of the roof. "We won't roll off, will we? If we fell, we'd bounce right off the tracks and over the wall and end up on the field. Is having your own personal ice-cream cone worth the risk?"

"I love risk." He reached over and pulled her to him. "And I hope you see yourself in the ice-cream-cone role." He put his mouth close to her ear. "You'll be safe. I'll take care of you."

With that assurance, she forgot about the game and the thousands of people watching it, to concentrate on the man. His dark hair shone in the sunlight and his eyes had a slumbering-predator gleam. She couldn't resist; she skimmed her fingers the length of that hair. The strands felt silky and warm from the sun. "Bet you're ready for a nap in the sun after all you ate."

"Not until I get my ice cream." He kissed the sensitive skin behind her ear. "And I have plenty of incentives to stay awake."

Up till now she'd kept her hands occupied with food.

They were empty now. So she touched his body. And felt righteous doing it. Wasn't there something about idle hands doing something? Well, her hands wouldn't be idle.

She closed her eyes so she could enjoy every tactile sensation as she ran her fingers over the side of his face. He clenched his jaw. *Patience, patience.* Then she followed the pull of gravity along the side of his neck and down over his collarbone. She had to open her eyes to zero in on exactly the right spot. His male nipple drew her. She traced a path around it with the tip of her fingernail and then leaned over to flick it with her tongue.

He didn't move. He didn't gasp. But his reaction was so powerful she felt it as a ripple of sensation in her own body, as though someone had touched *her* nipple. She *did* gasp. What was that about?

"I can't do this." He spoke through gritted teeth. "I thought I could stay still while you grew comfortable with me, but I don't have that kind of strength." He put his fingers under her chin and tilted her face up. Then he lowered his head.

She was ready for his kiss, a precursor to better things to come. But as he traced the curve of her lower lip with the tip of his tongue and then took her mouth in a heated plundering that seduced all her senses, she readjusted her opinion of it as merely a precursor.

His lips were firm yet soft, smooth, warm and, as she explored his mouth, she tasted his need. As strange as it sounded, she also tasted the darkness in him. His scent of aroused male stirred something primitive in her that had lain dormant for a lifetime.

Even the smooth slide of her tongue across his fangs was sensual. Fangs? His *fangs*? She broke the kiss and raised her gaze to his. In another world she would've run screaming, but this place, this time was different. "Vampire?"

He nodded, his expression wary.

"Let me see."

He curled his lip, exposing the fangs. She traced each one with the tip of her finger. Real. "How? Why?" *How can you possibly exist? Why don't I feel afraid?* But in some half-forgotten corner of her brain, she remembered him. And that was the craziest thing of all.

"I said I was magic." He reached out tentatively to brush a strand of hair from her face.

She didn't flinch. "Vampires can't lie in the sun."

He smiled, inviting her to feel, to taste his magic. "I walked into the sunlight for you. Will you walk into the darkness for me?"

She didn't understand the question, yet she knew it was important. "I don't know what you want."

"You will. Soon." He breathed the answer as he speared her with a stare that burned down to her soul.

It was one hell of a stare, because it not only burned all the way to her soul, but took her clothes with it. She glanced down. She was as bare as he was. "Magic?"

"Magic." He ran his fingers through her hair even as he lowered his mouth to her breast. He nipped her gently before drawing the nipple into his mouth.

She sucked in her breath. Obviously he was drawing her strength out through that nipple, because she couldn't remain upright any longer. She lay back, feeling the warmth of the roof seeping into her, along with a multitude of other sensations. All magnified by his magic mouth.

The woman she'd been would simply lie back and let the pleasure come to her just like her fave TV programs.

She wasn't a proactive kind of person. But she wasn't that woman anymore.

As he started to lower his head once again, she stopped him. "Me first." She sat up and then gave him a gentle shove. With a grunt of frustration, he lay down. The frustration wouldn't last long if she had anything to do with it.

She would've liked to give equal attention to every part of the male body spread out for her enjoyment, but this was only a nine-inning game. She had time limitations.

So she licked a path across both nipples and down the center of his chest and stomach, forming a kind of sexy seven. His moan probably meant he'd gotten over his frustration.

He lifted his hips, pointing her toward her next destination. She kissed a path along his inner thigh, reveling in the heat of his flesh beneath her lips and the awareness of tension thrumming through him. She'd never thought power would be a turn-on for her, but she got a real rush from knowing how every touch of her lips, her tongue, her fingers moved him.

And along with her sense of power came a sense of responsibility. She wouldn't allow anyone to hurt him. The primal need to protect her mate roared to life. Its ferocity shocked her into stillness.

He started to push himself up, but she took a deep breath and moved on to her ultimate goal.

He was fully aroused. She circled his sacs with the tip of her tongue over and over until he shuddered and reached down to bury his fingers in her hair. Then he forced her head a little higher. Hey, she could take a hint.

Starting at the base of his shaft, she climbed him

with her tongue, circling and flicking and tasting. It was amazing how her tongue was attached to every sexual switch in her body, because one at a time they were all flipping on.

He massaged her scalp with fingers that shook. "Any minute now I'm going to explode and launch us right onto the playing field." He groaned as she finally reached the head. "The umps can give us an inside-the-park home run because we definitely scored."

While he was busy thinking up baseball metaphors, she was doing more exciting things. She gently nipped the head of his shaft before sliding her mouth over it. Tightening her lips to imitate muscles a lot lower, she took more and more of him in. And when he writhed and made noises of male pleasure, she withdrew while still keeping up the pressure against his flesh.

Up and down, up and down, she mimicked the motions of sex. Her breathing and heartbeats picked up the rhythm while she clenched her thighs to keep her own enjoyment from getting out of hand.

"Enough."

She could feel his guttural command vibrating through his body, sensed his control slipping further and further toward that inevitable moment. Well, she had nowhere else to slip, because her control had reached bottom first and was waving up at him.

He gazed at her from eyes that had turned completely black, and his fangs were on full display. When he saw her staring at them he turned his head away. "They're not part of this."

And before she could comment, he lifted her as though she were no heavier than, well, an ice-cream cone, and planted her on his shaft.

This was no playful knocking at her door and running off to hide. This was a kicking down the door and storming inside to announce, "I'm home, babe."

He filled her. Completely. But just to make sure, she wiggled and jiggled and bounced until he shouted, "Be still, woman."

Wow, his speech patterns changed with his emotions. This must be his "I'm this close to orgasm. Make another move and it's all over."

He might not be able to do any heavy breathing, but her breaths came in rasping gasps loud enough for both of them. Her heart pounded so fast she barely noticed the voice from the PA system.

"Strike one!"

He smiled up at her, exposing his fangs. "In baseball lingo, I'm ready to slide into home."

He wouldn't get an argument from her.

His gaze captured hers, black with heat and something else beyond passion. She lifted herself from him, feeling the delicious slide, the sizzling friction. The return journey was fast and hard. She wasn't in a gentle mood today. The primitive savage in her had scrambled from its cave and was rubbing two sticks together with wild abandon. The ensuing blaze wiped out all thoughts, all reason, all logic.

She rose and fell, clenching around the long thick length of him as he picked up her rhythm and rose to meet her on the way down.

Harder, harder, harder. And, oh God, faster, faster.

The heavy pressure low in her belly built with each of his thrusts.

Just. A. Little. More. Each word in her mind was accompanied by a blinding blast of light.

"Strike two!"

"Now!" He reached up and pulled her down on top

of his sweat-sheened body even as he continued to drive into her.

She felt his mouth on her neck and he was shaking uncontrollably. But she didn't feel the prick of his fangs.

He wanted this. Was she willing to give it? Could she walk into his personal darkness and accept that part of him?

"Taste me." She guessed she could.

He didn't ask if she was sure, but he did hesitate, waiting.

"I'm sure." Her voice was only a murmur, because that was all she could manage. All of her being was focused on her orgasm, building and building until it had nowhere to go, nothing that could contain it.

Everything happened at once.

He thrust into her one last time and she reached her tipping point. Sensation overload gripped her. She cried out as that first huge spasm rocked and twisted her, tying her into a double knot of tight emotions and then cutting her loose.

She felt the momentary sting of his fangs in her neck and then everything flowed into a spasm that threatened to rip her apart with the pure pleasure of it. Could an orgasm kill you?

She felt his own release shudder through him. She wrapped her arms around him and held on. If they rolled off the roof, they'd at least go together.

The crack of a bat.

"It's going, going, going, gone!"

"Guess Fosen gave up a home run."

His disgusted mutter barely registered as she trembled through spasm after glorious spasm.

Then the locomotive jerked into motion. It chugged

toward the end of its short track with its whistle shrieking and bell ringing, smoking and steaming its little butt off.

As the final spasm died away, she closed her eyes. "Oh, hell, I'm going to jail, and I don't even know your name."

# Chapter Sixteen

He watched as she sat with her eyes tightly shut and talked to herself. If he could, he'd stop her, but he was still trying to find his own way back. So he said nothing.

"Ohmigod, when this train gets to the end of the track, the police will take us away. My photo will be in the *Chronicle*. My family will see it. Grandma will think it's cool, but Grandpa's heart isn't too good. I'll lose my job. I mean, even if I can't seem to remember what it is, it's still my job." She twisted her hands in her lap. "I can't believe I made love with you. For God's sake, I don't even know your name. And I'm naked. Trespassing and indecent exposure. I'll have a rap sheet. I'll—"

Finally, he found his voice. "Open your eyes, Cinn."

"Cinn?" She grew silent, and then slowly blinked her eyes open. She looked around, dazed. "Wicked Fantasy? How did we get here?" Then she stared at him. "Dacian?"

"We never left here. Eric just took us on a wild fantasy ride." Dacian rubbed his hand across his eyes. "Wow. Just got a lot more respect for my old vampire buddy."

Cinn's eyes grew wide. "But it really happened. I lived every moment of it. It felt more real than this place." She waved her hands in the air. "In some demented parallel universe, it really happened."

He nodded. "I know." Dacian could still taste her, feel her muscles tight around his cock, hear her cries, and would always remember the scent of summer, baseball, and wild woman. "It really happened."

He tried not to stare at her neck, but he couldn't help himself.

She saw where he'd fixed his gaze and reached up to touch the spot. Her eyes grew even wider, if possible. "The wound is fading, but I can still feel it."

What the hell? The punctures were barely visible, but they were definitely there. How? He pushed that question aside. Even Eric didn't know the how of it, so maybe Dacian should concentrate instead on a more pressing issue.

Cinn looked up at him, and he saw the moment when her confusion faded and humor took its place. "I can see it on your face. You want to ask if it was as good for me as it was for you. Hey, it was better." Her smile faded and something tentative and breathtaking showed in her eyes. "Way better."

She glanced away and took a nervous sip of her drink. Was she remembering his little speech about walking into the darkness with him? Was she trying to think of a way to distance herself from the whole vampire thing?

At last she took a deep breath and looked back at him. "Maybe we can take in a night game sometime. I'd like to see the city lights." She sounded serious.

"Sure." He smiled while he tried to decide if there was a coded message he'd missed. Dacian never did come to a conclusion because someone opened the door in his mind. From Cinn's expression, she was feeling the intruder, too.

*"Perhaps you should come back to the greenhouse. There's been an incident."*

Asima didn't bother to elaborate, leaving both Cinn

and him to assume the worst. With a muttered curse, he stood and ran from the club, with Cinn beside him.

Dacian didn't know what to expect when he flung open the greenhouse door and stepped inside.

Asima sat on the table in the middle of the greenhouse. She looked as though she'd just gone through a windstorm and caught a lot of flying debris. The cot was upside down and the chair was lying against one wall, but other than a few leaves scattered around, all the plants seemed to be in one piece.

"What happened?" Cinn sounded breathless as she moved down the aisles, looking at each plant.

*"Airmid came. She thought I'd let her destroy the plants."*

"But you didn't." Dacian's opinion of Asima went up a notch.

*"I promised to protect them."* Asima looked militant.

Cinn returned to his side. "Are you okay?"

Asima nodded. *"I heal quickly."*

"How did you drive off a goddess?" What Dacian left unsaid was that Asima might be immortal, but she didn't have goddess power.

Asima's tail seemed to have a few kinks in it as she whipped it back and forth. One ear looked a little ragged, and bald spots here and there would give her lots of street cred with Galveston's alley cats.

*"I've been a messenger of Bast for thousands of years. I've learned to protect myself. Besides, Airmid is a goddess of plants, not a warrior goddess."* Her eyes gleamed with wicked satisfaction. *"And I fight dirty."* Her satisfaction was short-lived, though. *"She'll return."*

Cinn pressed her lips into a thin line. "I'll be prepared. Thank you for what you did. It couldn't have been easy to fight your boss's friend."

Asima groomed one paw. *"Sometimes you have to make a difficult choice and then be prepared to defend that choice."*

"We'll take over, Asima. Go get some rest. You deserve it." Cinn dragged the chair back to where it belonged.

Asima left in a hurry. Dacian watched her go before righting the cot. "I think I underestimated her. She has more power than I gave her credit for. Because no matter how dirty she fights, Airmid should've been able to bounce her off these walls."

Cinn sat on the cot. She sighed and her shoulders slumped. "Will this thing with Airmid ever end? I can't guard my plants forever, and I can't depend on others to do it for me."

Dacian sat on the chair. "You'll have to talk to her again, convince her to back off." His expression said he'd be there when that conversation took place.

"Yeah, I guess you're right."

Neither of them seemed willing to continue the conversation, so Dacian reverted to thoughts of the fantasy. He'd been sure the sunlight and food would share top billing with their lovemaking. After all, he could make love without a fantasy. He'd been wrong. Dacian couldn't even remember the taste of the hot dog, and the sunlight had hurt his eyes and made him sweat. He liked the night better.

But he remembered every smooth line of her body, remembered the warmth of her skin and the scent of *his* woman. There was possession attached to each memory. The realization had been sneaking around corners in his mind ever since he had first emerged from his rage to the sight of her round little behind. But it hadn't decided to come out of the shadows until the fantasy.

That was because Eric had made sure Dacian didn't bring along any of his normal baggage, all of his excuses for why a relationship wouldn't work. He couldn't love a human because she'd grow old and die. A woman wouldn't love him because of his fangs and liquid diet. Love couldn't survive as long as Stephan still walked the night. All legit reasons for running from Cinn, but none of them had mattered on top of that roof.

Time to cut off his thoughts before they really got dangerous. He might accept his feelings for Cinn, but he'd never act on them. And she might enjoy making love with him, but she had too much common sense to involve her emotions.

"Hey, I need to talk to Cinn." Wade's voice came before him as he pounded on the door.

Jerked out of his increasingly depressing thoughts, Dacian stood and opened the door. Wade strode in, bringing a blast of cold air and the promise of dawn. Damn.

Cinn didn't look too thrilled by the demon's visit either. "What's happening, Wade?"

The demon huffed and puffed and shuffled his large feet. "I was just walking back to my room and suddenly I remembered that I gave you a whole bunch of my fishing gear." He threw Cinn a confused look. "Can't figure out why I'd do that. You never said you liked fishing, and to tell the truth, I'd give away my granny—if I had one—before I'd give away any of that stuff." He did some more shuffling. "So I'm here to ask for it back." His eyes glowed as he waited for Cinn's decision.

Relief washed over her. Thank God, Wade's reaction to Eva's pollen had faded. That meant her two plants would return to normal—whatever normal was for them—in a little while. "You can have it all back." She nodded toward the corner where she'd piled everything on a small table. "I appreciate your generosity, but I probably wouldn't get around to using the stuff often." *Like ever.*

"Thank you for understanding." He hurried over to his things before she could change her mind. The door banged shut behind him when he left.

"Well, things are looking up." Cinn refused to acknowledge the herd of elephants still tramping around her greenhouse. She glanced at her watch. "You don't have much longer before dawn."

"I'm not happy about leaving you with someone else." Dacian stood and did some pacing. "I'm getting a bad feeling about things. I know Ganymede thinks he's got everything covered, but Stephan's had time to work on his strategy. He'll have every eventuality covered." His pace quickened. "The more I think about how everything fell into place, the more I see Stephan's hand in it."

"You're right. Too many coincidences."

He nodded. "First, my contact calls to say he's found out that Stephan knows where Taurin is and is coming for him. Then Ganymede gets a tip that I'm in Alaska." He stopped and his gaze sharpened. "We have a wizard in the castle who's way too powerful to ever want a job here. So what's he really after?"

"It only makes sense that someone in the castle is passing information to Stephan. Otherwise how did he find out about Taurin in the first place?" The informant could be anyone. She knew jealousy made Kyla's name pop into her head, but still, she'd check to see when the vampire had arrived at the castle.

"I wish the damn dawn weren't so close. I want to check on some things myself. Ganymede might be powerful, but that doesn't make him infallible."

Cinn was closest to the courtyard door when someone knocked. She watched Dacian grow still as he reached for the person's identity.

"Edge." He scowled.

She smiled. Maybe the jealousy bug was catching. She hoped so. Cinn opened the door.

"Damn, it's cold out there." Edge stepped in, bad temper stamped on his face. "You know, I'm getting tired of babysitting a bunch of plants." He glanced at Cinn. "I'll babysit you anytime. Too bad you're attached to the leaf-people."

The tension in the room shot through the roof. Great. Two large males with tons of testosterone in one small space was a formula for disaster.

Thank heaven Dacian had to leave before violence became an issue. With a surly nod toward Edge and a heated stare for her, he banged out of the greenhouse.

Too bad she'd been adjusting her sleeping schedule to Dacian's waking hours, because now she'd have to sleep while Edge hovered. Maybe a little small talk would put her more at ease. "If you were up all night, how will you stay awake to guard the greenhouse?"

His smile would make most women forget what he was. Not her. Strange, though, that she didn't have any trouble putting Dacian's fangs on the back burner.

"I had a good night. The right people died. I'm running on adrenaline right now. But Bain will take over later in the morning and I'll rest. Other than vampires, most nonhumans don't need much downtime."

So much for small talk. She didn't want a blow-by-blow description of how the right people had died. Cinn faked a yawn. "Well, I'm still human, so I'll say good night." Without meeting his gaze, she stuck a pair of earplugs in her ears so noise wouldn't wake her, stretched out on the cot, and pulled the covers up to her chin.

And somewhere during her rerun of the fantasy, she fell asleep.

* * *

If it weren't for the snow, Cinn would've been bored to death. She'd risen in the afternoon to find Bain peering at her plants. That was better than him peering at her.

Outside it was snowing. Hard. So hard she couldn't see a foot in front of her when she peeked outside. Even though she wasn't from the area, she knew snow was rare in Galveston. Not only was the white stuff sticking, but at least six inches had already accumulated and it was getting deeper by the minute. Weird. The weather report had predicted forty-five degrees and cloudy. Not cold enough to snow.

She felt grimy, but she figured she'd wait until Dacian woke up. Then he could go to her room with her while she took a shower and got clean clothes.

Coffee couldn't wait, though. "I'll be back in a minute. I'll just slip into the kitchen and—"

"Wouldn't do that if I were you." Bain turned to look at her. "Ganymede dropped in a little while ago to see how things were going. On the way through the kitchen he hopped onto a counter and stole a pork chop. Chef Phil got all bent out of shape. Guess he was worried about the Board of Health or something." Bain seemed to reconsider. "No, I guess it's just because Chef Phil is a cranky shithead."

Cinn didn't see what that had to do with her, so she headed for the door.

"Anyway, Chef Phil chased Ganymede in here. He was so pissed off he didn't even stop to put down the bowl of meatballs he was holding. He followed Ganymede all the way down to where your supersized Venus flytrap is."

Uh-oh.

Bain grinned. "That plant just dipped down and

scooped those meatballs right out of the bowl. Scared the crap out of Chef Phil. In between the running and the screaming and the cursing, I think I heard the chef say he quit. So I don't think you'll find a bunch of happy people inside the kitchen right now."

Cinn wasn't sure what to say about that. "Oh, God, I'll have to apologize to everyone for Carla."

"I think the chef already left the building, but I'm sure there're plenty of other people who'd like to see you do a little groveling."

"Thanks for your support." She didn't try to tone down the acid content of her comment. "I guess no one thought about warning the chef to stay away from the weed warriors."

He looked puzzled. "Why would I warn him when he was so much fun to watch? Broke up the monotony."

She wanted to pound on his gorgeous head. "Don't you have any sense of right and wrong?"

"Sure." He grinned. "Wrong is usually a lot more fun."

With a hiss of frustration, she left the greenhouse and strode into the kitchen. This was about the only time she felt safe without a guard tagging along. During restaurant hours there were always people around. Airmid would keep her distance.

But this afternoon the busy worker ants looked as though someone had stepped on their hill. Kitchen staff were running in every direction and bumping into each other more often than not. And above all of the din, a voice shouted.

"I need cream. Where's the cream? I asked for the potatoes an hour ago. Someone turn that burner off."

Sparkle? Cinn made her way to the center of the frenzy. Sparkle stood at her command post in front of one of the commercial stoves. She wore mile-high strappy platforms, skintight black pants, a sparkly gold top, and a cropped black leather jacket. To top everything off, she wore a diamond stickpin in her chef's hat. Chef Phil had never looked this good.

"I hear you have a problem." Cinn would start with the obvious and take it from there.

Sparkle tossed her red hair away from where it hung over one eye, and glared at her. "You think? You're lucky I don't pull your meatball-stealing bandit out by her roots."

Cinn winced. "Umm, I'm sorry about that."

Sparkle took a moment to yell at some worker ants who weren't scurrying fast enough. One of them rushed past Cinn, muttering, "The hell with Prada. The devil wears Hermés."

"Damn right I do." Then Sparkle focused on Cinn again. "You slept late. Must've had some great dreams."

Cinn squashed the urge to smile. Oh, yeah. Her dreams had been a replay of the game, and not the one on the field. "Want me to help?"

Sparkle stepped away from the stove and pulled Cinn with her. "I think I have everything under control. Luckily, there aren't many people eating in the restaurant." A crease formed between her amber eyes. "You know, there're a few things puzzling me. First, the hotel part of the castle is full. Not something you'd expect during a slow month like January. Second, where is everyone eating? There should be more people in the restaurant. I mean, where else can they go in this storm?"

An unexpected shiver worked its way down Cinn's spine. "What's the weather service's explanation for the storm?"

Sparkle shrugged. "Who knows? Cable and phone

service are both down. We can't even get local TV stations. Nothing but static on the radio. I guess we're lucky to still have electricity." Just then the lights flickered. "Oh, crap."

Cinn held her breath, but finally the flickering stopped.

"Holgarth has already shut down the park, but we still have to take care of the hotel's paying guests. If the electricity goes, we have generators, but it won't be fun for any of us. Don't worry, though, we'll get heat to your plants."

Cinn wanted to speed up the time until Dacian could be with her. It wasn't exactly that he made her feel safe. He made her feel complete.

Before Cinn could ask any more questions, Ganymede leaped into the room. His amber cat eyes had a frantic gleam to them.

*"Stop. No. Tell me you're not cooking for the guests, honey-pumpkin."* His tail whipped from side to side in a distressed frenzy.

"And who else was supposed to do it after you scared off our chef?" She went all slitty-eyed on him.

*"Hey, it wasn't me. The plant scared off Phil."* Ganymede avoided her gaze.

"Go ahead, blame it on an innocent plant." Sparkle tapped one Hermés-clad foot.

*"You're kidding, right? Have you seen that plant? She's a man-eater."*

Cinn couldn't let that pass. "Oh, for heaven's sake, Carla just took some meatballs. If you hadn't stolen the pork chop first, the chef never would've gone into the greenhouse."

Ganymede chose to ignore that truth as he returned to his whining. *"You can't do the cooking, babe. You know what happened the last time you cooked a meal."*

Sparkle looked sulky. "So? We paid everyone's hospital bills."

*"Why don't you let the rest of the kitchen staff do it? They have the routine down. You need to do other important stuff like . . ."*

Cinn could see the desperate look in Ganymede's eyes as he tried to think up some "important stuff" for Sparkle to do. Cinn wasn't in a mood to help the cat, but if he was right, then she didn't want to be eating Sparkle's culinary efforts either.

She hooked her arm through Sparkle's. "Let's go up to your suite and discuss how your character-building campaign is coming along."

Sparkle's expression cleared. "Great idea. And while we're there, we'll talk about your pitiful outfits. Other than the ones I loaned you, of course."

Cinn glared at her.

"Oops. I forgot that part of character building is learning to be charitable toward others. So we'll chat about your unfortunate clothing choices. Is that better?" Sparkle started to drag her from the kitchen.

"Wait. I have to let Bain know I'm with you." Cinn pulled out her cell and flipped it open. "Strange. It's not working, and I just charged it."

Sparkle shrugged. She glanced back to where Ganymede was eyeing a steak someone had put on the grill. "Let Bain know Cinn's safe with me."

*"Yeah, yeah."* Ganymede sounded as though he didn't care if Sparkle dumped Cinn in the first trash bin she came to, as long as his honey wasn't cooking dinner.

They'd almost reached Sparkle's suite when the lights went out. There was a moment of complete darkness before the emergency lights came on in the hallway.

And in their glow stood a man . . . or something. He was big, close to seven feet, with shoulders that seemed to fill the whole hallway. But that wasn't what made Cinn stare at him with unblinking horror. He had the stitched-together look of a Frankenstein, without any of the charm.

"Holy hell," Cinn breathed out on what felt like her last breath.

The man moved with a speed that pegged him as definitely not human. Cinn didn't even have time to suck in enough air to scream before he'd reached them.

Sparkle seemed frozen in place, and it wasn't until he grabbed her that she breathed a word. "Rabid."

Then both of them disappeared.

Cinn turned and ran. She didn't scream. Screaming would take breath and only attract humans who'd be useless. She didn't bother with the elevator. It would take too long. Instead, she lunged for the stairs. Cinn was halfway down when she realized where she was instinctively heading. Dacian's room.

But she needn't have bothered, because he met her before she reached the bottom of the steps. He wore no shirt and his feet were bare. His hair made a dark tangled frame for his face.

He was vampire. His eyes were solid black and his lips were drawn back to expose deadly fangs.

As soon as he saw her, Dacian stopped. She was okay. He fought to calm the explosive violence pushing at him. "What happened? Your fear woke me. I thought . . ." He didn't know what he'd thought. In fact, there hadn't been any thinking going on at all. Only his driving need to protect the woman he loved. Well, hell, now was a great time to throw the L word at him.

Her face was pale in the glow of the emergency light. "Someone grabbed Sparkle and disappeared."

She didn't get any further because Ganymede materialized on the step beside her. This wasn't the lazy, laid-back, big-appetite cat of a short time ago. His amber eyes glowed and something so powerful crouched in them that Dacian expected the staircase walls to explode outward.

Ganymede only said one word. "*Sparkle.*"

"We were walking down the hall. A big man appeared. Not human. He grabbed her and disappeared." Cinn put her hand on the wall for support as reaction set in.

Dacian reached up and dragged her down to the step he was on. He pulled her hard against his side. Ganymede remained on the step above them.

"*What did he look like? Did he say anything?*" Ganymede pinned his ears flat against his head.

"He looked all messed up, like someone had torn him apart and then put him back together without bothering to make all the edges match." She threw up her hands. "I know, rotten description." She raked her fingers through her hair. "Sparkle looked as though she was in shock. She didn't say anything until the man grabbed her. Then she just said one word—'rabid.' Mean anything to you?" She stared at Ganymede.

All the emergency lights in the stairwell shattered. But they weren't in complete darkness. Ganymede's amber eyes glowed, the promise of death in their depths. This was the badass Dacian had always suspected hid behind the easygoing fat-cat persona.

"*Oh, I know him. And yeah, I did a piss-poor job of putting him back together again. I won't even try this time.*" In one leap, he cleared their heads and landed on the step below them. "*We're meeting in the greenhouse. I've sent out a call already. Only the people I trust. Go get some shoes on, vampire. I don't want one of those assholes taking you out by stepping on your toes."*

Dacian opened his mouth to say, no, he wasn't leaving Cinn. But Ganymede beat him to it.

*"Take her with you. Taurin, Eric, and their wives have risen. They're waiting at your door."* And then Ganymede was gone.

"The night feeders are in the castle, aren't they? The . . . person who took Sparkle is controlled by Stephan, isn't he?"

Cinn sounded calm, but her hand shook in his as they hurried to his room. He squeezed her hand to give her confidence, a confidence he wasn't sure he felt himself. He'd planned to use the nonhumans in the castle to help him. Now Sparkle was gone. Had he made the right decision? Maybe he should've tried to lure Stephan somewhere else for their showdown. *What showdown? You can't kill your own maker, and Taurin isn't strong enough.*

His brother and Eric, along with Donna and Kristin, were already in his room. The two women sat on his couch, Eric paced, and Taurin leaned against the wall. At another time Dacian would've made a sarcastic comment about their coming in without an invite, but not now.

"You know everything?" Dacian glanced around.

"Yeah. Ganymede filled us in." Taurin pushed away from the wall.

Cinn dropped onto one of his overstuffed chairs. "Ganymede seemed to know who took Sparkle. What does that mean?"

"It means that not only has the enemy breached the castle, but Stephan has pulled in a few helpers who aren't night feeders." Dacian knew his expression was as grim as his thoughts.

"No chance that Sparkle's kidnapping isn't related to Stephan, that it was just an unfortunate coincidence?" Donna watched Eric pace, her eyes troubled.

"Not likely." Eric didn't stop pacing.

Dacian yanked a sweater over his head and pulled on his boots. "We'd better get our butts moving. Ganymede will be waiting."

No one spoke as they hurried to the greenhouse. Once inside, Dacian made sure Cinn was still at his side before glancing around.

"No one challenged us at the door. Anyone could've come in." Two centuries of hiding from Stephan had taught Dacian the value of caution.

"I've put a ward around the greenhouse. Only those Ganymede named are permitted through." Holgarth cast a dismissive look at Cinn. "I would advise Ms. Airmid to stay in here with her plants during the battle. I doubt she or her 'weed warriors' will be of much use against the night feeders and whatever ilk they've brought with them."

A glance from Cinn stopped Dacian from pointing out that if Holgarth's gargoyles had done their job, there wouldn't be any "ilk" in the castle.

Ganymede hadn't arrived yet, but otherwise it was the same group as before, except for three new men . . . no, not men. Demons. They stood next to Bain, scanning the room with predatory glances. The gazes of all three stopped at Cinn. One of them licked his lips.

Dacian growled low in his throat. The demon looked at him and then glanced away. But not before Dacian saw him smile. "Bain. I hope you have a tight leash."

Bain shrugged. "These three are lesser demons. Vicious fighters, but not too selective. They'll stay with me, and I'll point them in the right direction. They were the only ones I could get on short notice."

"Demons? They don't look as . . . human as Bain." Cinn sounded uneasy.

"Bain is more powerful, so he can put on a better show. But never doubt that underneath he's as merciless as them."

Bain smiled at him. "A compliment, Dacian? I get so few of them. See, now you've made me feel all warm and friendly."

"How did your demons get past the gargoyles?" Holgarth seemed to have pulled himself from his funk. His gaze was clear and sharp.

"They walked past. Your gargoyles are confused, wizard. They're not stopping anyone from coming through." Bain's smile hardened. "I wonder who was responsible for that trick?"

"The sorcerer." There was no doubt in Holgarth's voice.

"You mean the wizard who tried out for your job and woke the gargoyles?" Edge spoke for the first time.

"I prefer sorcerer to wizard. I'm sure there's black magic involved in his power."

Dacian figured that was what Holgarth wanted to believe. He could use that explanation to excuse the butt-kicking the stranger had handed out.

Holgarth straightened his hat, and Dacian wondered why he didn't get one that fit his head. Wait, maybe they didn't make them that big.

"I assume he wove a spell into his awakening of the gargoyles that countermanded my orders." The air seemed to go out of Holgarth, leaving him once again deflated and morose. "I should have sensed what he was doing."

And even though Dacian had no liking for Holgarth, he found himself trying to divert attention from the wizard's obvious pain. "Where's Ganymede?"

The greenhouse door crashed open with so much force that the whole greenhouse shook. And everyone's gaze was riveted on the figure standing in the doorway.

# Chapter Seventeen

Silence. A shivering sliver of deadly quiet. Outside, the wind howled and blew the snow into drifts that formed strange shapes against the greenhouse walls.

But inside, everyone waited. And those who had breath held it. Cinn thought she might never breathe again. Because breathing required a heartbeat, and she was sure hers had stopped the moment the door opened.

A man stood in the doorway while a cold blast of air and driven snow blew into the room around him. Then he slammed the door shut.

That seemed to jump-start everyone in the greenhouse.

"Who the hell are you? If you're not on Ganymede's list, you're dead."

Cinn had never seen Edge look this dangerous. Not exactly a hearty "Welcome, stranger."

"Cut the drama. It's me."

More silence.

"Ganymede."

"No way." Bain said it for all of them.

Ganymede was a chubby cat with a huge appetite. This man was . . .

Cinn wasn't sure she had words for what he was. Tall, about six five. Muscular with broad shoulders that tapered down to narrow hips. Strong-looking legs. He wore jeans tucked into calf-high boots that looked well broken in, a white T-shirt, and a tan suede jacket. His hair was a little too long and it curled, framing his face, making him look like a fallen angel who was enjoying the dark side a whole lot. The color wasn't just *blond* blond. It had a richness, shine, and depth to it that would make any woman want to rake her fingers through it over and over and over.

"What do you think, wizard?" Eric looked as though he wasn't sure whether to attack or accept.

"The voice belongs to Ganymede." Holgarth scowled. "Only Sparkle would know for sure. But this could be the nefarious work of the sorcerer."

"We don't have time for this crap. My babe is in danger. You want proof, wizard? How about if I drive your pointy hat through your thick skull? That proof enough for you?" The air vibrated with the power of his anger.

"Why did you take human form?" Cinn didn't know if this was Ganymede or not. But the woman in her couldn't look away from his face. The amber eyes were a given, but the rest of his features were a total surprise. The Ganymede who spoke in her head should have rough-hewn features, maybe a beard, probably bushy eyebrows and a jutting jaw. A scary tough guy.

"I need opposable thumbs so I can choke the life from Rabid when I find him."

Okay, so the scary part was still a go. But what an incredible face. Its spectacular lines and angles, combined with a sensual mouth and amber eyes framed by long lashes, should have looked almost too beautiful. But instead his face was strongly masculine.

Even though Cinn thought Dacian was the most gorgeous guy she knew, she was still part of the collective "woman." And that part of her couldn't help admiring Ganymede. She hadn't understood Sparkle's love for him before. Now she did. And yes, Sparkle would applaud her shallowness.

"Who is this Rabid?" Taurin seemed to have accepted Ganymede.

"A rogue cosmic troublemaker." Ganymede threw Dacian a pointed stare. "He creates insane rages in his victims."

Dacian made the connection. "He works with Stephan. *He's* the one who's causing my problem."

*"I don't mean to change the subject, but Airmid is near. I sense her. She's waiting for the battle to begin so she can slip in here and destroy the plants while everyone is occupied elsewhere."* Asima was lying next to Teddy. The cactus seemed calm tonight. *"I'll remain here to protect the plants."*

Ganymede nodded. "If we need you we'll call. Luckily, we don't have as many rooms as a regular hotel, so Stephan probably only got in a couple dozen of his vampires." He scanned the rest of his small army. "I asked Holgarth to check on something before he came here." He nodded at his wizard. "Tell them what you found."

"Almost all of those who've checked in during the past few weeks have been in groups of three. No nonhumans were around when they checked in so we can't verify if they are indeed human. I suspect not. Only one member of each group has eaten in the restaurant regularly. Perhaps the other two have eaten at another restaurant. I doubt it. During the time they've been here, they've asked that they be allowed to clean their own rooms. Fresh linens have been left outside their doors." Holgarth glanced at Ganymede.

"Translation: The night feeders checked in and brought their own takeout with them. They stayed in their rooms and their sorcerer wove some kind of crappy spell so we wouldn't sense their presence." Ganymede looked grim. "The night feeders alone wouldn't worry me too much, but they brought along two big guns. We can't even guess at how powerful their sorcerer is."

"And Rabid? What's his range of power?" Edge's expression hinted that he'd heard of the rogue.

"Not wide enough." Ganymede smiled, and everyone backed away from him. "We both go back almost to the dawn of time. I kicked his ass then, and I'll do it again. If he hurts my woman, I'll do it slowly and painfully. And if he kills her . . ."

The emergency lights flickered and went out at the same time the whole greenhouse shook and rattled. The power flowing from Ganymede seemed to fill the small space and expand outward. Cinn expected the greenhouse windows to explode in a shower of glass.

Ganymede's voice deepened, seemed to pulse with deadly energy as he spoke into the darkness. "I'll destroy him and drag his body into the bowels of the earth to rot like the piece of shit he is."

"The Big Boss destroys any cosmic troublemaker who takes the life of another of his kind." Edge sounded as though he were repeating a rule he'd memorized.

"To hell with the Big Boss."

Cinn didn't even know who this Big Boss was, but she instinctively cringed, waiting for the lightning bolt to take them all out. Nothing happened.

Suddenly, the emergency lights came back on. Ganymede looked calm, his eyes giving away none of the intense emotion that had manifested itself physically a moment ago. Cinn wouldn't want to be on the receiving end when he finally released all that repressed rage.

Holgarth filled the silence. "Oh, one more bit of information. The Mackenzie vampire, Kyla, checked in several nights before you brought Dacian to the castle. And a known night feeder left at the same time she checked in. I looked at the surveillance tape for that time period and found several frames showing them talking together in the parking lot." Ganymede let the implications settle in.

"She betrayed our clan." Eric sounded suddenly weary.

Taurin looked stricken. "All that talk about being worried about Dacian. Lies."

Dacian remained silent, but Cinn felt his anguish. She'd expected to feel triumph if this moment happened. Instead she just felt sadness for the three men who'd trusted Kyla.

Donna wisely changed the subject. "So what's the plan to kick their butts?"

"We'll keep it simple." Ganymede's expression said that ice cream and chips weren't anywhere on his radar now. "Rabid is mine. I'll find him and get Sparkle back. Everyone else stay away from him. Once he locks onto you, he can trigger the rage."

Ganymede met Dacian's gaze. "Sorry. Can't help you. He'll probably take you out right before they attack so you can't fight against them. And this time you won't get the usual warning from Stephan."

"I won't let you guys fight a battle that should be mine while I'm locked in the dungeon." Dacian spoke through clenched teeth.

Ganymede looked thoughtful. "I agree. That's why I'm bringing the chains here." Without warning, manacles and chains attached to an upright post appeared by his side. "At the first twinge, get yourself chained to that post. Yeah, I know the chains won't hold you for long, but let's hope they'll last until some of the killing frenzy fades."

Cinn was so busy being amazed by Ganymede's magic that she didn't realize he'd switched his attention to her.

"Cinn, stay here with Asima and Dacian. If for some reason you can't get the cuffs on him, Asima will try to control him until he comes around."

*Try* was the operative word. Cinn didn't want to believe Dacian would hurt her, but she'd seen the emptiness in his eyes that first time. No one home. She nodded.

"The rest of us will split up into pairs. Eric and Donna, Taurin and Kristin, Bain and his three demons, Holgarth and Edge—"

"Whoa, wait, stop." Edge raised both hands in the air. "I work alone. No wizards." He glared at Holgarth. "He'd run his mouth at me, and I'd end up killing him."

Once again the building shook as Ganymede visibly fought to control his temper. "Did I give you a choice? Don't remember that happening. Probably the most powerful weapon Stephan has is that freaking sorcerer. You think that's a real snowstorm out there? Bet our sorcerer friend whipped that up while he was brushing his teeth this morning. What do you think he could do if he really concentrated? Oh, maybe drop the castle on our dumbass heads."

Cinn swore she could hear thunder rumbling as Ganymede worked himself up.

"You think you can take him all by yourself, Edge? Bet you do. But you know something? I think you need Holgarth to help you. Neither one of you by yourself can bring him down. Holgarth's already tried."

Dacian evidently saw what she saw. Edge was working on his own power source, and he might explode into violence at any second. None of them needed the two cosmic troublemakers going at each other.

Dacian interrupted their stare-down. "Are there any humans left in the castle? If so, we need to do something with them. They won't survive the night feeders. Stephan's forces are always looking for an energy bar to keep them going."

Ganymede closed his eyes and cursed. "Damn, hell, shit, fuck, and son of a bitch. I forgot about them."

Edge evidently couldn't help getting some of his own back. "Thought the Big Boss banned your swearing. Bet you just pissed him off big time."

Ganymede opened his eyes and just stared at Edge. The other cosmic troublemaker subsided.

"Holgarth, bring them here. Tell them since we had to cancel the regular fantasies, Cinn will entertain them with tales of her amazing plants. Maybe even manage a surprise fantasy."

"She will?" Cinn knew she looked horrified. What tales?

Bain winked at her. "I could give you a few."

Dacian flashed fang.

Cinn widened her eyes as another thought hit. "You can't bring a bunch of humans in here. It's too dangerous."

"Tough shit. You think they'll be safer in the castle with all those vampires running around? When the bloodlust hits them, they aren't too selective about whose throat they rip out." Ganymede's expression said his decision stood.

Bain was still thinking about Cinn's plants. "You could tell them about the plant that—"

"Forget it." Dacian glared at Bain until the demon shrugged and glanced away.

"Do your three demons talk?" Cinn knew this might not be the time to ask, but she needed to steer the conversation to something safer.

Bain checked out his demon friends. "Nope. They just kill."

"Oh." Well, that was short and not so sweet.

"Okay, you all know what to do. Eric, create nightmare fantasies for them. Donna, take their heads."

Cinn wished Ganymede would be less graphic. Donna had just gone three shades paler.

"Taurin and Kristin, work as a team. You know how night feeders think."

Cinn could see worry for his brother in Dacian's eyes. God, she hoped this didn't end with one of them dead, not after they'd finally found each other.

"Holgarth and Edge, you might have the toughest job of all. Don't know what to tell you about the sorcerer." Ganymede turned toward the door. "If any of you need me, give me a mental shout-out."

"Some of the Mackenzies are on their way, but something's blocking my mental messages. And with cells and landlines dead, I don't know how close they are." Eric looked frustrated.

Ganymede shrugged. "We go with the people we have now. We can't count on getting help."

"Who'll be helping *you*?" Cinn knew she was probably the only one who could ask that. Ganymede wouldn't expect a human to have any sense.

Ganymede looked at her from eyes that shone with bloodlust. "I hunt alone, babe. I'll find Rabid. And I'll find Sparkle. Don't doubt it." And then he was gone.

Within seconds everyone else had left, too. Only Cinn, Dacian, Asima, and Cinn's plants remained.

*"Everyone's worried about Stephan, but what about the plants? No one cares if Airmid comes in here and makes tossed salad of them."*

"I care, Asima." Cinn took a deep breath to steady herself. But lord, she cared about Dacian more.

Dacian paced. "Not only useless, but dangerous to everyone around me." Self-disgust filled his voice.

"We'll deal with what comes." Cinn didn't want to think what would happen when Rabid struck. Would there be enough time to secure Dacian, and would those chains hold him? And how the hell would they keep a bunch of humans safe?

"Yeah, I know." He reached for Cinn and dragged her into his arms. "Promise me that if I get loose and come for you, you'll take one of those wooden stakes you use for your plants and drive it into my heart."

"You're kidding, right?" She knew he wasn't, and that was what horrified her. "Your fangs will fall out before that happens." He was getting ready to argue, Cinn could tell. "Besides, you'd rip that little stick out of my hand like it was a toothpick. No, if you get loose, all of us humans will hide behind Asima."

Just then Holgarth pulled open the kitchen entrance to the greenhouse and almost shoved a small group of hotel guests inside. Without saying a word, he left. The people all carried folding chairs and stood looking at her expectantly.

Oh, shit. She pushed away from Dacian and smiled at the newcomers. "You can put your chairs along the walls of the greenhouse."

Dacian muttered his opinion of Ganymede's keep-the-humans-safe idea. Some of his curses were in languages she didn't recognize, but she understood the feeling behind them just fine.

Cinn waited for all of the guests to be seated. Her mind was a spin cycle of worry about the coming battle. She couldn't begin to concentrate on making up stories about her plants. So she'd just tell them the truth. "Umm, thanks for coming."

"Didn't have a choice. That wizard guy yanked us outta our rooms and here we are. You better be good, gal." An old man glared at her from beneath bushy white brows.

"Well, okay." She mentally gave the old fart the finger. "The two plants to my right are Jessica and Sweetie Pie. They feed off of sexual energy."

"Huh. They'd be dead sticks in our room." A middle-aged woman with a bad perm cast her husband a disgusted look.

Wasn't this a happy group. Cinn sighed. "Umm, and the big pitcher plant is Becky. She eats things."

A man who looked like he should be teaching a bored class of college freshmen spoke up. "Like what? Unless I've forgotten my Plants 101 course, pitcher plants eat insects. There's nothing spectacular about that. Sure, this one is a lot bigger than the norm, but it's just a pitcher plant." Self-important professor guy had his superior stare going for him tonight.

Cinn smiled at him. "Your hand, if you're stupid enough to stick it inside her."

That wiped the superior expression from his face. He cast the pitcher plant furtive glances, and she knew he intended to test her claim as soon as he could. Cinn figured she was being mean, but Becky couldn't happen to a nicer guy.

Before Cinn could say anything else about her plants, Dacian interrupted.

"I think the wind stopped."

They all listened.

"You're right. And it doesn't look like the snow is still coming down. Maybe that means the sorcerer has his hands full with Holgarth and Edge." Cinn kept her voice to a whisper so the humans couldn't hear.

"It's too quiet." The lady with the nonexistent sex life said it for all of them. "Kind of eerie."

Dacian turned away from the audience and spoke quietly to Cinn. "Vampires and demons are quiet killers. The Mackenzies carry these big-ass swords, but they make silent kills. No guns. Things might heat up, though, when the two magic makers go at it. The cosmic troublemakers?" He shrugged. "Who knows?"

"Hey, lady, the wizard guy said we might get a surprise fantasy. When's that going to happen?" A young guy over in the corner evidently didn't get off on strange plants.

Dacian was looking down at her when she saw his eyes change. One moment they were warm, filled with everything that made her love him, and then they were black with no white showing.

"I'd say right about now." Cinn couldn't stop her voice from shaking as her heart skipped a beat and then began to race madly.

Dacian's last coherent action was to shove her away from him. She sailed into one of the counters and fell to the floor along with about five of her plants.

"Wow, cool." The young guy was finally entertained.

Asima leaped into action. Cinn didn't even see her move, but she was suddenly between them. Whatever power she flung at Dacian drove him backward until he was pressed against the post. *"Put the cuffs on his wrists and ankles while I hold him there."*

Cinn didn't waste time with words. She scrambled to her feet and rushed to the post. Asima had managed to keep Dacian from flailing around, but Cinn could almost see the energy the cat was expending to hold him immobile.

She cuffed his wrists and ankles and then stepped back.

Her audience cheered. They didn't have a clue how close to death they were.

"A bondage and discipline fantasy. Are you paying attention, Clyde?" The bad-perm lady was feeling it. Her husband? Not so much.

*"I can't keep this up, so I'm going to release him. Come stand by me in case he breaks the chains."*

Cinn didn't waste any time in getting behind Asima. Then she remembered the other humans. "Everyone stay behind the cat. She's the messenger of a goddess and has unspeakable powers. She'll keep us safe from . . . the mindless killing machine." That hurt to say.

The old guy was into the whole fantasy thing. "Woo-hoo! You go, kick-ass kitty."

Cinn stared with tears in her eyes at what Dacian had become. He growled and hissed at them, his eyes black and filled with hate, his lips drawn back to expose his fangs. He'd kill her without hesitating now.

"Vampire!"

"How'd they get those fangs to look so real?"

"Wonder where he got those neat contacts?"

Cinn ignored the comments floating around her. Dacian was in there somewhere, helpless. She'd just turned to look at Asima when the door crashed open and a strange vampire filled the doorway. Cinn could see others crowded behind him.

Asima didn't hesitate. Cinn felt the flash of her power

as she hit the vampire with it. He staggered back, but he didn't go down. He smiled, and it chilled whatever parts of Cinn weren't already freezing.

The human audience cheered Asima's efforts. Cinn wondered how long it would be before they realized this was the real deal.

"Interesting. What is the cat, Zane?" He moved aside so the man behind him could step in beside him. "Oh, and up your power. I felt that attack."

Cinn recognized the newest arrival. The sorcerer.

*"You don't have to ask him. I can speak for myself. I'm Asima, the messenger of the goddess Bast, and you are not welcome here, vampire."*

The vampire seemed to think that was a hoot. "Well, I'm Stephan, cat. And I'm not welcome in a whole bunch of places. But that doesn't bother me much."

"Stephan?" He'd caught Cinn by surprise. He didn't look like the description Dacian had given them. This guy had short dark hair and no mustache.

"I know, I know, you were expecting someone who looked completely different. But my good friend Kyla told me you had my description, so I simply changed a few things about myself."

Stephan waited while Asima hurled another blast. This one bounced harmlessly away from him. Zane had done his job. Frantically, Cinn sent out a mental cry for help.

"I'm blocking your Mayday, plant lady, so don't expect anyone to rush to your rescue. My people are keeping your people busy while I visit here. And I've brought a few of my special friends along." He moved farther into the greenhouse so the ones behind him could enter. When it didn't look like there was enough room for them, he swept some of her plants to the floor and shoved the counter aside.

Up till now, the humans had been cheering and boo-ing, enjoying themselves. Now some of them grew quiet.

Cinn had thought she'd felt hate earlier, when she'd found out what Stephan had done to Dacian. But it was nothing to what she felt now. Dacian wasn't the mind-less killer in this room. She tried to calm her mind, to think logically. Dacian and her plants were helpless. The sorcerer was neutralizing Asima. No one would bother with Cinn. They wouldn't expect a human to pose a threat. Hell, she probably didn't.

She watched Kyla step inside. Not a surprise. Then Rabid. Not a surprise. But the woman he held in his arms shocked Cinn. Sparkle. But this looked more like a wax figure than a real person. Pale and limp, with eyes closed, Sparkle already looked dead. Rabid brushed more of the plants to the floor and dumped Sparkle's body on the counter.

The rogue grinned at her, and it was the scariest thing Cinn had ever seen.

"I've helped myself to Sparkle's life force. But I didn't take all of it. I'm leaving a little for a bedtime snack." His laughter was an evil rumble that worked its way up through his massive body.

Stephan rubbed his hands together. "Now, what shall we do first?"

"I have an idea." Kyla sidled over to Dacian. She licked her lips as she pushed his shirt aside and drew her long nails down his chest, leaving bloody furrows be-hind. She glanced at Cinn to see her reaction.

Cinn met her gaze, mimicking the mask vampires seemed able to put on at will. It wasn't so easy for her. She was sure her hate and fury must be oozing from her very pores. But the creature watching her wanted a show of emotion. So Cinn showed none.

Kyla's moue of disappointment looked strangely feline. She shifted her gaze back to Dacian. He growled
and bared his fangs at her, but his black eyes showed no
recognition.

"Make Rabid take away his rage, Stephan. I want
Dacian aware when I drain him." She licked her full
lips, her expression equal parts pouty and sensual anticipation. "My lovers never walk away from me"—she
offered Cinn a phony woman-to-woman glance—
"alive."

Stephan looked at Dacian. "He's not going anywhere,
so we'll leave him till last." He grinned at Cinn. "Too
bad he'll never know the truth. All those centuries he
thought I wanted him to fight by my side, when all I really wanted to do was destroy him."

"For God's sake, why? He couldn't kill you. You're
his maker." She chanced a glance at Dacian. No help
there. Yet.

"True. But he was always more powerful than I was.
The night feeders would only follow the strongest."

"Idiot. He didn't want to lead the night feeders."

Stephan's expression turned ugly. "Be careful, bitch,
or your little life will end a few minutes sooner than I'd
planned." He seemed to have trouble getting his temper
under control. "In fact, I think I'll kill you first."

Zane spoke for the first time. "Why kill the human?
Send her on her way." He glanced at the wide-eyed audience. "Send them all on their way. This vampire is the
one you want. Let's take care of business and get out of
here."

"I have to make sure his brother dies, too, or else I'll
have to put up with centuries of tiresome revenge attempts." Stephan turned thoughtful. "This castle will
make a perfect Texas headquarters. We'll wipe out ev-

ery nonhuman and move in." He cast the humans a contemptuous glance. "The humans, too. We don't want anyone telling tales."

"I can wipe their memories." Zane didn't look as though he cared one way or another.

"But I enjoy the killing." Stephan wore the same pouty expression as Kyla had when she'd talked about draining Dacian.

Great. A match made in hell. Cinn hoped her disgust didn't show.

One of the humans giggled nervously, but none of them had panicked yet. Cinn recognized that most of them still thought this was just a particularly scary fantasy. *And about to get a lot scarier.*

"That wasn't in our agreement, vampire. You hired me to help destroy this vampire and his brother. That's all." Zane didn't sound happy.

A rift? Cinn dared to hope.

Stephan waved the sorcerer's comment away. "Then go when we've finished with the two vampires. I won't try to hold you."

"That's because you can't." An edge of threat ran beneath Zane's calm voice.

"You're right. I can't."

Cinn figured what Stephan left unsaid was that Zane had better not ever turn his back.

Rabid seemed to have heard enough of the bickering. "We don't have all night. Kill the woman because that's what you want to do. Then kill the vampire. Take care of the humans later. Zane can make sure they don't go anywhere."

Stephan shrugged. "I suppose so. Too bad I won't be able to take my time with her." He glanced around and then froze. "Where's the cat?"

Everyone looked at where Asima had been. She was gone.

A timid cry of, "Run, kitty, run," sounded from the audience.

"How did you let that happen?" Stephan was working up to another mad, this time at his sorcerer.

Zane shrugged. "I can't control everything at once."

"Fine. Let's get to it." Stephan reached for Cinn.

Cinn was no dummy. It was run or die. She raced for the door leading to the kitchen and . . .

Smacked right into Airmid, who'd suddenly appeared in front of the door. The goddess held Asima in her arms.

Airmid scowled at Stephan. "You will *not* murder this woman. She has a part of my godhead."

The audience cheered.

Zane looked intrigued. "A demigoddess? Cool."

To hell with the demigoddess crap. Fat lot of good it would do her. They all needed to get their butts out of here. And she wasn't leaving without Dacian.

She cut her glance to him and blinked. He was gazing back at her with awareness in his dark eyes. *He was back.* Quickly she looked away so Stephan wouldn't notice.

Stephan wasn't noticing much of anything because he'd finally lost his temper. "Fuck all of you. I'm killing the plant bitch and then I'm taking out the cat. And if you know what's good for you, big-shit goddess, you'll go back to Mount Olympus or wherever damn place you came from." He threw an order over his shoulder. "Zane, make sure the cat doesn't disappear again." He charged down the aisle toward them, clawed fingers extended and lips drawn back from his fangs.

The audience gasped.

Cinn watched him come, her mind a frenzied tangle of thoughts. She didn't have the power to stop him. She was going to die. And she could only hope Dacian would be able to break free and Ganymede would get here in time to save him. With death staring her in the face, or in this case, the throat, she could only regret that she hadn't told Dacian she loved him. How romance-novel-clichéd was that?

Suddenly, Stephan tripped. Surprised, Cinn looked down. Vince's pot lay cracked and broken beneath Stephan's boots. She pressed her hand across her mouth to hold back her scream. Unnoticed, Vince had dragged his pot into the middle of the aisle in a pitiful attempt to save Asima. Up until now, Cinn had held back the tears because crying didn't solve anything. Vince's bravery did her in, though.

Cursing, Stephan regained his balance and started up the aisle again, leaving the periwinkle crushed in the dirt.

But he didn't get far. Out of the corner of her eye, Cinn saw Teddy slowly bend back like some prickly slingshot. She couldn't imagine the effort it took for him to do that. Then he let fly.

It was an incredible act of self-sacrifice, because Teddy shot every one of his jointed arms at Stephan. Parts of Teddy hit and stuck everywhere on the vampire's body. His clothes didn't protect him, because Teddy had managed to put so much force behind his fling.

Screaming in pain and fury, Stephan changed his course. He reached where what was left of Teddy rested. Already insane from the pain, he tossed Teddy onto the floor and stomped on him.

"Hey, leave the plant alone."

Professor guy soared to hero status in Cinn's mind.

Then Stephan turned, a walking pincushion, and charged toward Dacian. "This is all your fucking fault. I should never have turned you. But I'll fix that right now."

Shouts of, "No! No!" erupted from the fully engaged humans.

Dacian had finally pasted all the pieces of his brain back into the right places. Once he'd realized what was going on, he'd almost panicked and made his move before he'd pulled his focus together.

Cinn was in danger. He wouldn't let Stephan touch her. When Cinn's plants slowed Stephan down, Dacian had a moment to gather himself.

Now with his maker bearing down on him, he'd run out of time. He heard Cinn's scream as he roared his fury and broke the chains.

The audience's screams blended with Cinn's.

Free. Dacian took a quick inventory of everyone else in the greenhouse. The sorcerer and the big guy who must be the rogue cosmic troublemaker—because he sure as hell wasn't a vampire—seemed to be enjoying the show. They weren't making any moves to interfere. Cinn seemed okay with Airmid and Asima. The hotel guests still lined the wall of the greenhouse. All alive. Good.

Why wasn't Asima trying to help? He glanced at the sorcerer.

The guy offered him a nod. "Yeah, I'm keeping the kitty out of the fight. Don't want her ruining the fun."

And then Stephan was on him. Dacian couldn't kill his crazed maker, but he could hold him off until he figured out what to do. Which was probably nothing. Unless one of the good guys showed up, he'd have to keep

Stephan at bay until dawn. Not an easy thing, since Stephan was going for the kill.

As Dacian backed up, he tripped over something. With a curse he went down, Stephan on top of him. Some of Stephan's cactus spines dug into him.

That was when he heard the sound of running feet. Glancing past Stephan's body, he saw a sight that scared him shitless. Cinn had picked up one of her plant stakes and was leaping toward Stephan's back.

He had a momentary impression of the shocked expressions on everyone's faces. She'd caught the sorcerer and Rabid by surprise. They couldn't stop her.

And before he could roar an order for her to stop, she drove the stake into Stephan's back. He screamed and rose from Dacian. Twisting, he made a futile attempt to jerk the stake out.

Everyone in the human audience cheered.

That was when all four walls of the greenhouse blew out and Ganymede strode over the wreckage. Others followed behind him. He met Dacian's gaze. "Lucky for you, vampire, Bain remembered his vision. There was only one post with a vampire chained to it in the castle. Now I have some dickheads to kill."

Outside, the snow was gone and a full moon was shining. The humans screamed as they scrambled out of Ganymede's path, but they didn't run away. Probably too confused.

Too bad. They should've run while they had the chance. Dacian leaped to his feet, searching for Cinn. He finally found her standing frozen as she stared at Stephan.

Crazed with pain, Stephan crouched to pounce on her. "Your little stake hurts, bitch. But not half as bad as you'll be hurting in a second."

"Wouldn't count on that." Dacian lifted Stephan high in the air before slamming him down onto the dirt floor. Then he held him there.

"You can't kill me." Stephan glared up at him. "Rabid, bring on the rage. Get this bastard off me."

A quick glance showed Dacian that Rabid had his own problems.

Suddenly, Taurin was by his side. "*He* can't kill you, but I can." He grabbed a sword from Eric, who stood behind him with four other vampires.

Stephan screamed as he saw his centuries-old existence was about to end.

The audience screamed with him.

Dacian watched, amazed, as his little brother lopped off Stephan's head.

"That's for my brother and two hundred years of hell."

For just a moment, there was dead silence from all the humans as they watched the spurting blood, and then the reality of what they'd witnessed sank in. You couldn't fake a head lying a foot from its body. They scattered, their screams fading away as they disappeared into the night.

Ganymede barked out an order. "Eric, track them down and change their memories." Then he got back to what he'd been doing.

Eyes glowing in the darkness, he stalked Rabid. "Take a last look at the night, bastard, because you won't be seeing any more of them."

Rabid laughed. "And you won't be seeing your woman anymore either." He hooked a thumb at Sparkle. "She's dying. Pretty soon you'll be lying there next to her. I couldn't take you last time, but that was thousands of years ago. I'm more powerful than you now."

"You have no idea what real power is." Ganymede's voice was a harsh whisper. "I've created black holes millions of miles wide, so I don't think I'll have a problem with a tiny asshole like you."

Rabid started to draw his power to him, and Edge spoke for the first time. "Need any help?"

"No." And then Ganymede's power exploded from him.

The ground rolled in waves like the surf beyond the seawall. Dacian reached Cinn in time to keep her from falling. They both clung to an upright from the greenhouse that still stood.

He pushed her behind him. "Don't watch."

She didn't fight him.

Flames rose up around Ganymede, swirling, snapping, and sizzling in a mad dance. Tongues of fire coated the ends of his hair in vivid reds and oranges, and as he stared from the flames with eyes as old as the universe, he looked like some demonic destroyer.

"Kill him." Ganymede's voice was a deep echoing boom that whipped the fire into a frenzy. The flames broke into separate streams that whistled and moaned as they gained speed. The streams of fire formed blades that flashed toward Rabid before he could even begin his attack. The searing blades sliced and diced until Rabid was no more than smoldering bits of flesh scattered over the ground.

Damn. Dacian could control fire, but not like that. He turned away. He was vampire, and he'd seen death before, but never such a complete one. He would never mess with Ganymede. Ever. Dully, he noticed Kyla's head lying nearby. Not attached to her body. The Mackenzies must've passed judgment and carried out the sentence.

Stillness settled over the scene.

And then someone began clapping. Slow, rhythmic. Dacian turned with everyone else to stare at the sorcerer, who stood where the courtyard door had been, applauding.

"Great show. See, if they put drama like that on TV, I'd stay home and watch it more." The sorcerer's face was still shadowed by his hood, but humor laced his voice.

Ganymede ignored him as he dropped to his knees beside the counter where Sparkle lay still and motionless.

Holgarth stepped from his place beside Edge to face the sorcerer. "What is your name?"

"Zane."

"Is that your true name?" No matter what Holgarth felt inside, his hand on his staff was steady and his voice rang with authority.

Dacian offered a nod of respect to Holgarth. The old guy had guts.

"It is today." The sorcerer shrugged. "Tomorrow? Who knows?"

"Will you continue the battle?"

Every person hung on the sorcerer's answer. Dacian figured if the sorcerer let his power rip, a lot of them wouldn't survive.

Zane shrugged. "The king is dead, long live the king. And he took my paycheck with him. I don't work for free." He started to turn away but paused. "Oh, and I'm withdrawing my application to be castle wizard. Too exhausting. You keep it, Holgarth. It suits you." Then he simply disappeared.

Holgarth managed to look strangely dignified in his crazy blue robe and pointed hat that once again had slid to one side. "He's right. The Castle of Dark Dreams does suit me. I'll retain my position."

By his last word, everyone had switched their attention to Ganymede.

He smoothed his fingers over Sparkle's hair. "If I could, I'd kill him again. Over and over and over for all eternity."

Then Ganymede looked up at everyone watching him. Emotion glistened in his eyes. "I'm taking her back into her castle. And when she leaves me, I'll . . ." He shook his head. "I don't know what I'll do."

"Perhaps I can help."

Cinn turned, startled. With the horror of all that had happened, she'd forgotten Airmid was still there. It didn't matter anyway. What more could the goddess do that hadn't already been done? Vince and Teddy were gone, and some of her other plants might never recover.

And Sparkle. She shouldn't have wasted the last days of her life trying to please someone called the Big Boss. Life was for living, loving, and enjoying those you loved.

Those you loved. Cinn looked up at Dacian. "I love you, you know."

His eyes lit with joy and wonder. He leaned down to just brush her lips with his. "In six hundred years of existence, I've never loved anyone more."

"I know I'll grow old and die, but I—"

He placed a finger over her lips. "Hush. Not now."

She nodded as Airmid slipped past her and stood beside Sparkle. Ganymede looked up at her, his eyes dead.

"I can help her."

No one breathed.

"How?" Ganymede's tone suggested that this had better not be a trick.

"I'm not a goddess of war, so I took no part in your battle. But I am a healing goddess. I can help bring her back." She motioned for Ganymede to move away, and then she pulled one leaf from a plant that hadn't been knocked to the floor. She held the leaf to Sparkle's nose. "Breathe in the life this leaf freely gives."

Everyone watched, riveted, as the leaf slowly shriveled up and turned to powder.

After what seemed like hours, Sparkle groaned and opened her eyes. She looked down to where only one shoe hung from her feet. Then she looked past Airmid to Ganymede. "Make sure you bury me with both Pradas, sugar-muffin."

Cinn turned away. This time belonged to Ganymede and Sparkle. A Sparkle who would live to shop again. Cinn had the deaths of two plants, who were so much more than plants, to mourn.

Cinn hung on to Dacian as she knelt down beside Vince. His pot was shattered, his soil scattered, and his poor roots exposed. He'd lost so many leaves, so many. Tears welled up.

Asima's keening cry rose up beside her, as the messenger of Bast mourned in her own way.

Dacian helped Cinn gather up what was left of him. Then she stood and stumbled over to Teddy. There was nothing left. Just an empty pot with pieces of cactus too small to even identify.

"*He loved me. He died for me.*" Asima's tear-clogged voice was a dirge in Cinn's mind.

Cinn sensed rather than saw Airmid standing behind her. "They gave their lives to save Asima, you, and me."

"I know." Airmid remained silent for a moment. "Because they showed their worthiness, I will allow you to keep the others in this greenhouse. Repot those that were thrown to the floor and they will again flourish."

The goddess reached out her hand for Vince, and Cinn reluctantly handed him to her. "This one will live again." She skimmed her fingers across his roots. "I've given him the strength he needs."

"Thank you." Cinn's hands shook as she took Vince back. "Teddy?"

Airmid's gaze was sorrowful. "His memory will be with me forever. He will truly be immortal. His is the sacrifice that must be. And think carefully, Cinn, before you experiment again. Raise many healing plants in your Teddy's honor."

Cinn could only nod, because if she tried to say anything, she'd dissolve into great gasping sobs.

Dacian held her tighter, giving her the strength she needed. She didn't care how long or short a time she had on this earth; she'd spend it loving Dacian. Teddy had taught her a lot about the value of time. It wasn't how much of it you had, but how you used it. And Dacian would simply have to put up with a withered old hag for a wife before he went on to the rest of his immortal existence.

"That won't happen, Cinn." Airmid sounded amused.

"What?"

"I read your mind, and you won't become a withered old hag."

Dacian murmured his assurance that he had a fondness for withered old hags.

"I don't understand."

Airmid sighed. "You share a part of my godhead. You're immortal, Cinn." She glanced from Cinn to Dacian. "I'd say you're well matched." The goddess knelt and scooped Teddy's remains into a small sack; then she stood and disappeared.

# Epilogue

Cinn lay in bed, thinking about what had happened since last night. She'd spent all day tending to her plants.

She'd put Vince in a brand-new pot and made him extravagant promises. First she'd buy an old two-story brick home with loads of character. Then she'd plant him beneath the big oak tree in the front yard. He could cover all the ground he wanted. Finally, she'd find him a sexy English ivy plant that could climb the brick walls and share his life.

Cinn had told Vince the English ivy represented female divinity for the druids. Because of the divinity connection, she figured it wouldn't take much tinkering to make her into the perfect companion for him. And since Airmid thought he was a hero, she'd probably look the other way this time.

Vince had weakly thanked her. He had no memory of having loved Asima. Cinn found that kind of sad. Not for Vince, but for Asima. She suspected the cat needed some love in her life.

Cinn had also arranged to have a small statue of a cholla cactus made in honor of Teddy. It would have a place of honor in her future backyard. The statue would serve to remind her that courage came in many different shapes and sizes. And sacrifice wasn't reserved only for humans.

Now only one thing remained to make her dream home magical—a hot vampire.

Dacian slipped into bed beside her. She had a hard time believing this big beautiful man loved her, and that they'd have centuries to be together.

As he turned toward her, she blinked. "Wait, something's different." She drew her fingers down the side of his face and over his collarbone and chest. Her fingers shook. "Your scars. They're gone."

His gaze seared her with his love, his need for her. "I figured if everyone else could forgive me, then maybe I could forgive myself."

She threw herself at him, laughing as he rolled onto his back and pulled her on top of him. "I have something for you."

He ran his warm hand over her stomach and lower before sliding it between her legs. "I know."

"No, no, something else." She reached over to pluck an envelope from the night table. "Here. Read it. It's from Eric."

"This better be good, because I'm not a patient man tonight." He ripped it open and glanced over the few words. Then he grinned at her. "A night game? When?"

She lowered her head until her lips touched his.

"Now."

*New York Times* Bestselling Author

# NINA BANGS

## Eternal

Eleven Gods of the Night...
The only creatures more
deadly are the ones they've
been summoned to destroy.

## Pleasure

Kelly Maloy opens her car door to much more than a
great- looking stranger at the Houston airport. Terror, desire, and a horrible truth climb in with him. Kelly's only
supposed to drive Ty Endeka around the city for a few
weeks. Too bad no one tells her that once day fades she'll
become part of a battle fought with an enemy that isn't
human. And the sensual man who feeds her fantasies hides
a soul that gives new meaning to animal magnetism.

ISBN 13: 978-0-8439-5953-6

✂ # ☐ **YES!**

Sign me up for the Love Spell Book Club and send my
FREE BOOKS! If I choose to stay in the club, I will pay
only $8.50* each month, a savings of $6.48!

NAME: _____

ADDRESS: _____

TELEPHONE: _____

EMAIL: _____

☐ I want to pay by credit card.

☐ VISA   ☐ MasterCard.   ☐ DISCOVER

ACCOUNT #: _____

EXPIRATION DATE: _____

SIGNATURE: _____

Mail this page along with $2.00 shipping and handling to:
**Love Spell Book Club**
**PO Box 6640**
**Wayne, PA 19087**
Or fax (must include credit card information) to:
**610-995-9274**
You can also sign up online at **www.dorchesterpub.com**.
*Plus $2.00 for shipping. Offer open to residents of the U.S. and Canada only.
Canadian residents please call 1-800-481-9191 for pricing information.
If under 18, a parent or guardian must sign. Terms, prices and conditions subject to
change. Subscription subject to acceptance. Dorchester Publishing reserves the right
to reject any order or cancel any subscription.